A Time to Tell

by

Maria Savva

First Edition published in paperback by: Pen Press (2006) ISBN -10: 1905621272 ISBN 13: 978-1905621279

This edition: Second Edition Published by:

Rose & Freedom Books P.O. Box 55285 London N22 9EU England, U.K.

Copyright © Maria Savva 2015

Cover design by Aeternum Designs (http://aeternumdesigns.com/)

A catalogue record of this book is available from the British Library

ISBN: 978-0-9928345-1-7

acknowledgements

Thanks to Pen Press (now indepenpress) for believing in "A Time to Tell" and for publishing the first edition back in the days when there were no online self-publishing tools available.

Thanks to everyone who ever read and reviewed the first edition of the book.

Thanks to Susan Buchanan at Perfect Prose Services: http:// perfectproseservices.com/ for the excellent editing advice.

Thank you to Darcia Helle for eagle-eyed beta reading and invaluable suggestions/comments.

Thanks to Laura Smith, Jenny Hilborne, and my cousin Marina for continued support and for taking the time to beta-read the novel.

Thanks to Julie Aldridge for being a life-saver and proofreading the final version for me!

Thank you to Kat at Aeternum Designs for the amazing cover design, and for helping out with the blurb (and for being so patient)!

Last but not least, thanks to all my readers for encouragement, support, and inspiration.

PROLOGUE

Cara opened her eyes and saw a young man with a kind face and spiky ginger hair.

'Are you all right?' she heard him say.

He took off his jacket and wrapped it around her like a blanket. 'It was quite a fall. You're lucky to be alive.'

Lucky to be alive. The words resounded in her head. She did not feel lucky to be alive. Trembling with fear as well as cold, Cara looked up at Stoneleigh Cliffs. They were even more imposing from below than they had been before she'd jumped. Her mind boggled thinking about what she had just done.

The young man distracted her: 'Someone's gone to call an ambulance. Hold on, it won't be long now,' he said softly.

Rubbing her eyes to ease the sting of the salt water, Cara stared up at the cliffs again, as if needing to confirm where she was. As she did so, it occurred to her that Frederick might be up there. For a second, she wished he was. Then, feeling nauseated, she remembered what he'd said to her. Turning her head slowly towards the stranger sitting next to her on the stony beach, she struggled to expel the painful memories.

He smiled sympathetically. 'I'm Billy. What's your name?'

'Cara.' She turned away self-consciously. Did he know she'd tried to take her own life? Shivering at the thought of what could have happened, she gripped the jacket that lay over her shoulders, pulling it closer, trying in vain to dispel the chill emanating from deep inside. Fear and regret taunted her. She didn't want to die. When she'd landed in the violent, unforgiving sea, she had fought for her life, battling the powerful waves.

Watching the grey sea as it lashed mightily against the shore, Cara feared for her sanity. She sobbed loudly, her heart full of self-pity and remorse.

Billy's arms tightened around her. 'Don't cry, love. You're safe now,' he said.

In the distance, she saw the lights of an ambulance approaching them. It was true, she realised, she was safe now, but seeing the ambulance drive onto the beach and the paramedics emerge, she knew her real nightmare was only just beginning.

FIFTY YEARS LATER...

CHAPTER ONE

Cara stared out of her bedroom window, through the net curtains. She had a good view of the avenue from where she sat in her bed, a pillow propped up behind her. She watched as the young mother with the small green car struggled to persuade her two children to get into the vehicle. The boy, who appeared to be about five or six years old, was wearing a smart grey school uniform and stripy green and blue tie. He was pulling the little girl's hair. The two children looked almost identical with their coffee-coloured hair: miniature versions of their mother.

Cara felt as if she knew this woman and her children. They did not know her. They'd never met, but for the past few months the young woman had often parked her car in the avenue when taking her children to school and collecting them. Cara witnessed it all from her view out of the bedroom window.

Her thoughts turned to her granddaughter Penelope. She usually arrived home, bringing the boys back from school, about five minutes after the small green car had driven away.

Most days were the same for Cara now. She often felt lonely sitting in bed for hours on end. She would follow the daily rituals of the people in the world outside the window. Some she recognised, such as the neighbours or regular visitors to the avenue like the young mother in the small green car, others she did not. They were all unaware she watched them.

For five years, she'd stared out of this window. She was bedridden, due to illness, having been diagnosed with multiple sclerosis over thirty years earlier. The doctors told her there was no cure for the condition and it would probably get progressively worse. Her only obvious symptom over the next twenty years was that she'd suffered from a slight limp. People had sometimes said she seemed drunk, as she'd walked unsteadily at times. Not being the sort of person to dwell on an illness, Cara had led a more or less normal life for many years.

In the past ten years, her mobility had gradually reduced. She put it down to the worry over her son's disappearance and her husband's death. Those stresses, no doubt, had weakened her immune system.

No longer able to look after herself, she lived with her granddaughter Penelope. As much as Cara loved her granddaughter, she often wished she could leave this place. She could not bear to hear the constant fights.

Almost as soon as Penelope's husband, David, walked through the door after work, the shouting would begin. Cara often heard things being thrown around downstairs, and the sound of furniture and crockery breaking. Penelope never talked about it. Cara wondered whether the girl had perhaps convinced herself that her grandmother couldn't hear the noise from her room upstairs.

At just seventeen years old, Penelope had married David Truman. They were a happy young couple, in love with each other—at least that's how Cara remembered it.

It seemed like only yesterday that she'd stood beside Penelope in front of a mirror, both of them beaming with pride.

'It fits you perfectly.' Cara discreetly wiped a tear from her eye as unexpected emotions assailed her. 'It could have been made for you.'

'Thank you so much, Nan, it's the most beautiful dress I've ever seen. It's amazing it survived for all these years in such perfect condition.' Penelope stroked the silky white fabric of the skirt and kissed Cara's cheek. 'I can't wait until Dave sees it!'

Memories of her own wedding day fought their way to the forefront of Cara's mind. She recalled the bright smile on Billy's face as she'd walked down the aisle towards him wearing this very dress.

⏳

Cara had established a routine of switching on her portable television as soon as David came home each evening, turning up the volume in an attempt to smother the sounds coming from the rooms below. She suspected Penelope might need help, but she didn't want to be seen as nosy or interfering.

On one occasion, two years before, when she had been truly worried after hearing loud banging noises downstairs during the night, she'd tried to broach the subject.

'Is everything all right between you and David, dear?' asked Cara, when her granddaughter brought her breakfast tray.

'Yes, fine,' Penelope said.

'I heard a noise last night...'

'A noise?' Penelope shrugged. 'Maybe it was the boys; they're always getting up to mischief.' She turned around quickly, heading for the door.

Cara watched her go, wishing she would stop and talk. Penelope did not look happy but, more than that, she'd once been so proud of her appearance.

The brown sweater she wore today was tatty, and she'd worn the same grey skirt for the past few months, alternating between that and an old pair of jeans. She didn't wear make-up anymore and didn't bother dyeing her hair, which was starting to turn grey.

As she grasped the door handle ready to exit the room, Cara called after her: 'Penny, if you ever need to talk, you know I'm here.'

Penelope remained rigid facing the door.

'I hear him shouting sometimes,' a last-ditch effort to keep her granddaughter in the room.

Penelope faced Cara and rolled her eyes. 'Dave and I are fine,' she said with an extended sigh. 'He has a bit of a temper. He works hard and he likes to let off steam when he gets home.' She didn't meet Cara's eyes, but before leaving she looked back at her and said, 'I'd rather you let me make my own decisions in my marriage. If I need your advice I'll ask for it.'

After that, Cara resolved to let matters lie. Penelope's two sons, Carl, eight, and Andrew, six, did not appear to be disturbed or affected by any of their parents' arguments. She felt comforted by this: if there were real problems, surely the children would show signs of distress.

Whenever she was feeling low, Cara couldn't help pondering whether Penelope and David's marriage had been all right before she'd moved in. Would they really have offered to let her live with them knowing she'd hear their fights and quarrels?

One morning, a few months back, Cara tried to talk to Penelope again, without mentioning her concerns about the arguments.

'Are you sure this house is big enough for me to stay here with you, dear? The boys are growing up so fast, and soon they'll need their own bedrooms.'

She saw something in Penelope's eyes then. Was it fear?

'I love having you here, Nan,' Penelope had said, sitting on the bed and taking her hand. 'Promise me you'll stay with us for ever.' It sounded like a plea.

Since then, Cara had suspected that Penelope *needed* her there.

Given the choice, Cara would have left. If she were far away she could pretend Penelope and David were happy.

She often thought of asking one of her children if she could move in with them. But how could she? She didn't want to upset Penelope, and she wasn't sure they would have room for her or even be able to make time to look after her.

Unable to find a solution to the dilemma, Cara stared out of the window as if searching for an answer in the street below.

CHAPTER TWO

'Please, try to keep your voice down,' said Penelope meekly, unable to meet her husband's hard stare, fearful of what his reaction might be. 'Nan will hear you.'

'Huh!' David slammed his fist down on the dining room table, causing the gravy boat to spill some of its contents onto the white tablecloth. 'That's what you always say.'

'W-well... it's true,' she stammered, eyes down, as she soaked up the spilt gravy with a napkin.

'Why did you ask that old cow to come and stay here in the first place?' He leaned across the table.

'I didn't ask her,' she said, slowly, quietly, in an attempt to calm him down. The edges of her lips trembled as she tried to hide her fear with a smile. 'She had nowhere else to go.'

'Don't make me angry, Penny. Don't treat me like I'm thick.' His voice was gradually rising.

She instinctively looked up towards her grandmother's bedroom.

David had started complaining as soon as he got home because his dinner was not on the table. She told him the food would be ready in a few minutes, but that didn't placate him. Recently, he picked on every little thing he could find to argue about. Weary and afraid, Penelope was at her wits' end. Nothing she said or did made a difference.

Penelope heard the sound of her grandmother's television, which had become louder since David came home.

He followed her eyes. 'Are you worried the old bat's gonna hear me? You must be as crazy as she is. She's fuckin' deaf. She has her TV so loud! What the fuck's wrong with her? I'm gonna complain about the noise. It's about time I said something. I didn't want her to come and live here anyway. It's my bloody house!'

'Dave, don't...' Penelope took a sharp intake of breath.

He turned around, his features contorted into a gnarled grimace. 'She's been living with us for five bloody years, and I've had enough. If she can't respect my need for peace and quiet when I come home from a hard day at work, she's out! D'you hear me?'

Penelope shivered. 'Dave, stop!' she called out, as he opened the door.

'What?' he shouted, turning back to face her.

The look in his eyes was the one she associated with the beatings.

As he approached, her whole body tensed up as if waiting for the punch, not quite sure when it would come.

Just then, their eight-year-old son, Carl, walked into the room.

Penelope's shoulders loosened slightly. There was one thing she could count on: he wouldn't hit her in front of the children.

'Daddy!' The boy grinned.

'Carl, my son.' David's whole posture changed and he became a loving dad. It was a Jekyll and Hyde transformation.

She wished she could freeze this moment so he'd remain this way: smiling and calm. He acted like a wild animal sometimes. Uncaged and dangerous. She shook her head, as if to discard the memory of what had just occurred, and went into the kitchen to serve the supper.

As she walked away, she remembered his threats to Cara. She would never forgive herself if he hurt her grandmother. She'd taken Cara in to her home hoping David might change his ways if someone else was living with them.

It hadn't always been this way.

Penelope met David at college where she was taking a secretarial course and he was training to be an engineer. She'd noticed his eyes first; they were the deepest shade of blue she had ever seen—deep and mysterious. He usually sat outside the college on a bench under an old oak tree to have his lunch, alone.

Whenever she walked past him, they exchanged a glance. They were strangers, and she felt sad about that. This boy intrigued her. He was distant, withdrawn. She grew increasingly curious about him.

One lunchtime, she joined him on the bench with her sandwich. She said hello, and he nodded back but remained silent. They sat there not saying a word for a whole hour.

He'd said hello to her the next morning. 'My name's David,' he said, smiling.

'I'm Penelope... er... you can call me Penny,' she offered.

They shook hands.

'It's nice to meet you.'

'Likewise. I'll see you on the bench at lunchtime then, Penny,' he'd said as he headed off in the direction of the engineering block.

'Okay,' she said, but he had already walked quite far ahead and wouldn't have been able to hear her. His behaviour confused her, but she assumed that maybe he was shy.

About three months after they'd first started dating, Penelope and David were sitting in a park on the grass enjoying a lazy summer's day...

David took her by surprise when he asked: 'Do you think I'm odd, Penny?' His blue eyes squinted in the bright sun.

'Odd?' She laughed, then screwed up her nose. 'In what way?'

He picked at the corners of his nails in what appeared to be a nervous motion. 'Different,' he said, his gaze still fixed on his hands.

'Well, yes, you are different, but that's why I love you.' She reached out to hug him, but he pulled away and she felt rejected.

'If you knew the truth about my family, you'd run a mile.' David laughed.

His laughter seemed out of place and it unsettled her. 'Wh-what do you mean?' She held a hand against her forehead to block out the sun so she could see him more clearly.

He stared straight ahead. 'Why are you with me, Penny?'

'I ju-just said why: because I love you. Dave, you're acting weird.' It was the first time he'd spoken about his family; she realised she didn't know much about him.

'My family is different,' he said cryptically.

'In what way?' she asked, now looking at her own hands, fearing that soon they'd have to discuss her family. She hadn't seen her father since he fled the family home, over four years ago, thinking he'd killed her mother after another one of their fights.

'My mum hates me,' said David. 'She says I'm like my dad.'

'Oh, look at that dog over there.' Penelope pointed, trying to change the subject. Flashbacks from the past assailed her mind, the dark secrets she kept locked inside.

'Dog? What dog?' He twisted around where he sat, looking behind him and then back at her. 'I'm spilling my bloody guts here, and you're more concerned about some fuckin' poodle!'

She'd never seen him angry. 'S-sorry,' she stuttered, finding it hard to meet his gaze as his deep blue eyes bore into her.

'My mum used to hit me a lot,' he stated. 'Always did, as far as I can remember. She can't now, though, because I'm too strong for her. She drinks too much.'

Penelope ran her fingers through the grass to distract herself from the painful recollections triggered by his words.

'Are you listening to me, Penny?'

'Yes.'

'Well? Aren't you shocked?'

'All families have their problems. There aren't any perfect families,' she

15

murmured.

'My dad's usually in prison,' he said, 'but when he's home, they fight a lot. He drinks too.'

Everything slotted into place: the reason he was such a loner. It all made sense to Penelope and drew her closer to him. It had helped her to hear she was not the only one who had suffered.

'I'd understand if you don't want me as a boyfriend.'

'Don't be silly, Dave, of course I want to be with you. I love you.' *A desire to protect him from any more hurt erupted in her heart. She punched him playfully on the arm.*

His reaction was to grab her arm and twist it hard. It was a spontaneous, almost defensive action. His eyes showed no emotion.

'Dave!' *she screamed.* 'You're hurting me!'

Letting go, he turned away.

Her arm felt sore as she instinctively rubbed it.

He didn't apologise.

They left the park in silence.

Penelope and David were married the following year.

'We're married!' *said Penelope, twirling in delight. It was the morning after their wedding day.* 'I'm Mrs Truman!' *Jumping onto the double bed, she grinned at him still lying there covered with the green duvet.* 'It's great, isn't it, Dave?' *Her smile faded slightly when she recognised a look in his eyes: one she'd seen before. His eyes darkened and his countenance became inscrutable. He'd last had that look when he first told her about his parents' violent relationship.*

She gazed down at the gold ring on her finger and then touched it, as if in doing so she might somehow dispel this cloud of misery that hung over them.

'What's wrong?' *she asked, touching his hair softly.*

He sat up slowly, avoiding her eyes. 'I suppose I find it weird, you being so happy.'

'Aren't you?' *She sighed and slouched.* 'You looked happy enough yesterday.'

'I don't know.'

Did he regret marrying her? Would he leave her? Tears formed in her eyes. She walked over to the wardrobe, pulling her dressing gown closer around her, a hollow feeling in her gut. Opening the wardrobe door, she moved a few hangers as though she were looking for something to wear, but it was just empty actions. She was distracted, waiting for him to speak again to make it all better;

she couldn't focus on anything else.

Hearing a rustling of sheets, she turned to face him and watched as he walked quickly out of the room. The bathroom door slammed shut; the unexpected sound made her shudder. Hesitantly, she shuffled towards the bathroom. 'D-Dave, are you all right?'

'Yeeeessss!' he roared.

Retreating, Penelope made her way to the bedroom, absent-mindedly twisting her gold wedding ring with a trembling hand.

Perplexed by his mood, she sat on the bed and thought back to the night before. He said he was tired when they arrived home, and went straight to bed. At the time, as she felt tired too, she was content to simply curl up next to him and sleep. Maybe she'd missed more signs of his regret. She blamed herself for being so caught up in the preparations for the big day: if only she'd paid more attention. A deep gloom pervaded her thoughts.

Shortly, David returned and walked over to the wardrobe. He took out a pair of trousers and a shirt.

'Dave, what's wrong? Please tell me.'

'Stop asking me that.' He had his back to her, the sound of fury in his voice.

'Why did you marry me if you didn't want to?' Her voice broke with emotion.

'Stop going on about us being married!' he said, turning to face her, anger searing his cheeks, colouring them red.

Penelope's mouth opened and closed, a silent scream, as tears slid down her cheeks.

He dressed quickly, as if in a hurry to leave.

'You regret it, don't you? You regret marrying me.' A sniffle followed the question.

After buttoning up his shirt, he stood facing her. 'Maybe I do.'

She peered up at him.

'It just feels strange, Penny, like we've stepped over into this new life, grown up and married.' He sat on the bed.

She took his hands in hers. 'Nothing's really changed. You're still you and I'm still me.'

'Everything's changed,' he moaned, pulling away. 'I'm scared we'll end up like my parents... Or your parents.'

'Dave—' She wiped her tears on the sleeves of her dressing gown.

'History repeats itself.' Rocking backwards and forwards as he spoke, he

17

continued, 'The abused becomes the abuser. Don't you know that?'

'We won't end up like them.' Penelope rubbed her hands together nervously, disturbed by his words and the glazed look in his eyes.

'How can you be so sure?'

Before she could answer, David took her face in his hands and turned her head towards him, a bit too forcefully.

'Ow! What did you do that for?'

'It could easily happen.' He glared at her, his eyes becoming darker.

'You're sc-scaring me.' She stood up to release herself from his hold.

He grabbed her arm and she recalled an incident not so long ago when he'd gripped her this way, hurting her. She trembled.

'Sit down.'

The force he used tugging at her arm compelled her to obey.

'Don't ever turn away from me when I'm talking to you!'

He loosened his grip.

She got to her feet and rubbed her arm where he'd twisted it. 'Dave, what's wrong with you? Why—'

The next thing she knew, she'd landed on the bed, where he'd shoved her before walking out of the room. Although he was no longer there, an intense fear remained. The dark, hard stare of his blue eyes burned into her memory; a warning that had come too late.

Over the years, she put up with the violence holding firm to the belief that she could change him. Sooner or later he'd see that what he was doing was wrong. Her love would help him overcome all the rage he held inside, she felt sure of it. Whenever he hit or punched her it still came as a shock, as if unexpected, almost as though she'd blanked out past incidents of violence. She always forgave him. It wasn't his fault he behaved this way: his parents were to blame. However, the violence became more and more frequent. The courage and strength she'd found within herself at the start of their relationship was slowly dying. With every punch, every kick, she grew smaller and smaller inside. Her self-worth faded a little more whenever she allowed him to treat her that way. Gradually, her self-esteem was whittled away to nothing and she became unable to stand up for herself, losing the will to fight. This was now her way of life.

The year before Cara moved in with them, Penelope became pregnant for the third time. David doted on their two sons, so she held out hope that another baby might help their marriage. She was overjoyed to learn from the hospital scan that the child would be a girl.

David seemed pleased too.

One evening, a few months into the pregnancy, he arrived home from work in a foul mood and began pushing her.

'Stop it! You'll hurt the baby,' she'd pleaded. He smelt of alcohol.

His response was to push her even harder.

Tripping over the coffee table in the living room, Penelope fell onto the linoleum-covered floor, landing on her stomach. She heard David slam the front door on his way out of the house. The telephone was on a side table near the sofa, about three metres from where she'd fallen. It took all the strength she had to drag herself along the floor.

As she phoned for an ambulance, she prayed the baby would be okay. The pain was unbearable.

By the time she arrived at the hospital, having lost a lot of blood on the way, Penelope knew something was wrong. A black mood fell over her that wouldn't shift for months. Her baby had died.

When David heard the news, he cried. Penelope was amazed at how repentant he appeared to be. His personality switched; he changed so completely as to make him almost unrecognisable from the man who had abused her. 'It was the drink,' he'd say, tears streaming from his eyes, begging forgiveness. Penelope hated seeing him like that. He gave up alcohol, made a promise never to hurt her, remained teetotal for months.

She felt torn between wanting to get as far away from him as possible and wanting to help him. She knew he grieved over the loss of their unborn daughter as much as she did.

Shortly after this, she learnt that Cara's multiple sclerosis had progressed. The family talked of putting her into a residential care home. Penelope offered to take care of her. It was a kind of blessing: she'd no longer have to live alone with David. There would be someone there to make sure he treated her right. But her plan failed.

It wasn't long before he reverted to his old ways, leaving Penelope in a constant state of anxiety always anticipating the next punch. To make matters worse, she had now committed to helping Cara; she had to stay there in that house, day after day, hoping David would leave. He never did.

CHAPTER THREE

Cara switched off the television. As she settled down to sleep, she hoped Penelope and David had stopped arguing downstairs.

It was late. Quiet. She prayed she would fall asleep without hearing another sound to disturb the silence.

As she said a prayer for Penelope and the children, she also asked God to keep Benjamin safe, wherever he might be. He was always on her mind. Not knowing if he was alive or dead proved a terrible burden to bear. She still prayed for him every night, hopeful she would see him again one day. He hadn't been perfect, but she loved him as a mother loves her child: unconditionally.

Benjamin, Penelope's father, had been missing for nearly sixteen years. On the night he disappeared, Cara and her husband, Billy, had rushed to the hospital to see Margaret, Benjamin's wife. When they arrived she was wearing a neck brace. Penelope and her sister, Jemima, were sitting next to her bed, wearing coats over their pyjamas.

Cara did not know why Margaret ended up in hospital, only that there had been a "domestic incident".

'Where's Ben?' she asked, looking at the two girls and then back at Margaret.

'He's gone,' Margaret replied, closing her eyes for a second.

'Gone? What do you mean?' Could he be dead? Had they both been involved in a terrible accident?

'Can you take the girls home with you tonight, Cara? I'd really appreciate it.'

'But where has Ben gone, dear?'

Margaret let out a heavy sigh. 'I don't know and I don't care.' The redness in her cheeks betrayed her anger.

Margaret's eyes swivelled towards where the children were seated and she appeared to regret her sudden loss of control. She smiled at the girls and tried to turn her head to face them, but it seemed like an arduous task.

'Penny, Jemima, you'll be good girls for Nana and Granddad now, won't you?'

'Yes,' said Jemima, who sat cradling an old black and white teddy bear. Cara recognised it as Benjamin's childhood toy.

Penelope only nodded, didn't speak; her large brown eyes remained in a shocked, unblinking stare.

'I'll take the girls outside, leave you two alone for a while,' said Billy.

'Thanks, Bill,' said Cara; perhaps now she would get a chance to find out the truth about what had happened.

When Billy and the children left the room, Cara repeated her question: 'Please tell me, dear, where has Ben gone?'

Margaret broke down in tears and told Cara about the many beatings she'd suffered at the hands of a drunken Benjamin and how he often disappeared for weeks with no word. This time she doubted he'd be back: 'He probably thinks I'm dead.' She sniffed, wiping her eyes. 'The fall from the stairs knocked me out. I can't remember a thing after that. The nurse told me Penny called the ambulance.'

'Oh dear, poor little Penny.'

'I'm glad he's gone,' said Margaret, battling tears. 'I hope he's gone for good. I never want to set eyes on him again.'

Margaret was paralysed from the waist down. The doctors were confident she would walk again, but the prognosis was years, rather than weeks or months, for her to regain all her motor skills.

The children were still young, and Margaret thought it would be unfair for them to take on the responsibility of being her carers.

Cara and Billy offered to take care of Margaret and the children. They were living alone in a four-bedroom house—much too big for only the two of them. Catherine, their daughter, had moved out the year before, and James, their younger son, lived in his own house with his wife, Emily, and their newborn son, William.

When Cara first heard about Benjamin's violence she didn't want to believe it. Although she took Margaret and the girls in to live with her, she still had reservations and preferred to keep a distance. After all, she reasoned, Margaret could have exaggerated things.

Gradually, she realised that her refusal to accept Margaret's version of events stemmed from not wanting to face up to the possibility that her own son could have done such an abominable thing.

After spending weeks and months with Margaret, her perspective slowly changed. She'd known Margaret as a bubbly teenager and here in front of her stood a withdrawn woman who carried a great burden. All the evidence pointed to Benjamin being the cause of that.

Consequently, for a long time, Cara hated Benjamin for what he'd done to Margaret and more so for his cowardice in running away.

As the years went by, however, with no word from him, Cara became concerned. Margaret said he'd left home drunk that night. Did he have a drink problem? What if he'd been involved in an accident or even killed himself?

Increasingly, Cara would find herself remembering him as a small boy: a loner who never joined in with his siblings' games. He'd been silent and moody, forever getting into trouble at school.

Whenever she remembered that side of his personality, she dearly wished she could talk to him and find out why he became such a bitter man.

She felt responsible. If she'd instilled in him the morals he needed for life, if she hadn't failed as a mother, he'd be here.

Cara could think of only one possible reason why Benjamin should have grown up to be so different from her other children. She alone knew that she may have treated him differently from the others when they were growing up, not deliberately but perhaps subconsciously.

He was *different*, after all.

Had she spoilt him a little more than the other two because he reminded her of her old love? Had she shouted at him a bit too much when he misbehaved, taking out on him the anger and resentment she held against the man she'd loved and lost?

CHAPTER FOUR

On the twelfth day of August 1952, eighteen-year-old Cara Hughes first set eyes on Frederick Johnson. Up until that date, she had not believed in love at first sight. She'd never imagined she would meet someone and immediately know she wanted to spend the rest of her life with him.

On the day in question, she was having lunch with her friend and work colleague, Annabelle. They were dining in The Horse and Dragon, a local public house. As chance would have it, Frederick had also decided to have lunch there.

Cara noticed him as soon as he walked through the door, partly because Huddlesea was such a small town and she didn't recognise him but mostly because he was tall, well built, with thick black hair and dark dreamy eyes. She could not help staring, in awe of his good looks. When his eyes met hers and he smiled broadly, she turned away blushing.

He approached the table where Cara and Annabelle were seated, introduced himself, and offered to buy them a drink.

'No thanks,' Annabelle said, glancing at her watch. 'We've just finished our lunch and have to get back to work.'

'Where do you work?' he asked Cara.

'Across the road, at the solicitors' firm,' she replied.

Annabelle glared at her.

Cara continued to gawk at Frederick.

He smiled and she felt insanely happy, flattered by the attention.

'As I said, we have to go,' muttered Annabelle, standing up and nudging Cara.

Cara did not want to leave; she could lose herself in this man's eyes for ever. Reluctantly, she picked up her handbag and followed Annabelle.

As she walked to the door, Cara could not resist turning back to steal another look at him; to her delight she saw that he was still watching her. A satisfied smirk on her face, she made her way out of the pub. Once outside, her feet refused to move any further, and she held on to the door unwilling to close it completely.

'Come on, Cara, we'll be late,' grumbled Annabelle. 'And why did you tell that man where we work?'

'Why shouldn't I have?' Cara asked. 'He was handsome, don't you think? He looked like an actor or something.'

'Yes, but he's not from Huddlesea. You shouldn't make a habit of talking

to strange men. Do you want to get a reputation?"

Usually she would agree with Annabelle when they discussed such matters, but today was turning out to be quite a curious day. Annabelle—dressed in a dull brown suit, her long mousy brown hair in a sensible plait—suddenly represented to Cara everything she hated about Huddlesea: the small-mindedness of the residents, the stuffy conservatism. The same people drove her best friend, Beattie, to her death through their lack of compassion and understanding. Ever since the day Beattie died, Cara had been searching for a way to escape the chains of living in this small town with its closed minds and staid rules restricting her freedom.

A sense of rebellion took hold. 'Annabelle, I'll see you back at work, I need to go to the toilet,' she said as an excuse to re-enter the pub.

Walking into the pub, Cara saw Frederick seated at the bar, his back to her. His smart suit made him stand out. Gazing at him in wonder, she racked her brain trying to find something to say that would make her sound sophisticated.

As Cara hesitated in the doorway, the door opened and she felt herself being pushed forward.

'Sorry, dear,' said a croaky voice, which sounded as though it belonged to an old man. A strong smell of cigar smoke filled the air.

Cara turned around and saw Barry Higgins, the owner of the tobacconists that was situated across the road from her father's grocery.

'Hello, Cara.'

She nodded at him, feeling guilty, as if he knew why she'd returned to the pub. Then George, the barman, looked in her direction, and her cheeks reddened.

'How are you today, Cara?' asked Barry Higgins.

'Fine, thanks,' she said, not wanting to get into a conversation with him, worried Frederick would spot her. She smiled at Mr Higgins and quickly walked past him, making her way to the ladies' toilets, praying Frederick wouldn't notice her. Her heart began to beat faster and she was physically shaking as adrenaline coursed through her veins. Everyone in this place knew her. How could she speak to Frederick with all of them gawping and gossiping?

Catching a glimpse of herself in the mirror in the ladies' toilets, she saw her cheeks were flushed. She took the hairbrush out of her handbag and ran it through her long red hair with a trembling hand, breathing deeply to settle the nerves that rattled inside her.

As she replaced the hairbrush, she remembered that she had some lipstick in her bag. The lipstick was still in there from last Thursday when she'd been out for a meal with the girls from work to celebrate Carrie's fortieth birthday. She did not usually wear lipstick, except on special occasions like weddings or parties. Taking it out of the bag, she carefully ran the pink colour over her lips.

She walked back into the bar area, heart racing, trying to avoid making eye contact with anyone.

Deliberately brushing past Frederick, she turned her head to face him. Her cheeks were burning and she prayed they didn't look as red as they felt. Above the pitter-patter of her heartbeat, she heard him speak.

'Are you sure you won't let me buy you that drink?'

She almost accepted but knew she couldn't risk being late for work. 'I have to go.' As she uttered the words she wished it wasn't true, wanting to spend the rest of the afternoon with Frederick. Might this be the last chance she would have to get to know him?

'We can meet up later,' he said, breaking into her thoughts and answering her question.

She beamed with delight.

'I'll be in here at seven o'clock,' he said. 'I'll see you then.'

⌛

Breaking with Huddlesea's traditions, Cara met Frederick that evening at The Horse and Dragon. She'd told her mother she would be staying at a friend's house. She embraced the freedom her rebellion brought her, but it also tore at her conscience. Meeting a man who was not from Huddlesea, without her parents' consent, made her a traitor of sorts. She knew that. Yet, there was a part of her that yearned to be independent and ever since meeting Frederick Johnson that part was battling to be heard.

Frederick drove them to a wonderfully secluded seaside spot on the outskirts of Huddlesea. As they walked hand in hand along the beach, he told her he had come from out of town for work. She listened intently to every word, loving the sound of his voice, so deep and soothing.

It was liberating to escape the stifling town and the sense of paranoia that pervaded it: eyes always watching, ready to report back to her parents. Here no one knew her; she was able to relax. She felt invincible.

Cara and Frederick stayed at a hotel and spent a passionate night together.

He drove her home early the next morning.

Reminiscing about the evening's events, Cara found herself mystified. The girl swept away by Frederick seemed like another person: the person she'd always dreamed of being. Somehow, the time she'd spent with Frederick outside Huddlesea had given her the courage to make her dream a reality. She could think of nothing but him: his face, his eyes, his smile.

Frederick told her she was beautiful. She mused over how she'd occasionally been called "pretty", often as an afterthought by some insensitive relative or friend of her parents who might have been openly complimenting her sister, Gloria, on her beauty whilst ignoring Cara. Gloria stole the limelight: everyone commented on her good looks, and Cara felt quite plain in comparison. Cara had run-of-the-mill ginger hair, whereas Gloria's was a deep auburn colour; Cara's eyes were an unremarkable shade of green but Gloria's were a searing ice-blue. Cara hated her freckles, envious of Gloria's flawless porcelain skin. Somehow, hearing 'You're beautiful, Cara,' from Frederick's lips, made up for all the years of insecurity about her appearance. He was, in her eyes, the most beautiful person she had ever seen.

Thinking back to the night before, she could hardly believe she'd slept with Frederick. What scandal it would cause in Huddlesea if anyone found out. Her brow creased as she brooded over how narrow-minded they all were. She couldn't wait to see him again.

When Frederick wasn't with her, Cara was dreaming about being with him, anticipating their next date.

'You look like you're keeping a secret,' commented Annabelle when they were leaving the office one evening.

Cara noticed her friend's serious expression. She secretly hoped Annabelle would find someone like Frederick, someone to bring her a bit of happiness.

'You're always smiling,' said Annabelle.

Cara's smile widened even more as she became aware of it. 'Aren't I allowed to smile?'

'Hmm... of course, but people usually need a reason to smile. Are you keeping something from me?'

'No.' Cara avoided her friend's questioning gaze.

'If I didn't know better, I'd say you're in love.'

Cara skipped ahead of Annabelle, making her way to the old bridge where Frederick said they should meet after work. 'I am in love.' She giggled as she turned to face her friend.

Annabelle stared at her, aghast.

'I'm in love with life!' Cara twirled like a ballerina, and then ran *towards the bridge.*

Cara and Frederick met most weekdays after work: always away from Huddlesea, the town that may as well have had four walls such was its claustrophobic atmosphere. The nights they spent together were romantic and passionate. She wanted to tell everyone about him, but he said people would talk.

'People don't understand love, Cara. You've told me how small-minded the people in Huddlesea are. We can't tell them yet.'

She was about to ask him when they could tell, but he lifted her up in his arms and kissed her. All else was forgotten.

Cara asked him why they couldn't spend weekends together and he explained he had to work long shifts at weekends.

Consequently, weekends became the worst time of the week for her. If she ever did lose her constant smile it was on a Friday evening, knowing she would be going home to her parents' house and wouldn't see Frederick for two whole days.

'Most people look forward to the weekend when they get a couple of days off work, Cara,' her mother commented one Friday. 'You mope around the house as if you've lost a pound and found a penny.'

Now and then, Cara wondered why Frederick never took her to his house, but not being quite sure where they would end up spending the night made their meetings more exciting and added an element of adventure.

She finally told Annabelle about Frederick a few weeks into the relationship.

Annabelle, recalling the meeting in The Horse and Dragon, looked up from her typewriter and frowned. 'I didn't like the look of him.'

'But he's gorgeous!' exclaimed Cara.

'I don't mean he isn't handsome, but just because someone's handsome doesn't mean they're to be trusted. The way he came straight over and offered to buy us a drink, makes me think he's one of those men who makes a habit of asking young women out, if you know what I mean.' She raised her eyebrows disapprovingly.

'He's really nice, Annabelle.' Cara thought about Frederick and smiled to herself. She loved his self-assuredness.

'I'm sure he is nice, but I... I don't know. He's older than us, isn't he?'

27

'He's not much older.'

'You should be careful. He's not even from Huddlesea. He could have all sorts of skeletons in his closet,' warned Annabelle, appearing stern, momentarily reminding Cara of her mother.

'I like the fact he's not from Huddlesea. Everybody knows everybody in Huddlesea: if I was to go out with someone from here, I'd know everything about him already. That's what's great about Freddie; there's so much I don't know about him, so much to learn.'

'All I'm saying is, I'd prefer to know a little about someone before I go out with them,' said Annabelle.

Cara regarded her friend in her plain grey suit, long brown hair tied up as usual in one tidy plait. It was easy to see Annabelle wasn't the adventurous type.

'I don't want to be a secretary in Huddlesea for the rest of my life,' retorted Cara. 'Anyway, the whole point of courting is to find out about the other person.'

'So where does this Freddie come from?' quizzed Annabelle.

'I don't know exactly—'

'And have you met many of his friends?' she asked, before Cara could elaborate.

'No, not yet. They don't live in Huddlesea.'

'What job does he do?'

'I'm not quite sure,' Cara said, shrugging.

'Well, you haven't found out much about him,' snorted Annabelle, sarcastically. 'What exactly do you do when you're together?'

'We go out. You know, we... spend time together. We do all the things normal couples do.'

'What do you have in common?'

'Lots of things.'

Annabelle rolled her eyes. 'But you'd have far more in common with someone from Huddlesea.' She spun around on her chair, turning her back on Cara, and carried on typing.

'Freddie's sophisticated, not like the men here. I mean, do you know any eligible bachelors in Huddlesea?'

'There must be some. What about Peter Jones?' Annabelle glanced over her shoulder. 'You used to fancy him at school, remember? I've heard he's still single.'

'Why aren't you pleased for me?' Cara wished Beattie was still alive. Beattie would have liked Frederick. Cara had shared all her secrets with her best *friend, who was always so enthusiastic. 'I'm happy,' she said. 'Freddie is so... so wonderful.'*

'He struck me as the type who just wants a bit of fun.' Annabelle adjusted her glasses at the end of her nose.

'He's not like that.'

'Has he talked about marriage?' She spun around in her chair to face Cara.

'Not yet, but it's early days.'

'Have you told your mother about him?'

'No, not yet.'

'Probably because you know she wouldn't approve.'

'I think you're jealous, Annabelle Smart.'

'I am not!'

But Cara didn't believe her: she would have been jealous too, if Annabelle were courting Frederick. She carried on with her work, a satisfied smile dancing about her lips.

After dating Frederick for nearly two months, Cara felt sure the relationship was progressing well; she decided to tell her parents about him. They asked to meet him.

'No daughter of mine is going to be gallivanting about town with a strange man. What will everyone say? Remember what happened to Beattie,' warned her mother.

On hearing her once best friend's name, Cara closed her eyes against the raging in her head she knew she could not express.

When Cara told Frederick her parents had asked to meet him, he changed. From that moment their relationship went downhill.

For nearly two months they'd hardly spent more than a couple of days apart, but now he didn't contact her for a whole week, and she had no way of contacting him, didn't even know where he lived. He'd never given her his address and she didn't know where he worked. Cara felt lost and alone, unable to concentrate; then, to make matters worse, she missed a period. The first thing that sprang to mind was what had happened to Beattie.

Cara was desperate to talk to Frederick: being older he would know more about such matters. If she was pregnant, she feared she'd be ostracised just as Beattie had been. She tried hard to convince herself that she was just panicking, after all, it wasn't so unusual for her to miss a period; it had happened once before.

Then one day Frederick called her at work, unexpectedly.

'I'm so sorry I haven't been able to see you recently,' he said. 'I've been really busy. I miss you. Let's meet at Turner's Bridge after work. We can go for a drive to a nice little hotel I know.'

Cara floated on an emotional high for the rest of the working day. It appeared she'd read too much into his absence from her life. He even sent an enormous bunch of roses to her office. She noticed the envy written on the faces of her colleagues when the flowers were delivered.

'I'm the luckiest girl in the world,' said Cara as she sat in the passenger seat of Frederick's car that evening.

'Yes, you are. Just remember that.' He flashed his broad, cheeky smile, and she felt a familiar tingling in her stomach. She truly loved this man. They were "just right" for each other. They fitted. They could get married and everything would be all right. She breathed deeply, taking in the fresh early evening air, savouring their time together.

'I love being with you,' she said.

'Of course you do,' he said. 'That's only natural.'

'Stop it, Freddie, you're supposed to say you love being with me too!'

'I don't have to tell you that, do I?' He laughed and winked at her, then fixed his gaze on the road ahead as he drove.

'I think we were made for each other,' she said.

A brief silence followed.

'Freddie?'

'Yes, dear?'

'Won't you reconsider what I said? I'd love you to meet my family.' How could she broach the subject of her possible pregnancy? 'We've been seeing each other for a while.'

He did not reply but slowed the car and parked at the side of the road. 'I can't meet your parents.'

'Oh, Freddie, they don't bite!' The tense atmosphere made her voice shake, but she laughed to cover her nerves.

Frederick didn't join in with the laughter. He seemed distant, as if he had something weighty on his mind.

'And you're going to have to meet them one day,' she persisted in a higher-pitched voice, anxiety getting the better of her, 'especially if we're going to get married and spend the rest of our lives together.'

'I'm so sorry.' He held his forehead. 'I can't marry you, Cara.'

'Why ever not?' Her question was a half-whisper as she inwardly kicked herself for mentioning marriage. Perhaps he would have preferred to be the one to ask her, when the time was right; that would explain his reaction. She tried to reassure herself with these thoughts, but an odd sense of insecurity had taken over. She bit her lower lip waiting for his reply.

'I'm so sorry, Cara.'

'You said you loved me. You said—'

'I know. It was all true, everything. I do love you.'

'Well, why...?' She blinked away her tears.

'I'm already married.'

A gasp left her lips before she could fully digest the sentence. Already married? She tried to respond, but her question stuck in her throat and no sound came out.

Frederick fidgeted in his seat. He reached for her hand, but she pulled it away as if scalded.

His eyes were wide as he pleaded with her. 'Please, listen... My marriage isn't working, but I have two small children; I can't leave them. I have to stay with my family. But I do love you. I would like to carry on seeing you.'

A stray tear fell onto her hand. She wiped it immediately, not wanting him to see. 'A-a-all this time... w-why didn't you tell me?'

'I'm sorry, Cara. I never meant to hurt you.'

Her mind screamed. How could someone who had been her whole world have done this? Recollections of his lies, so easily told, taunted her. All her dreams of their future together were gone in an instant. He had changed. Everything had changed. I hate you, Freddie Johnson! She couldn't say it out loud, as much as she wanted to, didn't want him to know he had clawed his way so deeply into her heart.

She pushed frantically at the car door and it sprang open suddenly, almost flying off its hinges. Pausing before getting out of the car, maybe in the hope that he would say something... anything... to change the situation, Cara felt her heart beating so hard she thought it might burst. As she had expected, Frederick didn't protest... didn't plead for her to stay. I have been such a fool!

She jumped out of the car and began to run.

After running for what felt like an age, she saw the sea beckoning. A strong wind blew as she walked nearer to the cliff edge. The gusts behind her were urging her forward. Tears streamed down her cheeks, and the rain lashed against her face. She walked steadily onwards and remained standing for a *while at the extreme edge of Stoneleigh Cliffs, staring down into the sea, which in the fading light of dusk appeared agitated and malevolent, reflecting and magnifying her mood.*

She took one more step.

Landing in the sea with such force she struggled to breathe, Cara was battered by the waves.

Cara's pregnancy was confirmed by her doctor in January 1953.

By then, she had been married to Billy for two months. She'd never had any actual proof that she was pregnant before she met him; she kept telling herself that and pushed all thoughts of Frederick as far away as possible.

Cara caught her breath at first sight of her newborn son; there was no mistaking his full head of black hair, just like Frederick's.

When Billy, with his shock of ginger hair, came to visit her and the baby at the hospital, Cara searched his face for any signs of suspicion but could only see a proud father gazing at his newborn son. A sense of shame caused her to tense up, and she found herself willing him to leave in case he commented on the child's features. However, to her surprise and relief, he said, 'He's got lovely dark hair, just like my mother's.'

'He's beautiful,' she agreed, feeling able to breathe again.

As the months and years went by, she convinced herself that Benjamin could just as easily be Billy's son. The links in her mind became more and more disjointed until at long last she was able to look at Benjamin without automatically remembering Frederick.

CHAPTER FIVE

Benjamin's violent tendencies were evident at a young age, as early as when he was at primary school.

At the age of about ten or eleven years old, he came home from school one day with a bloody nose. The front door opened and closed quietly as he entered the house.

Cara had been looking out through the front window and saw him walk up the path covering his nose with a blood-soaked tissue.

'Ben! What's happened?' She waited for an answer, standing at the entrance to the living room, gaping at her eldest son who remained by the front door, his back to her.

Without warning, he turned around quickly and ran past her through the hallway and into the kitchen, slamming the door behind him.

Cara rushed after him and tried her best to open the door, but Benjamin was pushing against it from the inside.

'Ben,' she said softly. 'Please tell me what's happened. Have you been in a fight?'

'No,' he snapped. 'Go away.'

Not long afterwards, Billy arrived home from work.

'Hello, love,' he said, kissing her.

Cara did not respond, her eyes still fixed on the closed door.

Billy raised an eyebrow and took a step backwards. 'What's wrong?'

She let out a sigh. 'It's Ben; I think he's been in a fight at school. He won't talk to me about it. Maybe you'll have more luck.' She pointed at the kitchen door.

Billy shrugged, and tried the door handle. 'Ben, open up,' he demanded.

The sound of shuffling feet could be heard from the other side of the door.

Billy tried the handle a second time and it opened.

Cara felt envious of how Benjamin always listened to Billy.

She chewed her fingernails as she waited for her husband and son to emerge from the kitchen, unable to hear what they were saying from behind the closed door.

After a few minutes, Benjamin exited the kitchen holding a tissue over his nose.

Billy followed him.

Benjamin nodded awkwardly at Cara and ran upstairs before she had a chance to talk to him.

'It was a nosebleed, love,' said Billy in his usual nonchalant way.

'So why didn't he tell me?'

'He was probably afraid you'd think he was acting like a girl if he made a fuss.' Billy chuckled. 'Our boy's growing into a man.'

His reply didn't satisfy Cara.

⏳

That Sunday, as they sat around the kitchen table at lunchtime, seven-year-old James asked a question. 'How come Ben's got black hair when we've all got ginger?'

Billy's eyes met Cara's for an instant and she held her breath, fearing his response, but he just smiled at her.

'We've talked about this before,' said Billy to James. 'My mother had lovely dark hair. Ben's taken after his grandmother.' He regarded Benjamin proudly.

Benjamin never allowed his face to betray his true feelings, especially sensitive emotions, but his expression softened as he looked at Billy then.

'Our teacher said if both parents have ginger hair the child will most likely have ginger hair too,' piped up nine-year-old Catherine, who, with her round spectacles and her hair tied back in a tight ponytail, exuded an authoritative air. She sounded like a young scientist lecturing on an important fact.

Benjamin appeared embarrassed and carried on eating his meal in silence.

'That's nonsense,' said Cara, trying not to sound overly critical as images of Frederick flashed through her mind. 'We have living proof it's not true.' She laughed and hoped to bring that particular discussion to a close. 'Cathy, pass me the salt, please, dear.'

'Yes, but my teacher told me the gene for ginger hair is quite strong,' persisted Catherine.

'It is,' said Billy. 'I've read about it. But just because both parents have the gene for ginger hair, it doesn't necessarily follow their child will be born with ginger hair.'

Cara shifted in her seat. Why had Billy been reading about this? Had he been suspicious?

'Why are we talking about jeans?' asked James. 'What have trousers got

to do with hair?'

'Not those types of jeans, silly,' said Catherine, laughing.

James shrugged and carried on eating.

Cara prayed they would change the subject.

'Edward King said Ben must've been adopted,' said James, breaking the silence.

'Yeah, and Ben punched him!' Catherine laughed.

'Shut up you two!' Benjamin scowled at his brother and sister.

Cara wanted to tell him to behave, but she also wished Catherine and James would stop going on about his hair.

'When did all this happen?' asked Billy, stern-faced.

Cara braced herself, concerned about how much longer she could hold her composure.

'Last week,' explained Catherine. 'Me, Ben, and Jamie met up after school to go home, and Edward King—who's the school bully—followed us. He started picking on Ben because he's got black hair and we've got ginger. They had a fight.'

'We didn't have a fight!' said Benjamin, red-faced.

'Yes you did,' chorused James and Catherine.

'Children can be cruel,' interjected Billy. 'Being adopted is no reason to pick on someone.' He glanced at Cara.

She felt the colour rush to her cheeks and, faking a cough, picked up her glass of water.

'This Edward King sounds silly; he obviously hasn't been brought up with any manners,' added Billy.

'He just looks for anything he can use to pick fights,' said Benjamin.

'Hmm... Well, you know it's no good to fight, Ben, don't you?' said Billy, softly.

'He started it,' said Benjamin, standing up. 'I'm not hungry, anyway.' He stormed out of the room.

'Ben's always getting into fights,' said Catherine.

'Yeah, everyone picks on him,' said James. He laughed and carried on eating.

CHAPTER SIX

Penelope's mother, Margaret, had been opposed to her relationship with David. She thought Penelope far too young to be getting so serious with a man, and she told Cara that David reminded her too much of Benjamin.

'He's already started telling her what she can and cannot do,' Margaret confided one evening, as she, Cara, and Billy were watching television together. David and Penelope had left for a night out at the cinema. 'That's how Ben started, then he tried to control everything I did,' she added.

'He loves Penny, it's plain to see. He only wants what's best for her,' argued Billy.

'He told her to take off her make-up and she did,' said Margaret. 'Am I the only one who thinks that's wrong?' She looked at Cara as she spoke, as if seeking an ally now that Billy had made his opinion known.

'She was wearing quite a lot of make-up, dear,' replied Cara gently.

'She only wanted to look nice.' Margaret's green eyes welled with tears. 'She was so happy with her make-up before he came round. She showed it to me,' she said in a shaky voice.

'Don't upset yourself, Maggie,' said Billy. 'They're only young. He doesn't mean any harm.'

'But have you noticed how he never talks about himself? They've been seeing each other for a couple of months and we haven't met his family yet.'

'Well, we know his family don't live locally, so it's not surprising we haven't met them yet,' said Cara.

'Yes.' Billy nodded his agreement.

'I don't like him, there's something not quite right.' Margaret shook her head.

Cara and Billy didn't read anything deep into David's behaviour. If he came across as a little reticent at times he was probably just shy, they reasoned. After all, he was young and they'd only recently met him. They were not analysing anything. The more Margaret criticised him, the more they defended him, attempting to convince her that not all men were the same as Benjamin. Their words were not getting through, however. Margaret could not be swayed.

Penelope left home and moved in with David not long after they'd first started dating, much against her mother's wishes. Cara remembered

Margaret saying he had "stolen her away".

Margaret would use every opportunity when speaking to her daughter to tell her she should leave him.

That Christmas, when the whole family were gathered at Cara and Billy's house, seated around the kitchen table for dinner, Penelope and David announced they were planning to marry.

Margaret, who had by then regained her ability to walk, rose from her chair, red-faced, and said: 'Over my dead body!' With that, she left the room.

Penelope felt embarrassed and tried to talk to her mother about it, but Margaret refused to discuss it. She would only say, 'If you marry him, I'll never speak to you again.'

Over the next few months, as the wedding arrangements were being made, Margaret's attitude caused great tension in the house. She would ignore David and Penelope when they came to visit, and she pleaded with Cara and Billy to stop the wedding.

Cara last saw Margaret the night before Penelope's wedding. She had not seen her for most of the day, being busy with the preparations. At about nine o'clock, she knocked on Margaret's bedroom door.

'Maggie, are you in there?'

Cara listened at the door, sure she'd heard a shuffling noise and the sound of Margaret blowing her nose. She opened the door slowly and saw her standing next to the bed, packing clothes into a suitcase.

'Maggie? What are you doing?'

She turned to face Cara; her eyes were red and puffy from crying. 'I'm leaving. I have to go.'

'Go where?'

'I'm taking Jemima and we're going to Jersey to my parents' house for a while, and then... Who knows?' Margaret resumed packing.

'But you can't leave, not now.'

'You've made it more than clear that I've outstayed my welcome.'

'That's not true!' said Cara. 'I want you to stay here.'

'Please, don't try to pretend you care,' sneered Margaret, twisting around to face her.

Cara placed a hand over her heart. She knew Margaret opposed Penelope's marriage plans, but she hadn't complained in the past few days. Cara had dared to hope she'd finally accepted, albeit reluctantly, that the marriage would go ahead with or without her approval.

'Y-you are going to the wedding, aren't you?'

'Of course I'm not!' snapped Margaret, turning back to zip up her suitcase. 'That's the reason I'm leaving... As if you didn't already know.'

'But Penny will be devastated if you're not there!' Cara put a hand on Margaret's arm.

'She knows I won't be there. I won't watch her throw her life away.'

'But... But you're her mother; you have to be there! She doesn't have a father to give her away. Stay for the wedding at least. If you still want to leave afterwards, I won't stop you.'

Margaret picked up her suitcase and placed it on the floor at her feet before facing Cara, arms folded. 'If I go, it will be like saying I'm giving her my blessing, and she'll blame me when it all goes wrong.'

'How are you so sure it will go wrong? Can't you give David a chance? You've never tried to get to know him; he's not that bad—'

'I've made up my mind.' Margaret picked up her suitcase.

'Wait!' Cara held out a hand to stop her. 'This is your eldest child and it's one of the most important days of her—'

'Maybe this will make her think twice,' said Margaret, talking over Cara. 'She knows where I'm going. I've told her she can come and stay with me when she sees sense and leaves him, but as long as she's with him I've washed my hands of her.'

'That's a bit harsh, isn't it? Do you want her to think that you don't love her? She'll never forgive you for not going to the wedding. She'll hate you.'

'Perhaps.' Margaret looked thoughtful. 'But I'd rather she hates me for not going to the wedding than hate me for letting David Truman ruin her life.'

'But Maggie, you won't stop her getting married by not attending. She'll still marry him. You know how much Penny loves David.'

'What about me?' Margaret's shoulders dropped. Sitting on the bed, she placed the suitcase next to her feet and blinked away a tear. 'Doesn't she love me?'

'Of course she does.' Cara sat next to her and put an arm around her.

'I've been through so much to make sure my girls have everything they need,' she sobbed. 'This is the gratitude I get.'

'Please don't cry.'

'I expected more from you,' she said, glaring at Cara.

'W-what could I have done?'

'You never backed me up when I talked to Penny about David, about what he's really like. You and Billy... you treat me like a fool.' She stood up.

'That's why the wedding is going ahead.'

'No, you're wrong. The wedding is going ahead because Penny loves David.'

Margaret turned on her heel and practically screamed the words, 'Yes, and I loved Ben once!'

'You can't live someone else's life for them, Maggie. Everyone has to make their own mistakes.'

'And you're willing to sit back and watch it happen?' Margaret flung an arm out in front of her. 'Well, I'm not!' Bending down, she picked up the suitcase again. 'I've booked a taxi for me and Jemima.'

'Please don't go, Maggie.'

Anger coloured Margaret's cheeks, and tears fell that she did not bother to wipe away. 'I'm sorry it had to end this way. I used to think of you and Billy as my second set of parents, but now I feel so betrayed. You could have helped me to stop this wedding and save my little girl, but you didn't even try.' With that, she departed.

Cara felt torn in two. She hated to see Margaret leave this way, but how could she destroy Penelope's wedding day? As much as she loved Margaret, she couldn't leave Penelope with no one to support her.

Cara wrote to Margaret a couple of months after the wedding, hopeful that by then she would have thought everything over and forgiven her. The letter came back in the post a few days later, marked: "Return to sender".

CHAPTER SEVEN

Cara turned up the volume of the television to smother the usual noises coming from downstairs. She watched the news: news of wars in faraway countries, news of terrorism and murders and deaths. She hated the news. When it finished there was an advertisement for a programme that would be televised in a couple of weeks. The details of the programme didn't interest her, but what caught her attention was the date. *Is it that time of year already?* Tenth of June: a date she could never forget.

On the tenth of June 1992, ten years earlier, she had still been quite mobile. While she was doing some weeding in her back garden, the front doorbell rang.

It was a few minutes after six o'clock in the evening: the time Billy usually arrived home from work. As Cara approached the door, she wondered whether he had forgotten his keys.

'Mrs Edwards?' There were two police officers at the door, a male and a female.

'Um... Y-yes,' she stammered.

'May we come inside?' asked the policewoman.

'Y-yes, of course.' Cara took off her gardening gloves and gestured for them to enter.

They walked into the front room.

'Please sit down, Mrs Edwards,' said the policeman. He removed his hat and sat on the sofa.

Cara trembled. Her mind recollected television programmes where things like this happened. Someone must have died, *she thought to herself.* Please let Billy be okay, *she prayed.*

'Are you the wife of William Patrick Edwards?' asked the kind-looking policewoman, as Cara seated herself on a chair.

'Yes. Billy. What's happened to Billy?' She stood up quickly.

'Please, don't upset yourself, Mrs Edwards,' said the policeman, standing up and approaching her. He put his hand on her shoulder. 'Please, sit down.'

She did as she was told.

'Has he been in an accident?' He drives too fast. I'm always telling him he drives too fast...

'Yes, I'm afraid he has. His car collided with another vehicle,' explained the policewoman. 'We'll take you to the hospital so you can see him. He's had to have some surgery. It was quite a serious accident.'

The policewoman started to relay the details of the incident, but Cara had tuned out, not wanting to acknowledge that this was actually happening.

As the policewoman ushered her into the police car, Cara remained silent. Her mind raced with fearful imagery of what could have happened.

She recalled the conversation she'd had with Billy that morning: 'Can you buy some milk on the way home?'

'Yes, dear,' he'd replied. 'See you later.'

He had kissed her as he did every day before he left for work.

Had he perhaps made a detour to buy the milk on his way home? Was that the reason he'd ended up in an accident?

The policewoman, who had by now introduced herself to Cara as WPC Jenny Holmes, accompanied her into the hospital building. They entered through the glass double-doors at the front, labelled in large red writing: "Accident and Emergency".

As they neared the reception desk, Cara trembled.

Jenny asked the woman behind the desk for directions to Billy's ward.

Cara looked at the receptionist, a middle-aged woman with greying blonde hair that had been tightly set with rollers. The woman's hair reminded her of a judge's wig and this temporarily distracted Cara from her worries.

'It's along the corridor, then to the left,' said the woman. 'Take the lift to the third floor. There'll be someone on the third floor who can direct you to ward three-C.'

Cara could not take in the directions. Words sounded as incomprehensible as a foreign language.

Jenny's deep-set grey eyes regarded her sympathetically; she seemed to realise that Cara would have difficulty locating Billy's ward on her own.

Jenny took her by the arm. Cara surmised she was perhaps the same age as her daughter, Catherine, though there were a few lines at the corners of her eyes and some speckles of grey dusting her mahogany-brown hair. Jenny's demeanour gave the impression that she kept her emotions in check, her poker face not giving anything away: even when she smiled, Cara sensed a distance between them. She felt sorry for the young girl; it could not be easy doing a job like hers.

The large building reminded Cara of a maze. With endless corridors all painted white and grey, she found it impossible to tell one from the other.

'Here we are, Mrs Edwards,' said Jenny as they exited the lift on the third floor. 'I'll have to leave you now. You just have to go to that reception desk there and ask for ward three-C.' She pointed to a desk that was labelled "Information".

41

'Ward three-C,' repeated Cara, in a whisper. Peering at the grey walls, she turned to the WPC and said, 'Yes, dear. I'll be fine. Thank you for bringing me this far. I'm sure I would have got lost without you.'

'You'll be fine from here on your own,' said Jenny stiffly. 'Don't worry. I hope your husband is all right.'

'Thank you, dear.' Cara watched Jenny walk back into the lift.

Taking a deep breath, she forced herself to approach the desk that Jenny had pointed to.

The tall man at the information desk greeted her. He appeared to be of African origin. The man wore a nurses' white coat, with a silver name badge. Cara couldn't make out the name on the badge as she wasn't wearing her reading glasses.

'Hello, madam, can I help you?'

She was squinting, trying to read his name: wanting to be polite and address him by his name. Suddenly that became the most important thing in the world to her; she inwardly scolded herself for not bringing her glasses with her.

'Madam?'

She looked up at him, realising that she had not answered his question. Why was knowing his name so important? The absurdity of her thoughts disturbed her. She knew she could just ask his name. Why not just ask? But somehow that wasn't enough. She wanted to read it. To do that. To do something. Anything. To take her mind off what she was really here for. The fear she felt inside was strangling her perception and making her obsess about the littlest thing.

The man had now emerged from behind the desk. He touched her arm gently. 'Madam, are you all right? Would you like to sit down, perhaps? There are some chairs over here, and I'll get you some water.'

The name badge was closer now. Peter. That was his name. Such a nice name, she mused. An image of her uncle Peter sprang to mind and she recalled the fishing trips she'd been on with him as a child.

'Peter,' she said absent-mindedly.

The man's eyes followed hers to his name badge and he nodded awkwardly. He then took her by the arm more firmly. 'Come with me, madam. I will get you some water and you can take a seat.'

Cara knew all she was doing was delaying. Delaying seeing Billy. She didn't want him to be in hospital. He should be at home. Should have bought the milk and gone home. Why did I ask him to get milk? If only Jenny had stayed longer.

Closing her eyes, Cara took a deep breath and said, 'I'm fine, really, I'm *here to see my husband, Billy... er... William Edwards. He's in ward three-C.'*

The man let go of her arm. 'Okay, I'll just check the records.'

He walked away, glancing at her over his shoulder with a friendly smile. Once behind the desk, he studied a sheet of paper. When he looked at her again, his expression had changed from a smile to a frown. 'Mr Edwards has been moved to ward ten. I'll ask the nurse to take you to the right ward. Please take a seat.' He pointed to a trio of orange plastic chairs lined up against the wall.

In a daze, she walked over to the chairs, not wanting to sit, wishing she had company.

Shortly, a nurse appeared. 'Hello, Mrs Edwards,' said the petite, dark-skinned woman. 'I'll take you to see the doctor who operated on your husband.'

Once more, Cara was led along the grey and white corridors.

Soon they arrived at a door labelled "Ward 10 – Intensive Care".

The nurse led her by the arm into a small room. A large green rubber plant sat in the far corner, and a few grey plastic chairs were scattered around a grey plastic table.

'Please take a seat, I'll call the doctor,' said the nurse, turning the lights on as she left the room. Daylight was fading quickly outside.

Cara sat on one of the chairs, wrestling with her anxiety.

'Mrs Edwards,' said a deep voice.

Cara turned her head to see an ashen-faced young man wearing a surgeons' white coat walk into the room. His hair was brown, and thinning slightly on top. In his hands were a few sheets of paper. 'Please remain seated,' he said as she tried to stand up to greet him. He sat opposite her on one of the plastic chairs, his eyes lowered as if he were about to deliver some bad news.

'How is he?' she asked, clenching her teeth, fearing the worst.

'He's in a serious condition. A coma. I would say the next few hours will be critical.'

'I want to see him.' Her voice sounded extremely high-pitched, even to herself.

The doctor nodded his head but didn't stand up—apparently trying to decide whether it would be a good idea for her to see Billy. Eventually, he smiled sympathetically at Cara. 'Follow me,' he said.

She followed and was given protective clothing to wear before entering the sterilised environment.

Walking into a brightly lit room, Cara saw Billy lying on the bed. Even though she'd known he was in a hospital room, it still came as a shock to her that he was lying there, not moving, with an oxygen mask partially covering his face. For the tenth time that day she prayed this was some sort of dream and that she would wake up.

The nurse she had met earlier was inspecting one of the machines next to Billy's bed.

'Is there anyone else we should notify?' asked the doctor.

'I'm sorry?' Cara said, her mind blank.

'Should we notify anyone else about the accident?'

'Yes, yes,' she said. 'Our children.'

'Nurse, please take the details.'

Cara gave James's and Catherine's details to the nurse, then sat next to Billy's bed. He looked peaceful enough. Apart from a couple of scars on his cheeks and forehead she could not really tell that he had sustained any injuries. A sheet covered his entire body.

She listened for a while to the sound of his heartbeat on the electronic machine. The sound comforted her slightly; it meant he was alive.

'Try speaking to him,' said the doctor. 'It can help if they hear a familiar voice. We'll leave you alone.'

She watched him walk out of the room followed by the nurse. A strange fear overwhelmed her when she found herself alone in the room with Billy.

The doctor's words rang in her head: 'It can help if they hear a familiar voice.' *"They", as if Billy were part of some group of people who were different. She felt too distressed to talk.* What do you say to "them"? What do you say to people in comas?

'Billy,' she forced the word out. 'Billy, it's me, Cara.' Her voice broke, and tears formed in her eyes.

Unexpectedly, her mind went back to their first meeting at Stoneleigh when she'd been so frightened and he'd stayed with her until the ambulance arrived. He'd always been there for her ever since; she could not imagine life without him.

If he died now, he'd never know the truth about their meeting. She put a hand to her neck and sighed.

Soon tears were streaming down her cheeks. 'I'm so sorry... I'm so sorry!'

He lay motionless.

'I should have told you, Billy. You deserved to know the truth about me back then.' Should she tell him everything now? Would it make a difference? He was in a coma. Could he even hear her?

'Billy, wake up! Please wake up!' Her despairing cry rang out in the hospital room.

Unzipping her bag with trembling hands, she took out her packet of travel tissues. She wiped her eyes and face, breathing deeply, trying to compose herself.

    'Billy, can you hear me?' she ventured softly.

    There was no movement, nothing to suggest he'd heard her, but maybe...
'Billy, I love you. There's something I have to tell you. I should have told you
this before. This... This accident has made me realise that. I've been so selfish.
I'm sorry.'

    The words poured out. It made it easier that he couldn't respond, so she
could tell the whole story without him interrupting. 'Billy, when we met, you
thought you'd saved my life, but I jumped off the cliff. I didn't fall. I tried to kill
myself because I was in love with a man and found out he was married.' She
stopped, and put a hand in front of her mouth, aware her confession sounded
like a declaration of love for Frederick.

    The sound of Billy's heartbeat on the monitor remained unchanged.
Surely, if he'd heard such news, and understood, his heart rate would have been
racing.

    Watching him lying there, a compulsion to continue swept over her; this
might be her last chance to tell him.

    'Billy, it's possible Ben isn't your son. I didn't know it for sure at the
time, but—'

    A terrifying sound was emitted from the heart monitor. Cara felt faint, the
room becoming a blur of white and red as panic gripped her and she struggled to
breathe. She stood up, gasping, and the long bleeping sound became louder.

    'No!' she screamed. 'No! Billy! Help! Please, someone, help!'

    Stumbling towards the door, she pulled it open. The doctor was just
outside. Several nurses followed him into Billy's room.

    Cara froze. Too afraid to go back inside, she made her way into the
corridor. Please, don't let him die, please... *Her mind screamed. He couldn't*
die now*: not at the moment when she had told him everything. She needed an*
opportunity to explain the facts to him properly.

    I should have waited. I shouldn't have told him now... Maybe he
didn't hear.

    She sat on the bench outside the room, feeling like a criminal waiting for
the jury to reach a decision, already knowing what the verdict would be.

    'Mum!'

    Cara raised her head to see her daughter, Catherine, running along the
corridor towards her.

    'Where's Dad? Is he all right?'

    Unable to expel the sense of remorse, Cara stared blankly.

    'Mum. Is Dad all right? He's not... He's not... I'm not too late, am I?'

'No, no,' Cara assured her daughter, with fear in her heart. She reached out to hug Catherine. 'Thank you for coming.'

The young doctor walked out of Billy's room, visibly disconcerted. 'Mrs Edwards,' he said in a deep, sombre tone, 'please follow me.'

He led the way to the small room where Cara had first met him.

'Please sit down,' he said, pointing to the grey plastic chairs. After closing the door, he sat opposite them. 'Mrs Edwards, I am very sorry. We did all we could, but...'

Cara held her breath.

'Unfortunately, we couldn't revive him.'

'You mean he's d... He's d...' She could not bring herself to say the word.

The young doctor closed his eyes briefly, then said, 'Your husband died a few minutes ago. I'm so sorry.'

Cara and Catherine nodded dumbly.

'They're moving him to another room. You'll have a chance to go and see him, if you wish,' he added.

'Yes,' said Cara, a vacant look in her eyes.

The doctor stood up and approached the door.

'Excuse me, Doctor,' said Cara in a weak voice.

He turned to face her.

'Do you think he heard me when I was speaking to him?'

Catherine put an arm around her.

'Yes, Mrs Edwards. I'm sure he knew you were there.' He smiled and left the room.

'What happened?' asked Catherine, tears rolling down her cheeks. 'How did it happen? He was so healthy.'

'It was a car accident,' Cara whispered. She began to cry again, this time fearing the tears would never stop falling.

'Where's Jamie? Does he know?'

'Yes. Yes, the nurse was going to call him,' replied Cara through sniffles.

'He should be here, Mum! Dad's dead! He should be here!'

'He must be on his way.' Cara wiped her wet cheeks with the back of her hand.

Catherine produced a packet of tissues from her handbag and gave one to Cara, also taking one for herself.

'And Ben,' said Catherine, 'he doesn't know Dad's dead. Ben should be here too! We won't even be able to find him to let him know about the funeral.'

Cara recalled the last thing she had said to Billy. Maybe it had killed

46

him. *She began to shake.*

'Mum. Mum!' said Catherine. 'Everything will be all right, you'll see.'

CHAPTER EIGHT

Penelope sat on the sofa, trembling, holding Andrew in her arms. 'Look what you've done to your son!' she screamed.

David stood in front of her, staring at the boy; she could see the bewilderment screaming out from his eyes. Her conscience said she should forgive him. *It's not his fault... He needs help.*

'It's got to stop,' she said loudly, to smother the unwanted thoughts. Her tears fell onto Andrew's hair.

She always forgave David, every time—even when he caused her to miscarry their baby daughter—but now she felt ashamed... weak. If only she'd walked away *then*, this wouldn't have happened to Andrew.

Her mind became clear. If she stayed with David, she'd be condoning what he'd done. She had been wrong to forgive him in the past, and she could not forgive him now.

'This vicious cycle has got to stop!' she shouted. The television in her grandmother's room upstairs sounded louder than ever. A familiar sense of humiliation stirred within her. Usually, she would try to ignore it and fool herself that her grandmother turned up the volume because she was hard of hearing. Penelope could no longer deny the truth. Today she had come face to face with the reality she'd denied year after year.

David's eyes were glazed over in shock, but she fought the urge to comfort him. He often became upset after being violent, but this was different. He'd hardly moved since hitting Andrew. It was the first time he'd laid a finger on any of the children, and she had to make sure it never happened again.

'I can't go on like this... *We* can't go on like this, Dave.' She stroked Andrew's hair; the same straw-coloured hair as his father's. He had cried himself to sleep, his head on her lap. The tears were still fresh on his face. The red patch on his forehead where the blow had landed was slightly swollen. She touched it gently, worry painting her countenance grey.

'He'll be fine,' said David, suddenly appearing to recover the ability to speak and move. 'He'll have to learn to stand up for himself. You mollycoddle him. Do you wanna turn him into a mummy's boy?'

Carefully lifting Andrew's head from her lap, she settled him on the sofa and raised herself up to her full height. She wiped the blood from her nose where David had hit her before he hit Andrew. 'Get out, Dave,' she said as calmly as she could.

He shook at the sound of her voice, as if startled.

'I'll call the police, and I'll tell them what you did to your son.'

'I didn't do anything—'

48

'Get out!'

'You're a crazy woman, Penny. Don't worry, I'm going, but I'll be back when you've calmed down.' Even as he said this, his eyes were lowered, incomprehension and shame written in the lines etched into his brow.

He walked towards the living room door.

'If you come back, the police will be here waiting for you,' she warned.

He mumbled a few words to himself as he walked away.

She heard the front door slam shut and fought the little voice telling her that perhaps this would change him.

Penelope looked again at Andrew asleep on the sofa: her baby. Tonight's events echoed what had happened the night her father fled the family home.

David had arrived home from work late and became angry because his food was cold and because Penelope and the children had already eaten. He started pushing her. As usual.

Andrew came downstairs for a glass of water, walking into the room at the precise moment that David had punched her in the face. 'Daddy!' he'd shouted. 'Leave Mummy alone!'

Penelope felt a strange mix of emotions then: relief that Andrew had entered the room because she took it for granted that the beating would stop—David was usually calm around the children—but at the same time, horror that Andrew had witnessed his father's violence.

As she fell backwards onto the sofa, her nose bleeding from the blow, an image came to mind: that of her mother lying at the bottom of the stairs, her guilty-looking father standing over her.

David had approached Andrew. 'What did you say, son?'

'Stop hitting Mummy.' Tears fell down the child's face as he beseeched his father.

'I hit Mummy because she did a bad thing. It's okay to hit someone if they're bad, isn't it, son?'

Penelope, having by then regained her balance, had walked over to David. He'd punched her in the stomach. 'Can't you see I'm talking to my son?'

Andrew reached out then and tugged at David's arm: 'Stop it!' he sobbed.

Then, in an apparent knee-jerk reaction, David swiped out and caught Andrew on the brow with the back of his hand.

Andrew ran over to Penelope who was sitting on the sofa, reeling from the pain of the punches she'd sustained, one hand holding a tissue over her nose to stop the bleeding.

⧗

Penelope knew she'd have to act quickly if she wanted to get away. David was stunned enough to back off for a while. What he did to Andrew would have sparked his deepest fear: that he would *become* his parents.

After running upstairs, Penelope found her handbag, and opening the inside zip, she saw it: the card the policewoman had given her last month when the neighbours called the police for the third time in two weeks after hearing yet another row. She'd told the policewoman she didn't need help but had kept the card, unable to bring herself to throw it away.

As she dialled the number on the card, her hand shook. She trembled as she listened to the ringing tone buzzing in her ears.

'Hensley Police, can I help you?' The woman's voice with a soft Scottish accent sounded friendly enough, yet Penelope still considered hanging up the phone.

'Um...' she began. 'I need to speak to someone about...' She hesitated, doubting herself. Would anyone even take her seriously? So what if David hit her now and then? Maybe she deserved it. But recalling the fear in Andrew's eyes, his face wet with tears, she forced herself to continue: 'Domestic violence.'

'Hold on, I'll put you through to someone,' said the kind-sounding Scottish woman.

Penelope sat on the edge of her bed, the phone in her right hand, her left hand still holding the card.

'Hello, Lindsay Brown speaking.' This woman had a London accent and the tone of her voice was louder than the Scottish woman's. 'How can I help you?'

Penelope clenched her jaw, wanting to speak to the other woman instead; it would have been easier. This voice did not hold much compassion, as far as she could tell. 'Um... I spoke to a policewoman, um... WPC Perkins. She gave me this number,' said Penelope, ignoring the inner voice telling her to stop being silly, to put down the phone.

'Okay,' said Lindsay. 'Can I take your name for our records, please?'

'Penelope Truman.'

'Do you live locally, Ms Truman?'

'Yes, in Furley Avenue.'

'That's just behind the park, isn't it?'

'Yes, that's right.'

'I used to go to school around there,' said Lindsay. 'But that's enough about me. How can we help you, Penelope? You don't mind me calling you Penelope, do you?'

'No... that's fine.'

'So, I understand you're calling about a domestic violence incident, is that correct?'

'Yes.'

'Please tell me, in your own time, what happened.'

'My husband... he's violent... aggressive.' She felt an urge to end the call again, didn't want to be telling this stranger about her personal life, even worse over the phone. Paranoia took hold. Negative thoughts swam through her mind. She couldn't see this policewoman's face, couldn't see her reactions. Would she be rolling her eyes at the story, inwardly blaming her for letting David behave that way? After all, she was just another faceless domestic violence victim to Lindsay.

'Go on, Penelope,' urged the policewoman.

Penelope convinced herself more each minute that she was being foolish. *Lindsay would probably have left Dave years ago, not put up with all the beatings.* Her hand shook and she lowered the telephone handset, but then she remembered Andrew's tears. She knew she had to disregard this doubt and go on for his sake. 'I don't know what he'll do next.'

'Right. Where is your husband now? Are you in immediate danger?'

'I don't know. He's gone out. He usually disappears for a while after he's—' She stopped.

'Did he hit you before he went out?'

'Y-yes.'

'And has this happened before?'

'Yes, but today... I've never seen him like he was today: s-s-so wild.' She closed her eyes. 'He hit our son.'

'How old is your son?'

'Six.'

'Please elaborate. You say he hit him. Tell me about that.'

'He... He caught his forehead with the back of his hand. It's swollen.'

'When you say he caught his forehead, was it a deliberate action?'

'I'm not sure. It happened so quickly. I think he reacted to our son pulling at him; our son had seen him hit me and was trying to stop him. He wouldn't usually deliberately hurt the boys.' Penelope winced. There it was again, that part of her that was forever defending David.

'How many children do you have?' asked Lindsay.

'Two boys.'

'How old are they?'

'Six and eight.'

'Has your husband ever hit any of the children before?'

'No, it's always only me. He usually stops if the boys come in, but tonight...'

'Okay, Penelope. Have you ever taken any legal action against your husband for domestic violence—for example, an injunction?'

'No.'

'We can put you in touch with a solicitor in your area, and they can help you to get a court order to keep him away from you and the boys.'

'I can't do that! He'll go mad. He'll kill me.'

'He doesn't need to know. You can go to court tomorrow morning and get the order. As soon as it's served on him you'll be safe. If he comes within a few yards of you, you can take him to court.'

'But I don't know where he is. How can I have an order served on him? What about if he comes back tonight? The policewoman I spoke to before mentioned a women's refuge. I'd prefer to just leave. I don't want to get a court order. I don't want to see him again. I want to get me and the kids out of here, out of danger. It's gone on for too long. Dave's not normal. He won't care about a court order.' The words spilled out at a furious rate as Penelope felt hope dissolving into nothing.

'Don't worry, Penelope, don't upset yourself; we're here to help. We'll do everything we can to make sure you're safe. I need to assess your situation because there are so many types of domestic violence, some more serious than others.'

Penelope started to cry.

'Penelope, I need to ask you some questions to see if you qualify for immediate help. The number of rooms in the refuges, and other temporary accommodation, is limited.'

Penelope took a tissue from the box on the bedside cabinet and dried her tears.

'How many times have you had to call the police in the last month?' asked Lindsay.

'I don't usually call. The neighbours have called a few times this month.' What would Lindsay think about that? Penelope was cursing herself for not seeking help sooner, for letting David get away with all of the abusive behaviour. Seeing him hit Andrew had woken up a part of her brain that had been shut down, it seemed. She felt so removed from her former self and in disbelief that she had lived so passively for so long.

'And you haven't sought any help other than this phone call?'

She shook at the sound of Lindsay's voice. Hope was fading fast, 'No. Does that mean you can't help me?' Her fingers were tightly crossed —an old superstitious habit she had in times of despair. She remembered keeping her fingers crossed all night when her mother was in hospital after her father left home. She'd kept them crossed for so long that in the morning they were numb.

'Not necessarily,' said Lindsay.

Penelope let out a sigh.

'Why did you decide to call today?' asked Lindsay.

'I've already told you. Dave's out of control.' As she said his name, she could picture his cold dark eyes, the colour of night, boring deep into her soul.

'Dave? That's your husband?'

'Yes. David Truman. He hit our son. I'm scared he'll do it again. You have to help me. I've never been so frightened, and I'm sure that if my son hadn't walked into the room tonight, he would have killed me.'

'Okay, Penelope, you can come to the police station tonight for an interview with an officer in our domestic violence unit. If your case is as serious as you've outlined, we'll help you to be placed in a refuge or other temporary accommodation until you can organise some legal assistance.'

'Thank you.' Penelope finally allowed herself to uncross her fingers. She'd taken the first step towards the lifeline she had been praying for and wished she'd made this move earlier. Now these people were going to help her get away from all the fear.

Reality jolted her from this brief respite when she heard a burst of music coming from the television in Cara's room. How could she leave? Who would take care of her grandmother?

'Can you make your own way to the station, or do you need me to send someone to collect you?' asked Lindsay.

'I'll drive to the station,' she said, still worrying about what she was going to do about Cara.

CHAPTER NINE

'Aunty Cathy, hello, it's me, Penny.' Her hand trembled as she held the phone.

'Penny, hi, how's Mum? I've been meaning to come and visit but I've been so busy.'

'Aunty, I need your help.'

'Penny? Are you all right? You sound upset.'

'I can't go into it right now, but I'm leaving Dave.'

'Why? I mean—'

'I don't want to talk about it on the phone.'

Catherine remembered seeing Penelope and David a few weeks ago at Carl's eighth birthday party. They appeared happy: playing with the children and chatting with their friends. 'Okay, look, I'll come and see you soon and—'

'We don't have time for that,' snapped Penelope.

'Time? What do you mean? You're not making sense.'

'I'm leaving tonight, and I need you to come and take Nan to stay with you.'

'Er... I—'

'Please Aunty, don't ask any questions, just help me.'

'I'd love to help, but we don't have enough room.'

'Then make room,' Penelope said, uncharacteristically forceful.

'Penny, I can tell you're under some pressure, but we can't have Mum here. I... Tom and I, we work such long hours.' Catherine rolled her eyes, hating the lies.

Tom was sitting in the kitchen, in the same position he'd been in for most of the day. He suffered from depression and took medication to help his mood swings. Catherine knew that if there was no alternative, she could make room for her mother on a temporary basis, but how could she bring her here to see the way they lived their lives these days? She and Tom hardly spoke to each other, and she'd had to work extra shifts to cover the mortgage payments since he lost his job.

'I'm not asking you, I'm telling you,' grumbled Penelope. 'I'll be gone tonight, and someone has to look after Nan. She's your mum, for God's sake! We'll meet you at forty Furley Avenue in an hour.'

'But you live at number forty-three, don't you?'

'I'll explain it all to you later. Be there in an hour, or earlier if you can.'

'Number forty, you say?' She found a pen lying next to the telephone and wrote the address on a scrap of paper.

'Yes.'

'Okay, Penny, I'll think of something.'

Catherine placed a hand over her mouth when she hung up the phone. She had worked so hard at hiding her own problems from the rest of the family. If her mother came to stay, it would be virtually impossible to prevent her finding out about Tom's depression.

She picked up the phone again and dialled her brother's telephone number. His wife, Emily, answered.

'Hi, Em, it's Cat. It's been ages since we talked. How are you?' she asked, trying to bridge the conversation.

'I'm fine. Look, I'm sorry, Cat, but you've caught me at a bad time; I'm just about to go out.'

'It's Jamie I wanted a word with actually. I'm after a favour. Do you think you and Jamie could let Mum stay with you for a while?'

'Have you spoken to him recently?' asked Emily.

'No, not for a couple of weeks.'

'You should speak to him,' she said without further explanation.

'Is he around?'

'No, try his mobile.'

'Okay, but—'

'Bye, Cat.'

Catherine heard the humming of the phone line. Frustrated, she looked at her watch, aware time was running out; soon she would have to leave to collect her mother. Scanning the room, she wondered how she could rearrange everything, if her mother absolutely had to stay with them, to ensure Tom had as little contact with her as possible. She dialled James's mobile number.

'Jamie?'

'Hi, Cat.'

'Listen, would you and Emily be able to look after Mum for a while? Penny and David are going through some sort of relationship crisis.'

'What sort of crisis?'

'I don't know exactly, but it sounds serious. Penny's leaving home tonight, and she needs someone to take Mum.'

'Why can't *you*?' he asked.

'Where would I put her? We've only got one bedroom. Your house is big enough. You could put her in William's bedroom. He could sleep on the sofa for a while; it won't be for ever. I'm sure Penny and David will sort out whatever the problem is, and—'

'Sorry, I can't help.'

'You can be so selfish—'

'I don't even live at the house. I'm staying with a friend.'

'What?'

'I'm getting divorced.'

Catherine's mouth fell open. 'I knew you and Emily were going through a bad patch, but—'

'Well, now we're going through a divorce. And I might be taking this job in South Africa I told you about. If I do, I'm leaving the country in a few weeks. I'm going over there next week for a trial period.'

There was a melancholy tone to his voice. He was clearly burdened enough, and she didn't want to put pressure on him. 'What can we do about Mum?' she asked, thinking aloud.

'I don't know. Have you asked Aunty Glor if she can stay with her? She's been living all alone in that big house for years. She'd probably be glad of the company, even if she's never really got on with Mum.'

'But Mum and Aunty Glor haven't spoken to each other for... it must be at least twenty years.'

'Have you got any better ideas?'

'Absolutely not!' Gloria's shrill voice said from the other end of the telephone line. 'I won't have that woman in this house!'

'Aunty, please do this for me. We're desperate,' Catherine pleaded.

'There's nothing more to say,' said Gloria. 'It's not my problem.'

'Aunty, how old are you? Because, I have a five-year-old daughter who's more mature than you. This is your sister we're talking about. What if it were you?'

'She'd tell you the same. Anyway, I can look after myself, thank you very much.'

'That's cruel. I never understood why you and Mum couldn't make up your differences, but I'm starting to see you're probably the reason.'

'Huh! That's unfair,' retorted Gloria.

'Whatever happened between you was years ago, and Mum's upset you no longer talk.' Catherine knew that was untrue, but she prayed it would help to change her aunt's mind.

'Huh! I don't believe that for a minute. It's not a good idea, Catherine dear. It's for the best. Your mother and I have never been able to see eye to eye. We're as different as chalk and cheese. I can't see how that is ever going to change. I'm sorry.'

'Aunty, I'm not asking you to become best friends. Just let her stay with you until Penny and David sort out their problems.'

'No, I'm afraid I can't do that.'

'Well, tough.' Catherine sighed, no longer in the mood to be polite. 'I'm bringing her to your house tomorrow.' She hung up before Gloria could respond, astounded at how her mother's only sister could refuse to help her in a time of need. What could have happened to cause such animosity? *It's like one of them murdered someone,* she mused. Shuddering, she pushed the thought away.

Tom came out of the kitchen, holding a mug. His eyes were distant.

Catherine wondered whether he'd taken his antidepressants today. His memory had deteriorated recently and he often forgot to do things. His matted hair, which had long since grown out of any style, hadn't been washed in weeks; instead of the usual strawberry-blond colour, it was a horrible dirty-brown. The stubble on his face resembled not so much a beard as a greying shadow. In the past he'd always been so clean-shaven, buying the latest razors and aftershaves. She noticed a large stain on the knee of his grey jogging pants and realised he'd been wearing the same pair for days. He didn't even bother to change his clothes when he went to bed these days.

As he walked towards her, Catherine's eyes were drawn to their wedding photograph sitting on the mantelpiece behind him. His eyes had been so full of life and hope then, but now there were deep hollows and dark rings around them. He didn't really look like himself anymore.

She stared at the picture with longing in her heart: she wanted the old Tom back. How had things gone so wrong? She made up her mind to speak to his doctor again.

'Tom?' she said.

'What?' He scowled and then walked over to the sofa, turning his back on her.

'I need you to watch the children. I'm going to see Mum.'

'Whatever,' he said, sitting on the sofa in front of the television. The screen was blank yet he sat there and stared at it. It had become a habit recently.

'Shall I switch the TV on?' she offered, picking up the remote control.

He grabbed it from her. 'I can switch it on if I want to,' he blurted.

She felt torn, not sure if leaving the children with Tom was the right thing to do, but worried about how stressed Penelope had sounded on the phone.

Taking her handbag from the hook on the door, she made her way out of the flat.

CHAPTER TEN

Penelope knocked on Cara's bedroom door at just after eight o'clock.

'Hello, Penny.' Cara smiled, feeling happy to see her granddaughter. It was rare for Penelope to visit her at this time in the evening.

Cara lowered the volume on the television.

'I know it's a bit late, Nan, but Brenda from across the road has asked us over for a cup of tea. You remember Brenda, don't you? We haven't seen her for ages.' Penelope shifted her stance from foot to foot as she spoke, in a nervous manner.

Cara wondered why she hadn't mentioned the visit earlier. Wrinkling her brow, she peered at her granddaughter. 'Is everything all right, dear?'

'Yes, of course.' Penelope laughed, but the laughter was out of place and this heightened Cara's concern. 'I just thought it would be nice for a change, to get out of the house.'

Penelope walked over to the window and took a quick peek outside.

'The boys are quiet; are they asleep?' asked Cara.

'No, they're playing in their room.'

'Are you sure you're all right?'

'Of course I am.' Penelope laughed again, but it sounded forced. She opened Cara's wardrobe and took out a dress. 'Is this one okay for you to wear?' she asked, holding it up in front of her.

'Er... yes, dear.'

'Good.' Penelope placed the dress on the bed. 'Can you manage to get ready on your own, while I see to the boys?'

'Yes, of course, Penny.' Cara frowned. 'Where's David? Is he downstairs?'

'Um...' A momentary hesitation. 'No, he's at work.'

'This late in the evening?'

'Yes, well, his job is very demanding. You might have noticed he's not here half the time.' Penelope fiddled with her wedding ring as she spoke.

'I thought I heard him come home earlier.'

'He did, but he's gone back to work,' Penelope murmured, walking towards the door. 'I'll just go and get the boys ready, then we'll go.'

As Cara watched her leave the room, she could not help thinking of Margaret. Penelope's demeanour reminded her of Margaret whenever she'd turned up late at night, after yet another row with Benjamin, asking Cara and Billy if she could stay with them. Her eyes had that same faraway look, and she appeared terribly nervous.

⧗

Penelope returned to the bedroom after a few minutes. 'Are you ready to go, Nan?'

'Er... yes, okay.'

Walking over to the corner of the room, Penelope started setting up the wheelchair. 'I'm going to be going away.' She had her back to Cara as she spoke. 'I don't know how long for. A friend of mine has booked a holiday and has no one to go with her. She'd been planning to go with her boyfriend but they've split up.'

'Oh, that's a shame.'

'So I'm having to arrange for you to stay with someone else while I'm away.' Penelope glanced over her shoulder at her grandmother.

'But what about the boys, won't they have to miss school? And what about David? Is he going too?'

'I'm taking the boys,' Penelope said.

'So where am I going?' asked Cara.

'Aunty Cathy's meeting us at Brenda's.'

'What? Tonight? But it's the anniversary of Billy's death next Sunday,' said Cara, 'are we still going to visit the grave together?'

Penelope did not respond immediately.

When she turned around, Cara saw her eyes were red and wet with tears. 'Penny! What's wrong?'

'Nothing.'

'Please, come and sit down and tell me. What is it? Is it David or the boys? What's happened?'

'Nothing, Nan.' She walked quickly towards the bedroom door and left the room.

Cara cursed her legs when she heard Penelope going downstairs, wishing she could get out of bed and follow. She could feel her temperature rise as she became more and more anxious. Without thinking, she heard herself scream, 'Penny!' Her voice had a will of its own. There was no reply.

She continued to shout her granddaughter's name, not aware of how many times, but eventually she felt her strength wane. She took deep breaths in an attempt to calm herself.

Listening intently for any movement in the house, she heard a shuffling sound coming from Penelope's bedroom.

Cara picked up the bell from the bedside cabinet—the bell she

59

used when she needed to call Penelope. She rang it once and waited. After ringing it a second time, there was still no response. About to ring it a third time, she saw the bedroom door open slightly.

Penelope walked into the room.

'Nan... I lied earlier. Sorry.' She caught Cara's eye, then lowered her gaze. 'I'm not going on holiday. I'm leaving for good.'

Cara noticed that her granddaughter's jaw hardly moved as she spoke, and she appeared to be having difficulty getting the words out. She looked so small and scared standing by the bedroom door; like a child.

Cara was reminded of the twelve-year-old Penelope who had moved in with her; she had the same lost look in her eyes. Cara felt a desire to reach out and take her in her arms.

'I'm leaving Dave,' stated Penelope. 'I'm taking the boys. We can't stay here anymore, Nan. I'm sorry.'

'Wh-what's happened?' Cara feared she already knew the answer.

'It's Dave... He's dangerous.'

'But—'

'We're leaving. The police are going to help me. I'm going to find somewhere safe for me and the kids.'

All of Cara's suspicions were confirmed. She opened her mouth to speak but could find no words.

'I'm sorry, I wish I could take you with me, but it wouldn't be fair.' Penelope's arms hung limply, her eyes threatening to spill the silent tears they held. 'Aunty Cathy's coming to collect you.'

Penelope hung her head, then looked up at Cara. 'I should explain.' Closing her eyes, she continued, 'Dave left the house after h-he punched me.' She lifted her T-shirt to reveal a red mark, about five or six inches in diameter.

Cara gasped.

'He hits me a lot,' admitted Penelope. 'I didn't tell you before because I didn't want to worry you, but it's gone too far. Tonight he hit Andrew.'

'Dear God. I-is he all right?' Cara placed a hand over her mouth.

'Yes. Thank God. He's never hit the boys before, Nan. That's why I've made my mind up to leave. I can't risk him doing it again. I called the police and they're going to help me get into a women's refuge.' She spoke quickly, and her mood appeared to change from moment to moment; one minute she seemed relieved to be able to finally explain the pain to someone, the next she was straining to keep her composure as if she might crumble and fade away.

Cara, feeling stunned, did not speak as Penelope helped her off the bed, into the wheelchair, and then onto the stairlift.

Once Cara was back in the wheelchair, they left the house behind them, with all its secrets, and headed across the road to number forty, Furley Avenue.

Brenda, a kind, elderly woman, lived alone with three cats, a small dog, and a large aquarium of exotic fish. She kept up to date with the gossip in the street as she made a point of visiting her neighbours regularly, invariably taking with her some home-made cakes. She was quite a large woman and wore brightly-coloured clothes. Her neatly styled hair was the colour of freshly settled snow. Brenda had become quite friendly with Penelope, and when Cara first moved in she'd made a point of getting to know her too. Brenda's visits had been less frequent in recent years. Cara often saw her from the bedroom window, out and about on her daily shopping trips and knocking on various neighbours' doors.

Brenda greeted Cara and Penelope at her front door. 'Please come in,' she said politely, leading the way to the living room.

Penelope pushed the wheelchair into the room and told Andrew and Carl to sit on the sofa.

Tears welled in Cara's eyes.

'I'm going across the road to get your things, Nan; I won't be long. Boys, behave yourselves.' To Brenda, she said, 'I'm going to leave Cara and the boys with you for a while. I have to go and pack our stuff. I won't be long.'

'Right you are, love.'

Penelope hurried out of the door.

'Shall I put the kettle on, Cara, and make us a nice cup of tea?' asked Brenda.

'Not for me, thank you,' Cara replied.

'Well, I'll get some biscuits for the little ones. You'd like that, wouldn't you, boys?' She patted them both on the head, and they smiled at her.

The boys were dressed in identical clothes. Penelope liked to dress them in matching clothes. Whenever she went shopping for the children she bought two of everything. Today they were dressed smartly in their khaki trousers, cream-coloured shirts, and denim jackets.

'Please make yourselves at home,' said the neighbour as she left the room.

Cara surveyed the unfamiliar surroundings. She thought about the times she'd wished and prayed to leave Penelope's house, but she'd wanted to get away before she knew anything for certain so she could fool herself that David and Penelope were happy together. It was too late for that now. She would have to live with this knowledge for ever.

Cara looked at the boys sitting on the sofa. Noticing a bruise on Andrew's forehead, she remembered Penelope telling her that David had hit him.

Her eyes were drawn to the window; Penelope would be back soon with her belongings, and Catherine would arrive shortly to collect her. As she sat waiting, she could hear Brenda in the kitchen singing a joyful tune. Penelope had almost certainly not told the woman the real reason behind why she was leaving Cara and the children with her.

Brenda entered the room carrying a cup of tea and a plate of biscuits.

'They're home-made, of course. I made them fresh today. Chocolate chip. They're delicious, even if I do say so myself.' She smiled and offered a biscuit to Cara.

Cara took one to be polite, even though food was the last thing on her mind.

After giving a biscuit to each of the boys, Brenda sat next to Cara. 'I hear you're leaving Furley Avenue,' she said, as she placed the plate on the table in front of her.

'Yes.'

'That's a shame, I'll miss Penny; she always had time for a chat when I saw her on the street. She's such a sweet girl. You must be proud of her.'

'I am,' said Cara.

'It's for the best, I'm sure,' opined Brenda, dipping a biscuit into her tea. 'I always told her she shouldn't let David control her and break her spirit. She should have left him years ago, really.' She spoke freely even though the boys were sitting and watching her, as though she did not think they could understand.

Andrew got up off the sofa when he saw one of Brenda's cats enter the room. The black and white cat approached him and sniffed his hand as he reached out to stroke it.

'Ooh, he likes you,' said Brenda.

Andrew stroked the cat, a gleeful expression on his face. 'What's its name?' he asked.

'Toby,' said Brenda.

Andrew followed Toby over to the far corner of the room.

Toby jumped up onto the table to get closer to the aquarium and began pawing the glass as if trying to catch the fish.

'Look Carl, fishes,' said Andrew, pointing at the exotic multicoloured fish swimming in the glass tank.

Carl followed his brother.

'I'm so pleased she's going now, so the boys will be safe,' said Brenda, turning to Cara. 'I told her to leave him years ago, not long before you moved in. The boys were only babies. I saw an ambulance turn up in the middle of the night. I knew she was pregnant, but the baby wasn't due for a few more months.'

Cara frowned. Penelope had not, to her knowledge, been pregnant again after Andrew. Perhaps Brenda was referring to when she had been expecting Andrew.

'I went to see Penny after she came out of hospital and she told me the terrible news,' continued Brenda, dipping her biscuit into her tea as she spoke. 'I told her a man who hits his wife has a serious problem and she should be careful. She wouldn't listen to me. Said she loved him. I just knew it would end like this.' She raised her eyebrows. 'I mean, what man hits his wife? Especially his pregnant wife.'

Cara listened but was still sure Brenda must have got the story confused.

'Of course, I tried to look out for her after that,' said Brenda. 'I know her parents live abroad. I visited whenever I could, to make sure she was all right. You might remember I used to visit often?'

Cara nodded.

'Well, I stopped going because I got the feeling I wasn't welcome. I thought she'd be okay, though, because you were there. I still used to speak to her in the street, to try to get an idea of her state of mind. She didn't want to talk about any of it, though. I think losing the child really hurt her; she withdrew into herself. Especially as the scan showed it would have been a little girl. Can't say I've seen her smile much since then.' Brenda knitted her brow and sipped her tea.

Cara dropped the biscuit she was holding onto the carpet then looked at Brenda, eyes wide.

Brenda's gaze rested on the biscuit that had fallen onto the floor. She touched Cara's hand gently noticing her expression. 'Don't worry, dear, it's only a biscuit. I'll get a dustpan and brush to clear away the crumbs.' Checking the time on her watch, she said, 'I must be getting on with my chores, anyway. I've got all the family coming over tomorrow for lunch. So much to do, so little time.'

Cara watched Brenda float out of the room. Inwardly, she was trying in vain to erase from her mind what she had just been told. She hoped Andrew and Carl had been too busy counting the fish in the aquarium to have heard the conversation.

Only now was Cara beginning to appreciate the extent of the violence and pain her granddaughter had suffered at David's hands.

Penelope had been gone for about ten minutes. Cara recalled her frightened face and the bruise on her body.

As the minutes slipped by, she became increasingly anxious for Penelope's safety. Her imagination soon started to play tricks on her: every man who walked along the street could be David. She felt her palms perspiring.

A car pulled up outside the house. Cara breathed a sigh of relief when she saw Catherine emerge from the vehicle. Then she saw Penelope walking out of her front door carrying a large green suitcase. She watched as the two women hugged each other and stood talking for a short while. From the look on Catherine's face, Penelope was telling her about what David had done. Penelope placed the suitcase in Catherine's car and they both approached Brenda's house.

Once inside, Penelope sat on the sofa next to Cara. She touched Cara's cheek.

Cara instinctively reached up and held her granddaughter's hand.

'I'll miss you, Nan. The boys will miss you too. As soon as all the legal stuff has been sorted out and we're sure Dave can't hurt us, I'll be in touch, I promise.'

'How long will that take?'

Penelope shrugged. 'I don't know, Nan. A few months, maybe. A year or so.'

'There must be another way,' Cara spoke as if in a trance.

'There's no other way,' Penelope said sadly, her face hollow, eyes darker than ever as if all hope had been extinguished.

There was so much Cara wanted to say, but the words stuck in her throat. Nothing she could say would change the past.

'I'm so sorry, Nan, but you'll be all right, I've made sure of that.' Penelope stood up.

Cara kept hold of her hand, not wanting to let go. 'I love you, Penny,' she said.

'I know. Goodbye, Nan.' Her hand slipped out of Cara's.

'Goodbye, dear. Take care.'

'Boys, say goodbye to Nana, and come on.'

Andrew and Carl both kissed Cara and followed Penelope out of the door.

The sound of the door closing echoed in Cara's head, and tears fell from her eyes in silent protest.

'Don't cry,' said Catherine, putting an arm around her. 'It's so terrible about Penny and David! I was shocked when she told me what happened. I thought they were happy together. I had no idea. Why didn't she say anything sooner? Did you know about the violence?'

'No,' said Cara, then wished she had not answered so abruptly, fearing that the immediacy of her denial would arouse suspicion. She avoided Catherine's eyes. 'I didn't know. There were times I might have heard shouting, but all couples have a few arguments,' she said mournfully, 'and whenever I'd ask Penny she said they were fine.' Cara heard the emptiness of her words.

'Poor Penny,' said Catherine. 'I had a friend who had to go through the courts when she divorced because there was domestic violence involved, and her ex tried to get custody of the children. It took years to resolve.'

'Years?' said Cara. She felt a finality, an ending, as if she would never see Penelope or the children again.

'I can't take it in,' said Catherine, peering out of the window. 'Mum, we'd better go, in case David turns up.'

Brenda entered the room. 'Is everything okay?' she asked.

'Yes, we're leaving now,' said Catherine. 'Thank you for letting Mum stay here.'

'No bother at all; I'm just sad you can't stay longer. Won't you at least have a cup of tea before you go?'

'I'm afraid we're in a bit of a hurry,' said Catherine.

'Well, you're both welcome to come and visit anytime,' she said, then looked at the coffee table, 'Oh, you haven't finished the biscuits; I'll put them in a bag for you, and you can take them for your journey.' Brenda took the plate of biscuits and hurried into the kitchen, returning a few moments later with a plastic bag. 'I've put some home-made bread in there too.'

'Thank you,' said Catherine.

She wheeled Cara out of the house and helped her into the car.

Brenda waved at them from her front door.

As they drove away from Furley Avenue, Cara took one last look at her bedroom window from the back of the car. It was hard to believe she might never see the house again. It had all happened so suddenly. She had been desperate to leave that place, but this was all wrong. Tears rolled out of the corners of her eyes, and she felt unable to tell whether they were tears of relief that she was leaving at last, or tears of sorrow at the way it had ended.

CHAPTER ELEVEN

As they drove through Huddlesea town centre, Cara held back sentimental tears. It felt almost like taking a trip back in time, evoking in her a yearning to return to her youth. She recognised many of the old buildings. The solicitors' office where she'd once worked was still there, although the name had changed. The Horse and Dragon public house, where she'd first met Frederick, still stood proud at the corner of Haymart Street: a ghost from the past.

They arrived at Gloria's house at about midday. Catherine stopped the car outside the gate and turned to face Cara. 'Here we are,' she said, her forehead creased. 'You're not angry with me for arranging for you to come here, are you? You've hardly said a word since we left home this morning.'

'Don't be silly,' replied Cara. 'I'm just upset about Penny, that's all.'

'It's just that I know you and Aunty Glor never really got on well; we didn't make this decision lightly.'

Cara stared straight ahead out of the windscreen, not wanting to meet her daughter's gaze in case she noticed the tears forming in her eyes. Feeling unwanted and abandoned, unhappy at the prospect of having to live with Gloria, she knew the decision was out of her hands. There must have been, she supposed, some family discussion about where she would stay, and they finally decided to send her to live with her sister. Her children were aware she didn't keep in touch with Gloria, so she could not comprehend their decision.

'I wanted you to stay with me and Tom,' said Catherine, as though she'd read her mother's mind. 'It's so difficult because we're both working, and you saw how small the flat is. There'd be no one at home to look after you during the day.'

Cara thought back to the previous night. She'd only seen Tom very briefly. If she didn't know better, she would have sworn Catherine had tried her best to keep her in a different room from him at all times. 'Such a pity I didn't get a chance to speak to Tom last night,' she said.

Catherine coughed and then said. 'I'm sure there'll be other opportunities.'

'You must visit soon. Bring Tom and the children,' said Cara, staring out of the car window at the house she once knew so well. She felt almost fearful of venturing any closer to it.

'I hope he's remembered to make the children's breakfast,' said Catherine.

'What do you mean? Surely he'd remember that.'

Catherine placed a hand over her mouth. 'Um... oh dear, I didn't mean to say that out loud.' She laughed but seemed edgy. 'Don't mind me, I always worry too much about the children.'

'The sign of a good mother,' said Cara morosely, her own children's rejection uppermost in her mind. 'How's Jamie?'

'Um...' Catherine looked at her for a second then turned away. 'H-he's fine.'

'You don't seem convinced,' said Cara. 'Is there anything I should know?'

Catherine appeared to be pondering whether or not she should tell her something. Finally, she spoke, 'He might be leaving the country soon, that's why he couldn't offer you a room at his house: he's been offered a job in South Africa and doesn't know whether he'll take it. I'm sure he'll come and see you to explain everything. Anyway, maybe this is a chance for you and Aunty Glor to make up.'

Cara could not bear the idea of living with her sister, seeing her every day.

The sisters' relationship had been strained ever since Beattie's death. Thankfully, they'd only met up a few times over the years, mainly at family celebrations. In their youth they had made a few attempts to talk to each other whenever their paths crossed, but as they got older they mostly avoided one another, aware that any conversation would most likely end in an argument.

Cara resented being forced to call upon her estranged sister for help. She'd always hoped that it would be the other way round, that one day Gloria would need her help and have to apologise for all the pain she had caused in the past.

In Cara's mind, Gloria was nothing but a vindictive, spiteful woman who enjoyed hurting people.

She thought back to the last time she and her sister said more than a few words to each other. It was many years ago, when they'd both attended their cousin Ada's wedding. Cara's children were still young at the time. Gloria was quite nice to her at first.

'Cara, hello, how are you?'

Although Cara still felt betrayed by her sister, who now stood next to her smiling, she couldn't help but wish, just for a second, that things could be different. She knew they'd never be friends but decided to be civil, at least for today. After all, they didn't have to meet very often.

'I'm fine, Gloria,' she said. No thanks to you. *She scowled inwardly, but told herself to stay cool and calm. She focussed on her three small children*

and her strong husband who loved her dearly, then she looked at Gloria: a lonely woman, unable to sustain a relationship because of her bitter heart.

'I'm glad to hear it,' said Gloria cheerfully. 'It's so sad we don't see each other anymore. We really should try to keep in touch.'

Cara forced a smile.

'The children have grown.' Gloria pointed at James and Catherine who were playing with some of the heart-shaped balloons decorating the hall.

'Yes.' Cara nodded. Then, noticing the children destroying the decorations, she saw an opportunity to end the brief meeting with her unsavoury sibling. 'I'd better go and stop them ruining the decor!' Cara gave a fake giggle and took hold of Benjamin's hand, preparing to depart. 'Come on, Ben.'

Gloria turned her attention to Benjamin. 'Hello, Ben. You don't remember me, do you?' she asked, ruffling his hair.

He flattened his hair where she'd touched it. 'No, I don't,' he replied, wrinkling his nose.

'I'm your mum's sister.' She leaned closer to him: 'Listen, Ben, promise me you won't take after your mum and that you'll keep in touch with your brother and sister when you grow up.' She sneered at Cara. 'Your mum's terrible at keeping in touch, aren't you, Cara?' Gloria laughed, flicking back her long auburn hair.

Cara raised her eyebrows. 'You haven't exactly tried to keep in touch with me.'

'You're the one who should be making the effort.'

'Why's that?'

'Ever since that incident with Beattie Rogers, you've blanked me as if I'm the wicked witch.' She took a sip of her champagne.

'You're unbelievable,' said Cara.

'You still blame me after all these years, don't you?' Gloria's piercing blue eyes stared directly into Cara's. 'How sad, Cara. I'm your sister; your only sister.'

'What you did was unforgivable.'

'We're grown-ups, not young girls anymore. You should learn to forgive. You can't go around cutting people out of your life because they make a mistake. You'd have no one left.'

'A mistake?' Cara nearly retched. 'I think I have a right to feel angry with you, and I have a right to cut you out of my life after what happened to Bea.'

'I didn't do anything.'

'If it wasn't for you—'

'I didn't kill her.'

'No, but you might as well have.'

'Oh, Cara! You're still so melodramatic. I'm surprised you've got children of your own, you're behaving like one yourself.'

Noticing a couple whispering and pointing in her direction, Cara looked at the floor and mumbled, 'I think we've said all we have to say.' She felt the colour rise in her cheeks and began to steer Benjamin towards the other children.

Gloria followed her. 'It's funny little Ben doesn't look like the other two, isn't it, Cara?'

Cara glared at her sister.

'What?' said Gloria, shrugging. 'It's only a comment, unless you have something to hide. Weren't you courting a tall, dark, handsome man not long before you married Billy?'

Cara was eager to get Benjamin away. 'You're drunk,' she said, nodding at the champagne glass in her sister's hand.

'Not at all. Is that why you stick up for your trollop of a friend over your own sister? Because you're one yourself?'

Cara's eyes widened. 'You're an evil, acid-tongued gossip, Gloria Hughes, and I'm ashamed to call you my sister!'

'Huh! The truth hurts, doesn't it?' Gloria slurred, taking another sip of champagne and flicking back her long red hair.

Gloria's eyes were wild and glazed and she appeared to look right through Cara.

Scanning the room, Cara was relieved to see Billy in the far corner chatting with her uncle Ted: out of earshot.

Gloria smiled at Benjamin and leaned down so she was closer to his height. 'You're going to grow up tall, dark, and handsome, just like your father. What was his name, Cara? Freddie? Yes. Freddie. Tall, dark, handsome Freddie.'

'She doesn't know what she's saying, darling,' said Cara, as she hurried Benjamin away from Gloria.

A bemused eight-year-old Benjamin shrugged. 'Dad's name is Billy, isn't it, Mum?'

'Yes, dear, ignore her, she doesn't know what she's saying.'

⧗

Cara had last seen Gloria ten years before, at Billy's funeral. They hadn't spoken a word to each other on that occasion, and the only communication they'd had since was over the phone a few times—never by choice but when there was some family news that had to be conveyed.

'Aunty Glor is your sister,' said Catherine, interrupting her thoughts. 'You're both getting older. Wouldn't you prefer to patch it up before... Well, you know, before it's too late?'

Cara nodded while inside she wished she was miles away.

'I mean,' added Catherine, 'I bet you can't even remember what you were both so annoyed about now anyway, can you?'

'No,' Cara lied, knowing she would never forget.

'It's like wars,' mused Catherine. 'I'm sure there's usually some reason why everyone's angry at the beginning and they see war as the only answer, but then when they go on for years there are people out there fighting and not even knowing why or what they're fighting for, I'm sure. People need to learn to forgive more. The world would be a better place.'

Catherine helped her into the wheelchair.

'If you do find it difficult living with Aunty Glor, you can phone me and we'll try to make alternative arrangements,' she said in a half-whisper.

As they approached the house, Cara wanted to beg Catherine to stop and turn back. Tears pricked her eyes. None of her children knew why she and Gloria had fallen out.

⧗

It had been a hot summer, that much Cara could remember. Most of the detail remained misty in her mind, as if to remember the whole story would be to admit a deadly sin. It happened in 1950. In those days, Cara always looked up to her sister, Gloria, six years her senior. They were never really the best of friends, but Cara put it down to the age gap. To her, Gloria was beautiful, popular, and had an air of wisdom about her.

Cara spent most of her time with Beattie Rogers, her best friend. They shared all their secrets and grew up together almost like sisters.

That summer, at the age of sixteen, Beattie started a relationship with an older boy, Robert Jones. Young and naive, she fell head over heels in love, and it wasn't long before she fell pregnant...

'Cara, what am I going to do?' Tears streamed down Beattie's face as she stood in front of Cara in the tree house they'd discovered in the woods. She appeared tired and her eyes were red-raw, as though she'd been crying for days. Her brown shoulder-length hair, usually so shiny and neatly groomed, was unkempt. 'If my

parents find out, they'll kill me.'

Wrinkling her brow, Cara asked, 'How did you find out you're pregnant? Is that even possible?'

'Possible?'

'You're too young. I thought only older married people got pregnant.'

'Well, you thought wrong.'

'Do you know for sure?' Cara was still trying to make sense of it.

'Yes, of course.' Beattie rolled her eyes. 'I've missed my period. You mustn't tell anyone,' she pleaded. 'I haven't even told Robert.' She sat down on the log, which served as a chair in the tree house, and wiped her eyes on the sleeve of her dress leaving dark stains on the green velvet fabric.

'Here, Bea, use this.' Cara handed her a handkerchief from her handbag.

'Thanks.' Beattie sniffed. Her hands trembled as she took the handkerchief and wiped her eyes and nose.

Cara wanted things to remain as they were. Beattie was her oldest friend, with whom she shared years of memories. If she had a baby it would create a chasm between them, her friend stepping over into a whole new life of marriage and motherhood, leaving her behind.

'What should I do, Cara?' Beattie appeared desolate.

Cara felt a rush of panic, sensing Beattie waiting for her to come up with the solution.

'I'm not sure.' Cara sat down next to her and held her hand.

'Do you think Glor might know what to do?' asked Beattie. 'She's older...' Standing up, she walked to the other side of the tree house.

'Do you want me to ask Glor?'

Beattie did not reply but slowly turned to face Cara, worry lines set deep into her brow. 'No, it's probably best if we don't tell anyone yet. I need time to think.'

Cara walked over to where Beattie stood. A squirrel scurried along one of the tree's branches. 'Look Bea, a squirrel!' she said, in an effort to cheer up her friend. Usually Beattie tried to lure the squirrels into the tree house when she saw them, but now she didn't blink an eye.

'Maybe you should tell your mum,' suggested Cara.

Beattie looked at her, open-mouthed. 'My mum?'

Cara considered Mrs Rogers a kind, gentle woman. She found it easy to talk to her. 'She'll be able to help you, Bea.'

'Mum would send me to Aunty Beryl's until I have the baby and then she'd make me give it up for adoption. She'd be too ashamed about all the gossip in town.'

'What do you want to do?'

Beattie smiled through her tears. 'I want to marry Robert.'

Cara saw a spark of hope in Beattie's apple-green eyes. 'Are you going to tell Robert?' she asked, intrigued.

'I don't want to frighten him off. How do I tell him? We haven't known each other long. I'm not really sure how he'll react, but I love him and I think he loves me.'

'Well, you're going to have to tell someone soon. It'll be obvious you're pregnant in a couple of months, and won't you need to see a doctor?'

'Yes, yes, I know all that. I'm just confused. What should I do, Cara?' Beattie started to cry again.

'I don't know,' was all Cara could offer.

That night, Cara asked her older sister for advice. Gloria was more worldly-wise.

As they were getting ready for bed, Cara told Gloria about Beattie's problem.

'Cara, I forbid you to speak to that girl,' Gloria said as she brushed her long hair in front of the dressing table mirror.

'But she's my friend!'

'She'll be a bad influence. She shouldn't be doing that sort of thing at her age.'

Gloria sounded cold. Cara would have expected such a reaction from her mother, not from her sister.

'But she loves Robert, and he loves her.'

'Huh! Is that what she thinks?' Gloria scoffed, red-faced. 'Robert doesn't love her. He only loves himself. He's got a reputation, you know. Sleeps with everyone!'

'B-but Bea and Robert are in love.'

'Cara, you're so naive! Robert took advantage of her. He's much older than her. He's almost my age! Boys of his age are only interested in one thing. If she thought she could trap him by getting pregnant, she was so mistaken.'

'She's only sixteen. She didn't want to trap him, and she didn't want to get pregnant. She's frightened, and she's worried about what her parents will do if they find out. Robert doesn't even know about it yet. What do you think she should do?'

'She should have thought about the consequences before she got into bed with him.' Gloria stood up.

'She didn't know she—'

'Stop making excuses for her,' snapped Gloria as she pulled back her sheets to get into bed.

'Why are you being like this? You've had friends who've got pregnant.'

'They were married at the time,' Gloria retorted mockingly.

She got into bed and propped herself up on her elbow. 'About five years ago, another young girl got pregnant out of wedlock. Rosalind. She was about Bea's age. Do you remember the fuss everyone made?' Gloria appeared quite excited at the memory.

'No, I don't remember.' Cara screwed up her face as she racked her brain trying to recall.

'When this gets out, Bea will be seen as a bad girl.' Gloria smiled, but then her forehead creased. 'You'll have to keep away from her, Cara, for your own sake. You don't want people thinking you're like her.'

'But Bea's not a bad girl.' Cara's eyes filled with tears.

'Huh! If she wasn't, she wouldn't be unmarried and pregnant.'

'Wh-what happened to Rosalind?'

'Her family were forced to leave Huddlesea because of all the shame it brought on them.'

'B-but no one will find out about this. Robert and Bea can get married.'

'He won't marry her!'

'It's the best option.'

'When this gets out, Bea will have to leave town. Everyone will call her a whore.'

'Glor, you can be so cruel. I only asked for some advice for Bea. She's my friend and she's desperate.' Cara wiped her tears on the sleeves of her nightgown.

'Well, my advice would be for her to grow up!' said Gloria. 'What she has done is a disgrace, and I don't know how you can still be her friend.'

'I wish I'd never told you!' cried Cara. 'You won't tell anyone, will you? She made me promise not to tell anyone. If her parents find out, they'll make her give the baby up for adoption.'

Within a week, Beattie's pregnancy was common knowledge in town. Gloria made no attempt to hide the fact that she'd spread the news. Beattie and her family were outcasts.

Late one evening, Cara went to her best friend's house. As she approached the gate she considered turning back and going home. Beattie's parents would be furious that Gloria had spread gossip about their daughter. It took all her willpower to continue walking to the front door.

She knocked on the door and waited.

The net curtain flickered and Beattie's mother looked out at her from the living room window, glum-faced. As she turned to face her, Mrs Rogers shook her head and waved Cara away, as if in warning.

Just then, the front door creaked open and Mr Rogers, a tall imposing figure, stood glaring at Cara.

Warily, she took a step backwards. 'H-h-hello, Mr Rogers,' she stammered. Her voice came out sounding high-pitched. She was startled by the change in him. He usually greeted her with a warm smile and she was always treated like another member of the family. They'd often joked about how she spent more time at Beattie's house than her own. Today, his arms were folded in defiance, and his scowl emanated anger.

'I can't believe you have the audacity to turn up here,' he bellowed. 'Don't you think you've caused enough trouble?' His large round eyes and bulbous nose —features she'd once found endearing—made him appear frightening now, ogre-like.

'C-can I see Bea, please? I have to explain.'

'She doesn't want to see you.'

'But she's my friend.' Cara trembled. If she could only talk to Beattie, everything would be all right, she felt sure of it.

Beattie's mother joined her husband at the door.

Mrs Rogers was a quietly-spoken woman; Cara had often thought of her as a second mother. 'Hello,' said Cara, smiling, hopeful she'd receive a warmer reception from her.

'Cara, you should go home. You don't want people to start talking about you, do you?' said Mrs Rogers.

'Wh-what do you mean?'

'Bea has been a bad girl. She's going to have to leave town. She can't stay here. If you're found talking to her, people will think you're bad too.'

Gloria's words echoed in Cara's ears then. 'Bea's not a bad girl; she just didn't know what she was doing,' Cara murmured.

'Please leave, Cara,' Beattie's mother insisted.

Cara had never seen her so sad. Her eyes were black underneath, as if she hadn't slept for days.

'But please... I have to talk to her.'

'Maybe you're the one who led her astray,' said Mr Rogers, stepping forward. 'Our daughter was an innocent young girl until she became friendly with you.' He leant towards her.

Cara took another step back and gazed at the two people standing at the door, whom she no longer recognised. Her mind boggled as to what he meant about Beattie being an innocent girl until they'd become friends: they'd been friends in school since the age of four and grew up together. The past had been obliterated, all the good times replaced with another version of events fabricated by bitterness and resentment.

Mrs Rogers' mouth turned down at the edges when she saw tears form in Cara's eyes, but she didn't try to comfort her, just shook her head and then walked back into the house.

Mr Rogers took off his glasses and wiped the lenses with a handkerchief that he took from his shirt pocket. 'Don't come back. Ever.' His voice broke slightly as he spoke.

Cara watched as he turned around and closed the front door.

She walked backwards and looked up at Beattie's bedroom window, praying to see her friend. The curtain moved slightly. Cara craned her neck upwards. 'Bea!' she shouted, as loud as she could. 'Bea! Please come out!'

The front door opened and Mr Rogers stormed towards her. 'I've warned you to stay away!' he boomed.

Cara cowered as he approached.

'Go!' he said, pointing at the gate. 'Go on!'

Cara peered up in vain at Beattie's bedroom window, one last time, before turning on her heel and running out of the gate.

It started to rain.

Cara returned home distraught. 'Why have you done this?' she asked Gloria, standing in front of her in their bedroom. Cara's hair, dripping wet from the rain, left droplets on the carpet. 'She was my friend, she asked me for help. I told you not to tell anyone.'

'She's a whore, and now everyone knows it,' Gloria said calmly.

Her sister had always been outspoken and strong-minded, and Cara usually respected her for that, but now she felt betrayed. 'I didn't know you hated Bea. If I did, I would never have told you. Why did you do this, Glor?'

⧗

The following week, Beattie was admitted to hospital. Rumours were rife in town: some people said her mother had tried to help her to get rid of the baby and it went wrong, others said she'd suffered a miscarriage.

One day, as Cara walked past the butcher's shop, old Mrs Williams called out to her from across the road. She used to work as a dinner lady at Cara's former junior school and often stopped for a chat. Cara hadn't seen her since the scandal about Beattie's pregnancy had become the main news among the town's gossips.

'Hello, Mrs Williams,' she said hesitantly, not feeling in the mood for conversation or a lecture. The last two people who had stopped her to speak on the street that week—Rose Spencer from the grocery, and Angela Edgar who'd once worked for Cara's father—both told her what a "bad" girl Beattie had been. Those women were about the same age as Mrs Williams.

Mrs Williams walked across the road using her large black umbrella as a walking stick, as she usually did, carrying a bag of groceries.

Cara smiled at her and Mrs Williams glared back through large oval-shaped glasses.

'How are you?' asked Cara politely, noticing Mrs Williams' grimace.

'I hear your friend Bea Rogers has got herself into trouble,' said the old woman bluntly.

Cara coughed nervously. 'I have to go.' She started walking away.

Mrs Williams called out behind her: 'She's lost the baby because she committed a deadly sin; let that be a lesson to you! I hope you're more sensible than she is, for your own sake.'

Cara quickened her pace, ignoring the stares from the local people who had heard Mrs Williams' comments. She knew they were all thinking the same thing. They knew she and Beattie were best friends, and they all thought she must be a "bad girl" like Beattie. At that moment she truly hated Huddlesea.

Tears fell down her cheeks as she ran the rest of the way home.

In the end, Cara went to see Beattie at the hospital, uninvited.

Beattie appeared so pale and washed out, lying on the bed with its plain white cotton sheets almost the same colour as her skin. When Cara walked into the room Beattie opened her eyes, but it seemed to take an enormous effort to do so.

'Bea, hello,' Cara said, in a whisper, placing a bunch of pink carnations at her friend's bedside.

Beattie loved carnations. Cara remembered the time when she and Beattie were about eight years old and they picked all of the pink carnations from Mrs Fennel's garden. She hadn't seen the girls take them but made such a fuss about it around town for the next two weeks, even calling the police to say there was a flower thief on the prowl.

Cara and Beattie had stashed the flowers in their tree house and used them to play at pretending to be bridesmaids. *Images flickered in Cara's mind of how beautiful Beattie had looked with those pink flowers in her hair. A lump formed in her throat and she held tightly to her friend's hand; it felt cold and lifeless.*

'This is all your fault,' said Beattie slowly, her voice so quiet it was practically inaudible.

'Bea, I...' She wanted to explain. She knew Beattie saw her as the person responsible for everyone finding out.

'Please,' said Beattie. 'Just go.' Her voice sounded louder, but the three words she'd managed to speak had apparently drained all her energy. Her eyes closed and she took a deep breath, two tears trailing down her cheeks. On opening her eyes again, she fixed her gaze on Cara.

'Bea, I was only trying to help.'

'I trusted you.' Her voice grew louder, as if she had regained her strength: 'You betrayed me.' The words echoed in the room. 'I told you a secret. You weren't supposed to tell anyone. I was going to marry Robert, but his baby is dead and it's all because of you.'

Cara shivered.

'I hate you, Cara Hughes; you've ruined everything.'

'But I—' Cara stopped herself. She was going to say it was Gloria's fault but could not deny that if she hadn't told her sister, none of this would have happened. 'I'm sorry, Bea,' she said, wiping away hopeless tears. 'I shouldn't have told Glor, but I thought she could help.'

'It's too late,' Beattie said. She appeared to be asleep, but her voice sounded clear.

Cara remained beside the bed, tears streaming from her eyes, until Beattie drifted off to sleep.

She left the room quietly, dragging with her the weight of her sorrow.

Beattie died blaming Cara. Gloria didn't comfort her and never accepted any blame for what had happened to Beattie, not even as they watched her white coffin being carried to the cemetery.

Cara could not find it within herself to forgive her sister, especially when she recalled her last meeting with Beattie, in the cold hospital room with the too-bright lights. Her friend's eyes had looked lost and haunted. *'I hate you, Cara Hughes...'.* Those words left a deep scar within her soul.

CHAPTER TWELVE

The outside of the house had hardly changed in the past thirty-odd years; the old iron knocker was still on the door, and the ivy still grew around the windows. Everything held connections to the past.

The last time Cara had been here was when she'd attended her father's funeral. Gloria invited everyone back to the house for a drink. Cara was reluctant to go, but Billy persuaded her.

'Cara, you have to go. What will all your relatives think if you don't?'

'I can't think of anything worse than being stuck inside the same four walls as Glor. Haven't you noticed she's been ignoring me all day?' Cara glared at her sister, who stood at the other side of their father's grave. Gloria's face was partially obscured by her hat's black netted veil. She looked suitably upset, but Cara suspected her forlorn appearance was merely an act put on for the benefit of the rest of the mourners. In her mind, the real Gloria was a cold, hard-hearted woman.

'Cara, I know you and your sister have had your differences in the past,' said Billy, putting his arm around her, 'but let's go to the house and have a drink for your father's sake. You don't even have to speak to her if you don't want to.'

So they had gone. Cara remembered sitting on the sofa in the living room of the old house, feeling out of place and holding a glass of red wine, of which she may have taken one sip. All she had wanted was to be anywhere else.

⧗

'This is so annoying,' said Catherine.

They had been waiting for Gloria to answer the door for a few minutes.

'I've knocked on the door three times already.' Catherine walked over to the window to the left of the front door and pressed her face against the glass, in an attempt to see inside.

'Maybe she's gone out, dear,' said Cara, hopefully.

'She knew we were coming,' huffed Catherine.

Shortly, a shuffling noise could be heard from inside the house and the front door opened. Gloria looked as glamorous as ever, immaculately dressed in a smart navy-blue dress. Her thick, wavy hair was cut in a short, neat style and dyed dark auburn—similar to the natural colour of her youth—she was the picture of perfection.

All of Cara's insecurities rose to the surface. She lowered her eyes and slouched as old feelings of inadequacy asserted themselves. Why had life been so good to Gloria when she was so cruel? The worst thing was, Cara felt quite sure she must look much older than her sister. Cara had stopped dyeing her own hair years ago; it was now completely grey.

'Hello,' said Catherine.

Gloria didn't acknowledge them, instead she turned and walked back through the hallway leaving the front door open.

'Huh! She hasn't changed. Do you see how rude she is?' said Cara.

Catherine frowned and helped Cara into the house before returning to the car to collect her suitcase.

'I'm going to have to leave straight away,' she said, glancing at her watch as she carried the suitcase into the hallway. 'I can't leave the children with Tom for too long. You know what men are like; they have no idea when it comes to children.'

'I'm sure you're underestimating him, dear. It will be good for him to spend some time with them on his own.' It was more of a plea for Catherine to stay.

'No, I really have to go, Mum. Bye, Aunty,' she shouted into the house, then walked towards the front door.

'Wait,' said Gloria, who'd suddenly reappeared in the hallway.

'I have to go, Aunty.'

'Can I have a word with you?' Gloria asked sternly; it was more of a demand than a question.

'Okay,' said Catherine, twisting around to face her aunt.

'In private,' said Gloria.

Catherine looked at her watch again. Shrugging, she followed Gloria into the kitchen, leaving Cara in the hallway.

'I've already told you it's inconvenient for me to have her staying here.' Gloria's cheeks were bright red.

'It won't be for long, Aunty; I'm sure Penny and David will get back together soon,' lied Catherine.

'I'm not happy about this.'

'Neither is Mum, but you don't have a choice, so get over it!' Catherine headed towards the door.

'Well, I can see that you're your mother's daughter. How dare you speak to me like that in my own home!'

Catherine faced her aunt and let out a sigh. 'Look, I'm sorry; I shouldn't have snapped, but we're all stressed out. We didn't plan this. Mum was very happy living with Penny, and if she had the choice she'd still be there.'

'One week,' said Gloria.

'What?' Catherine raised her eyebrows.

'She can stay here for one week.'

'Aunty, this is as much my mum's house as it is yours.'

'No, it isn't,' Gloria replied stiffly. 'My late father left this house to me in his will. I have all the paperwork to prove it.'

Catherine blinked exaggeratedly. 'Whatever happened between you and Mum must have been pretty bad if you can't forget it after all these years.'

'She can stay for a week.'

'Please, Aunty, she has nowhere else to go. I can call you next week and check that everything's okay.'

'One week should give you ample time to make other arrangements,' said Gloria, scowling.

Catherine eyed the kitchen clock. 'I really have to get back to the children.'

As she passed Cara on her way out, she gave a sympathetic smile. 'Bye, Mum. I'll be back to see you soon.'

After watching Catherine depart, Cara sat alone in the empty hallway. The house was no longer familiar enough to be called home. Tired after the long journey, all she wanted to do was lie down on her bed and sleep. Her own bed was miles away, though, and she doubted she would be able to sleep in a strange bed in a house full of reminders of a traumatic period in her life, under the same roof as someone she had hoped she would never see again.

The longer she sat there, the more Cara felt lost and humiliated. *'If you do find it difficult living with Aunty Glor, you can phone me,'* Catherine had said. Cara wanted to shout as loud as she could for Catherine to come back and to take her home.

The light had begun to fade due to heavy cloud, so not much light filtered through the glass in the front door. It seemed clear that her sister intended to avoid her all day. Eventually Cara coughed, to assert her presence.

Gloria emerged from the kitchen and walked over to her, grasped the wheelchair's handles and pushed the chair into the living room. She switched on the television and left the room without uttering a word.

Cara stared at the screen vacantly, not really interested in watching it. Where had Gloria gone? Even having an argument would be better than this. It filled her with dread to think she might be living this way for the foreseeable future.

Soon, she felt the need to go to the toilet. Her wheelchair wasn't easy to manoeuvre, designed to be pushed, and her arms were too weak for her to attempt to move the wheels herself. She knew she should call out for Gloria, but would she respond? Cara tried to distract her mind from wanting to go to the toilet, but soon the urge became too great.

'Gloria!' she shouted, swallowing her pride. There was no sound. Had she gone out? Cara waited, feeling sure her sister would ignore her even if she was still in the house. 'Gloria, where are you? Please come here, Gloria!'

Gloria walked into the room and stood before her, arms folded.

'I have to use the toilet. Could you help me, please?'

Gloria didn't speak but took hold of the wheelchair's handles.

'Thank you, Gloria.'

Her sister wheeled the chair through the hallway and lifted her onto the toilet seat. 'We'll have to unpack your suitcase, and I suppose you must be hungry.'

'Yes, thank you.'

Somehow, the small act of helping her go to the toilet had altered Gloria's perception in some way. Her attitude noticeably changed in just a few minutes.

Cara watched as her sister took out the clothes from the suitcase and placed them into the old wardrobe in the bedroom. Gloria did not speak, but every now and then she smiled at her sister, as one might smile at a stranger.

This transition in Gloria's behaviour made Cara feel more positive. Perhaps it wouldn't be so impossible to live with her, after all.

That night, Cara lay awake in bed in the room she and Gloria had shared as children, on the ground floor at the back of the house.

Some of the original furniture was still in situ, including the mahogany dressing table and the wardrobes she'd used as a girl. Some features had changed: there was only one single bed, instead of two. It wasn't her old bed, which had iron bedposts and springs; this modern one had a wooden headboard and comfortable mattress. The walls had been repapered with a peach-coloured, floral-design wallpaper. She could still remember the deep burgundy tone of the old wallpaper and felt glad it wasn't there anymore; the bedroom looked different enough not to cause her to dwell too much on the past.

Unable to sleep, she sat up in bed in the darkened room and drew the velvet curtain so she could see outside. The view was of the back garden.

With no real view to keep her occupied and no television or even a radio, how would she spend her days?

Although more comfortable in Gloria's company this evening, they were still far from becoming best friends.

Peering out of the window, Cara noticed the pathway leading to the forest where she and Beattie had discovered the tree house. She wondered whether the tree house still existed. Sighing at the retrospection, she closed the curtain.

She settled herself down on the bed to sleep but felt edgy. Closing her eyes, she tried to imagine being back at Furley Avenue. 'Oh, Penny!' she said under her breath.

As she recalled her granddaughter's harrowed face, tears welled in her eyes. She prayed Penelope, Andrew, and Carl would be safe and that David would never find them.

CHAPTER THIRTEEN

Cara woke up the next morning, disorientated. Sleep had evaded her for most of the night. She'd forgotten she wasn't in Penelope's house and consequently had to take a moment to find her bearings on opening her eyes in the unfamiliar environment.

Her thoughts were invaded as the bedroom door slowly creaked open and Gloria walked in followed by a small-framed young girl. The girl wore a long purple dress that appeared to be too big for her. Her frame was childlike and Cara guessed she could be no more than a teenager. Her long blonde hair was tied up in a ponytail, which only served to accentuate the fact that her cheeks and neck were red, caused by her apparent shyness or nervousness.

Cara tried to compose herself, running a hand over her hair and inwardly cursing Gloria for not knocking on the door before entering with the stranger.

'Good, you're awake,' said Gloria. 'I'd assumed you would be sleeping. I can introduce you now.'

She walked over to the window and drew the thick beige curtains. Afterwards, she returned to where the girl was standing. 'This is Rosetta. She's going to be your carer.'

The young girl smiled and her cheeks reddened even more, colouring her prominent freckles a deep red-brown. 'Hello, Cara,' she said politely.

'Hello,' replied Cara, still trying to digest what she'd heard. This girl was going to be her carer? She doubted Rosetta had any experience in caring for anyone.

'Rosetta lives in Hammond Street, so she's nice and local,' said Gloria. 'She'll be here from nine to six each day. She'll be responsible for your meals, and she can take you out around town.'

Cara nodded. Suddenly, the rest of her life flashed before her. The predictability of it. Sentenced to live out the rest of her days in misery. Alone and unloved.

'Right, Rosetta, let's go to the kitchen. I'll show you where everything is.' Gloria led the young girl by the arm.

'Gloria,' Cara heard herself say.

Gloria, already outside the bedroom, turned her head and looked in from the doorway.

'I need to talk to you,' said Cara.

'All right, we'll be right back when I've shown Rosetta the kitchen.'

'No, I need to talk to you in private.'

'I'll be back in a few minutes.'

She did not return. Instead, Rosetta came back half an hour later carrying a tray containing Cara's breakfast.

'Where's Gloria?' Cara asked impatiently as Rosetta struggled to place the breakfast tray on the bed without spilling the contents.

'She's gone out.'

'Out?' Cara sighed deeply.

'She said she had to buy some groceries,' explained Rosetta, smiling as she sat down on a chair next to the bed.

Frustration creased Cara's brow. She wanted to speak to Gloria about finding alternative living arrangements. Having a carer made her feel even more estranged from her family and heightened her sense of abandonment.

'It's a lovely day today,' said Rosetta. 'Later, we'll go out and I'll show you the town. Gloria said you haven't been here for years.'

Cara forced a smile. It would be difficult to find an opportunity to talk to her sister: she suspected Gloria had employed Rosetta as a way of avoiding contact with her.

Picking at her breakfast, Cara glanced up at Rosetta and her frown was greeted with a warm smile.

'Gloria told me you lived in London before moving here,' said Rosetta, transcending the abyss of silence.

'Yes, that's right.' A deep feeling of loss and sadness engulfed Cara. When Rosetta mentioned London, it felt as though she had reopened a fresh wound. Despite it having only been a day or so since she'd last seen Penelope, the distance between them made it seem like a much longer period of time. Cara had seen her granddaughter every day for the past five years, yet now she might never see her again.

'I've got a friend who lives in London,' said Rosetta.

Cara heard the front door open and close: Gloria had returned.

'Rosetta,' said Cara.

'Call me Rosie. Everyone else does.'

'All right. Rosie, could you remind Gloria I want to speak to her?'

'Of course.' The young girl left the room.

Cara heard her speaking to Gloria but could not make out the words.

Shortly, Rosetta re-entered the bedroom. 'Have you finished your breakfast, Cara?'

'Er... Yes, dear.'

'Good.' The girl walked over to the bed and took the breakfast tray. 'I'll take this to the kitchen, then we'll go out.' She smiled and turned to leave.

'Roset—, sorry, *Rosie*, did you tell Gloria I want to speak to her?' Cara asked, an anxious tone to her voice.

'Yes, I did,' said Rosetta, looking back over her shoulder, 'but she says she's too busy. She'll pop in to see you later, when I go home.'

Cara's mood darkened as she became aware that she was doomed to spend another day, perhaps even another week in this place, until one of her children got in touch so she could ask them for help.

⧗

Cara breathed in the fresh air as Rosetta pushed the wheelchair along Cheshire Road. She was glad to be out of the house and away from the simmering tension it held. It was a bright, sunny day, the atmosphere quiet and calm. She could not help feeling more relaxed.

When they reached the corner of the road where it adjoined the high street, someone called out from across the road: 'Rosie!'

'Mandy! Is that you?' Rosetta sounded thrilled and the wheelchair sped up. Cara turned her head and saw a young girl, with very black hair, running towards them.

'Mandy!' said Rosetta again when the girl came to a halt beside the wheelchair. 'You've dyed your hair black! I nearly didn't recognise you, and you've pierced your nose!'

'Yeah! I told you I would. And...' She opened her mouth, laughed, and stuck out her tongue to reveal another piercing.

Cara blinked in surprise.

'Through your tongue? Wow! Did it hurt?' asked Rosetta.

'Nah,' said Mandy, waving her hand to dismiss the idea.

'Well, you've become trendy now you're living in London,' said Rosetta, giggling. 'And how come you're back in town without telling me?'

'I sent you a text this morning,' Mandy replied.

'Oh, I forgot my mobile at home,' Rosetta grumbled. 'We've got to get together. How about tonight?'

'Yeah, I said that in my text!' Mandy laughed.

'So how long are you gonna be in Huddlesea?'

'A few days; Uncle Paul has a job in town, so we came with him.' She looked at Cara, appearing to have just noticed her.

Cara smiled at her, and Rosetta introduced them.

'I'm working as a carer,' she explained to her friend.

'That's nice,' said Mandy. 'Okay, Rosie, I have to go, because I'm meeting Uncle Paul for lunch. I'll call you tonight and we'll arrange something, okay?'

'Yeah, great!'

After Mandy left, Rosetta told Cara about her. They were best friends at school, but Mandy's family moved to London over two years ago as her stepfather, whom she called "Uncle Paul", found a job there.

'We keep in touch by phone and I knew she wanted to come back to Huddlesea, but I had no idea she would be here today. It's so great.' She wheeled the chair further along the high street.

Cara's mood became nostalgic as she recognised parts of the town. She saw the water fountain in the centre of the main square and smiled at the sculpture of the angel playing a harp in the middle of the fountain. She recalled the day when the statue was first placed there: everyone in town had gathered to watch a fireworks display that night, shortly after the Second World War. Having never seen a proper fireworks display before, Cara had been fascinated by the waterfall of colours cascading from the sky above.

Further along the high street they passed the old library and the town hall. The buildings were a little weathered with age but otherwise just the same as Cara remembered them. There were many new shops replacing the old ones lining the high street of her memory. There were restaurants serving all types of exotic foreign cuisine. At times, she felt as though she was in London as they meandered further along the street full of modern shops and bars.

'Are you all right, Cara?' asked Rosetta, after a brief silence.

'Yes, dear, I'm enjoying the sights.'

'Good, I'm glad.'

Rosetta pushed the wheelchair at an even pace, stopping from time to time outside shop windows.

Without warning, the wheelchair came to an abrupt halt in front of a restaurant. Not having expected to stop there, Cara was forced to hold on to the arms of the wheelchair to avoid falling out.

'Look, Cara, there's Mandy and her uncle Paul having lunch!' Rosetta laughed and waved, trying to catch her friend's attention, as she peered through the smoked glass restaurant window.

Cara saw Mandy sitting at one of the tables towards the rear of the plush Chinese restaurant, next to a man. He turned towards the window but did not appear to notice Rosetta, who had stopped waving. The man looked familiar to Cara.

She squinted, in an attempt to see him more clearly. He wore dark glasses and had a beard.

Surely not! It can't be. Adrenaline raced through her veins.

The man removed his glasses, turning back to face Mandy. They were talking to each other, studying the menu. Something about the way he moved, the tilt of his head, triggered long lost memories.

Rosetta steered the wheelchair away. 'Shall we go home?'

'All right, dear,' Cara replied distractedly. Why had Rosetta and Mandy called him Paul? Was it possible two people could look *that* similar? She'd only seen him for a short time, but she felt quite certain: the man in the restaurant was Benjamin.

⏳

Back at the house that evening, after Rosetta went home, Cara sat alone in her bedroom. Most of the afternoon she'd been lost in a daydream, unable to concentrate on much. Rosetta had tried her best to initiate conversation but all attempts had mostly been met with silence or nods from Cara. Cara feared the girl may have been left with the impression she might be ill or, worse still, senile.

The image of Mandy's uncle, Paul, was burned into Cara's mind. She'd now convinced herself that the man was definitely Benjamin.

For years, Cara had waited for a sign. She preferred to imagine he'd fled abroad. Although this did not stop her worrying about him, it soothed her to some extent, being more of a real reason why he didn't keep in touch. Living abroad he could not easily visit, could not send her letters or phone her if he was concerned about the police tracking him down.

She did not want to face the possibility that he'd never wanted to contact her, but Mandy said she lived in London and had travelled from there with her uncle. If he lived in London, her theory about him being a "man on the run" was no longer plausible.

Cara had often pictured the day when they would meet again. In her dreams he was thrilled to see her, he hugged her and told her he'd missed her. These dreams seemed unrealistic in light of what she had learnt. He'd been living in the same city as her but not once thought of getting in touch.

Going back to the pain of not knowing what had become of him would have been preferable to knowing she didn't matter to him.

Gloria walked into Cara's bedroom later that evening and sat on the chair beside the bed. 'You wanted to talk to me,' she said, without looking at Cara. Her demeanour suggested she'd rather be anywhere else.

Cara lowered her eyes. Gloria had always been spiteful whenever their paths crossed in the past. Was it her way of dealing with the guilt over Beattie's death? Cara doubted that. In her opinion, Gloria didn't have a conscience.

Gloria peered at her through cold and distant ice-blue eyes. 'Well?'

Cara remembered how badly she'd wanted to talk to her sister in the morning about making arrangements to leave the house, but in the course of just one afternoon everything had changed. How could she leave now?

'Um... I just thought it would be nice to have a TV, or a radio in the room, if you have a spare one,' she improvised.

'Right. I will have a look.' Gloria yawned. 'I'll say goodnight then.'

Cara watched her sister stand up and walk towards the door, then said: 'I know you didn't invite me to come here and you can't stand to be around me; you've made that quite plain. Just so you know, I wasn't exactly overjoyed about having to come here.'

Gloria turned to her, apparently surprised by what she was hearing.

'I'm not happy I had to leave my home,' continued Cara, 'to come here and be treated like an unwelcome guest. I didn't choose it. I'm hoping I won't have to stay here much longer. I'll be gone soon enough; we should try to put aside our differences while we have to live together.'

Gloria walked slowly to the chair and sat down. 'Oh, Cara,' she said, raising her eyes sheepishly. 'I'm so sorry.'

Cara spotted tears welling in Gloria's eyes. As far as she could recall, she'd never seen her sister become tearful or upset. In the past, Gloria only showed emotion when it was to revel in someone else's misfortune. Now here she sat with hunched shoulders, her face mournful and apologetic.

'I know I've been very unwelcoming, but it's not because I don't want you here.' Gloria wiped away a tear threatening to fall. 'You mustn't think that.' She sniffed. 'It just happened so suddenly... no warning. It's difficult for me; I'm not young anymore.'

'Well... I... '

'And the truth is,' said Gloria, taking a tissue from the box on the bedside cabinet, 'you brought the past back with you.' She scanned the room, as if trying to find an escape route. Practically cowering, she confessed in a small voice, 'Beattie's death has been on my conscience for all these years. It's not easy.'

A momentary feeling of relief washed over Cara, as though years of anguish had been lifted from her shoulders; finally her sister was admitting her part in Beattie's tragic end.

'I was young,' stated Gloria.

Young? Cara glared at her sister.

'I regret it... I do.' Gloria's voice sounded high-pitched and anxious. She paused.

Gloria may have been waiting for her to say something like 'it doesn't matter', but Cara had no desire to relieve her of any guilt.

'When you're young, you do things that—'

'The fact that you were young is no excuse for what you did,' huffed Cara, overcome by an urge to tell Gloria how she'd felt all those years ago about her betrayal of confidence. 'You haven't said you're sorry.' She spoke her thoughts as they raced through her mind. 'All these years have passed and you've never said you're sorry. You've always made out you didn't do anything wrong. This wasn't just a folly of youth; you ruined Bea's life, you killed a sixteen-year-old girl with your spite.'

'I am sorry, really I am. I'll never forget what I did. I know Beattie died because of me. It was my fault. My fault.' Gloria rocked backwards and forwards on the chair as she spoke, in an alarming motion. When she looked up at Cara again, a tear fell down her cheek and onto her skirt. 'But I had a reason.'

'A reason?' blurted Cara.

'Jealousy.' Gloria stopped rocking and sat upright.

'Jealousy? What do you mean?'

'I loved Robert.'

Cara's forehead creased. She tried to think back to that summer, long ago, but she could not recall Gloria having been in love with Robert. Her anger subsided slightly, replaced by a sudden interest to hear more.

'It's no excuse, I know,' said Gloria, closing her eyes. 'My jealousy killed Beattie. I know that. My feelings for Robert were real and nothing else mattered to me at the time. I wanted revenge, but I had no idea everything would escalate to such a scale.'

'You knew what the people in Huddlesea were like,' Cara interjected. 'I remember you telling me about another girl forced to leave town because she got pregnant out of wedlock.'

'I aimed to split Beattie and Robert up. That's all. You see, I had a brief relationship with Robert. He left me for Beattie. She was younger than me and more beautiful. Hearing she was pregnant with his child... well, that just threw me. I thought Robert loved me. We'd even talked about marriage. I know it sounds silly, but it was one of those all-consuming love affairs.' Her cheeks reddened. 'I... Oh, none of it matters now.'

Cara watched as Gloria changed before her eyes. This woman she'd considered incapable of love had suddenly transformed and revealed a hidden story. Was it part of some fanciful tale her sister had concocted to rid herself of blame? She hardly recognised this fragile woman, eyes wet with tears, full of remorse and regret.

'I didn't know she would die. When you're young you don't even consider things like that.'

'Why haven't you ever told me any of this before?'

'We've hardly ever been on speaking terms, have we?' Gloria took another tissue and wiped her eyes. 'I preferred to keep my distance from you because I blamed myself for Beattie's death, and you remind me of everything. I changed after she died, became a different person. I locked the pain inside. I didn't want to admit my part in her death, so I chose to forget.'

'How convenient.'

Gloria sighed. 'I don't mean I *forgot*; of course I can never forget. I mean I couldn't deal with it, so unconsciously I made a decision to put it all to the back of my mind. Blank it out.'

'So you could just carry on living as if nothing had happened, even though Beattie died?' Cara scowled.

Gloria took a deep breath. 'About twenty years ago, I used to drink heavily,' she said, staring across the bed and out of the window. 'I would drink late at night and I'd wake up the next day craving alcohol. I don't know how I survived. I was in a relationship at the time with a nice man, Walter. He convinced me to get some counselling, and slowly I got back on my feet. The psychologist told me my guilt over Beattie's death made me unhappy and led to me drinking too much.'

'But Beattie died over fifty years ago. If you only became an alcoholic twenty years ago, there must have been other factors in your life that made you start drinking,' said Cara.

'Yes, there were, but I... my therapist said they all stemmed from my guilt.'

'You carried on living your life after Beattie died for a good thirty years before your drink problem and I remember you showed little remorse for what you'd done.'

'Why do you think I never had children?'

'I imagined you didn't want any.'

'I wanted to have children. I used to dream about getting married and starting a family. I envied your life, Cara. But I couldn't have a proper relationship, I would always end up doing something to make them leave me. I didn't feel I deserved to be loved. My psychologist said I deliberately eliminated from my life any chance of having children or being happy because I felt I'd denied Beattie that chance.'

'But what about Walter, the man you mentioned who helped you with your drink problem?'

'Walter was a good man, he really cared about me. He loved me no matter what I did. I was difficult to live with, but he didn't care. I told him about Beattie. I was in love with him, trusted him completely. When I told him about what I'd done, it might have been a vain attempt to try to come to terms with it, but reliving everything sent me off the edge. I became depressed, so I started drinking to numb the pain. If Walter wasn't around I'm sure I would have killed myself.'

Cara shivered. 'Er... Do you still keep in touch with Walter?'

Gloria looked down. 'He died.'

'I'm sorry,' said Cara.

Gloria smiled through her tears. 'You know, I often told him that if we'd met when we were younger, we would have married and had children. I'm sure of it. Believe me, Cara, I haven't had an easy life; every day is a struggle.'

Suddenly, Cara was seeing her sister in a different light. Gloria's thin veil had cracked, revealing a deep well of pain that had etched itself into the lines on her face. The signs on Gloria's face were not quite hidden by the make-up she wore: wrinkles that had the effect of pulling her mouth perpetually downwards, and dark hollows around her eyes. Cara had been oblivious of this other side of her sister's personality during the years she'd held on to the blame from the past.

'Cara, I want you to know before it's too late, I didn't mean to hurt you.'

Her voice roused Cara from her musing. She noticed Gloria's tone of voice sounded melancholy.

'I was too proud to admit I'd done anything wrong. I'll carry that to my grave.' She opened her mouth to speak again but only shook her head, as if overcome by despondency. She stood up and walked away, then turned to Cara, her face still locked in gloom. 'Goodnight,' she said.

Cara nodded at her sister as she walked out of the bedroom door. What had happened with Beattie seemed so distant. They had been not much more than children, now they were old. Gloria would have to be a pretty good actress to convey the emotion she'd shown this evening if she didn't actually feel it. She had lived with the consequences of her actions for over half a century. Perhaps the time had come to forgive and forget.

Maybe Gloria wasn't such a horrible person. Maybe the real Gloria was the woman who had just apologised to her. After all, Cara had never really known her.

⧗

That night, Cara dreamt that Beattie came to visit her, dressed all in white and looking beautiful, just as Cara imagined an angel would look. Her appearance was so far removed from the girl she'd last seen lying on the hospital bed. Her eyes were no longer full of hate or bitterness. Beattie smiled at her; a warm smile bringing with it a sense of tranquillity. She led Cara to the old tree house. Cara floated towards the tree house, following her friend. She saw the trunk of the tree and their names carved into the wood. In the dream, their names were as legible as they had been the day they cut into the tree with their penknives as teenagers. Cara felt as if she were actually there, standing beside her best friend. Then Beattie disappeared.

When Cara woke up there was a peaceful atmosphere in the room. A tear fell from her eye as she sensed forgiveness from Beattie's spirit pervading the air around her.

CHAPTER FOURTEEN

When Rosetta arrived the next morning with the breakfast tray, all Cara could think about was Mandy's uncle.

'Good morning, Cara,' said the young girl, cheerily. 'Did you sleep well?' Placing the tray on the bedside cabinet, she helped Cara sit up in bed, adjusting the pillow behind her. 'You're quiet this morning.'

Cara snapped back to the present, pushing aside thoughts of Benjamin. 'Sorry, Rosie. I'm not very good in the mornings.'

Rosetta giggled. 'Don't worry, I'm the same; I can't function until I have a cup of tea! Here's your breakfast.'

'Thank you,' she said, watching as the girl placed the breakfast tray in front of her. 'By the way, I enjoyed our day out yesterday. It was nice to see the old town again. It has changed a bit since I lived here, but there are enough reminders of the past to make me feel quite sentimental.'

'We can go out today, if you like. It's bright and sunny. Very hot.'

'Yes, that would be nice. We might even bump into your friend Mandy,' Cara said, her words echoing her wishes. She sipped her tea and held her breath in anticipation of the reply.

'Yes, maybe we will. We went to the cinema last night. It was so great to spend time with her.' Rosetta sat on the chair next to the bed.

'How long is Mandy staying in Huddlesea, dear?'

'I'm not sure. A few days maybe. Her uncle is here on business.'

'What job does he do?'

'Um... it's something to do with buying and selling property, I think.'

Cara raised her eyebrows. Benjamin had been an estate agent.

'He works for Mandy's granddad. That's how he met her mum, Claire,' added Rosetta. 'They've got a little girl, Amy. She's eight years old; Mandy's half-sister. She's so cute.'

'Ben's daughter?' said Cara.

'Who's Ben?' Rosetta wrinkled her nose.

Cara felt the heat rise in her cheeks. 'Oh... er... sorry, dear. It's just when you said Amy. I know someone called Ben who has a daughter called Amy, that's all.'

Benjamin had a daughter she didn't know about; a grandchild she'd never met. She ate her breakfast in silence, thinking of her eldest son and everything she wanted to say to him.

⏳

Later that day, Rosetta took Cara around town, but much to Cara's frustration they did not bump into Mandy, or her uncle "Paul".

⧗

That evening Gloria carried a portable television into Cara's bedroom. Smiling, she placed the television opposite the bed, handing Cara the remote control. 'This television was in the kitchen, but I can watch the one in the living room,' she said, sitting on the chair next to the bed.

'Thank you.'

'It's the least I can do, really.' Gloria was wearing a floral blue and white apron over her dress. She reached into the pocket of the apron and pulled out a necklace. The chain held a silver locket engraved with the initial "C" in swirly script.

Gloria held it up in front of Cara. 'I found this in our room when I came back to live here,' she said.

Cara gulped.

'I should have returned it to you back then,' said Gloria, 'but we were so estranged. I put it in a trinket box and it's been in there for the past forty-odd years.'

Cara gaped at the shiny silver pendant as a multitude of memories were evoked.

Gloria held the necklace towards her, waiting for her to take it.

Did Gloria know it was a gift from Frederick? Was she about to use it as an excuse to make a spiteful remark? But the relaxed expression on Gloria's face did not appear to bear malice.

Cara reached out hesitantly and took the necklace. The cold metal in her hand still felt familiar. She'd worn it every day that summer and had never taken it off until the night she fell from Stoneleigh Cliffs.

Her father had collected her from the hospital. When he asked her what had happened, she'd made up a story about how she foolishly went for a walk on the cliffs not realising how windy it was.

Whilst getting ready for bed that night, she had noticed the locket when its shine reflected off the mirror. Frustration tore at her from the inside.

Fiddling with the clasp, Cara had practically torn the chain from her neck. Why hadn't it come off when she'd landed in the sea? Why hadn't it disappeared into the vast ocean? Like a curse, the locket remained.

She'd put it in a drawer that night intending to get rid of it, and she very nearly did.

Now, fifty years later, she sat marvelling at the necklace in her hand, mystified at how it had survived the fall from the cliff. It represented a link to the past. The urge to open the locket was great, but she resisted, feeling embarrassed that Gloria might see the contents.

Then she realised that Gloria must have already looked inside, and her heart skipped a beat.

'Well, I'd better get ready for bed,' said Gloria, standing up.

Cara somehow managed to pull her eyes away from the locket's spell so she could respond to her sister. 'Thank you,' she said softly, holding up the shiny silver pendant.

Gloria walked to the door, then she turned around.

Cara braced herself. Would she comment about Frederick's hair?

'I can tell that locket means a lot to you.'

'Yes, it does.'

'You know, Cara, you and Beattie were lucky to have such a strong friendship. I know it was cut short, but many people don't get the opportunity to have a good close friend even if they live into old age.'

Cara breathed a silent sigh of relief, glad the topic of conversation had changed but slightly confused as to why Gloria was talking about Beattie.

'Did she also have a locket with a lock of your hair in it?' asked Gloria.

Cara's frown transformed into a smile. 'I can't remember,' she lied.

When Gloria had left the room, Cara opened the locket and saw the strands of hair; unmistakably Frederick's hair. Jet black. She was surprised that Gloria had believed it was Beattie's hair, which had been brown. Cara recalled the day Frederick gave her the gift.

Frederick produced a piece of jewellery from his navy blue waistcoat pocket. 'This belonged to my mother,' he said.

They were seated opposite each other at a table outside a roadside café, some miles from Huddlesea.

'I'd like you to have it.'

His brown eyes appeared to be darker than ever, even though the late evening sun cast a light across his face.

Cara admired the fine silver chain and pretty oval locket. 'It's beautiful,' she said. Her mind went back to a conversation they'd had a few days after they first met: he'd told her, with tears in his eyes, that his mother had died the year before and how she missed her so much. He must really love me if he's giving me her necklace. The idea made her feel light-headed and dizzy. Soon perhaps he would ask her to marry him... She reached out to take the necklace.

He cupped his hands over hers and held tightly for a few moments.

Cara gazed into his eyes.

He loosened his grip and held the necklace up in front of him. Standing up, he said, 'Let me put it on you.'

Frederick gently placed the chain around her neck as she lifted up her long hair.

He returned to his seat. 'It really suits you, Cara.'

'Thank you.' She lifted the pendant to see it more clearly. 'What was your mother's name?'

'Caroline,' he said. 'She would have liked you. I'm sure you two would have got on really well.'

She grinned and then opened the locket. 'It's empty. I could put your photograph inside.'

'You don't need my photograph. I'm right here.' He chuckled.

'I have an idea.' Cara picked up her handbag from the chair beside her and unzipped it. She took out her nail scissors.

'What are you doing?' His forehead lined in confusion.

'I'm going to give you a haircut!' she said, standing up.

'Cara, please.' He narrowed his eyes at her, as if he thought she'd gone mad.

'Don't worry, I only need one tiny lock.'

Frederick placed his hands over his hair as she approached him. 'Cara, sit down.'

'Don't you trust me?'

'What are you doing?' he asked again.

Cara noticed the café's only other customer, an old man sitting at the table by the door smoking a pipe, was watching them. It didn't bother her. She felt carefree: didn't have to worry about anyone recognising her here. As she smiled at the old man, he turned away and carried on reading his newspaper.

She snipped some of Frederick's hair, despite his protests, and returned to her chair.

'What have you done?' He touched the back of his head, bemusement written in his crinkled brow. 'My barber won't be very impressed!'

'Stop making a fuss, Freddie.' Giggling, she placed the lock of hair into the little silver pendant and snapped it shut.

He screwed up his face.

'What I've done is make sure we'll always be together, no matter how far apart we are,' she said. 'I'll always have a lock of your hair. It's lucky; it

means we'll never part.'

⧗

Cara stared at the tiny strands of jet black hair, battling with the images tumbling through her mind. Closing the locket, she placed it in the top drawer of the bedside cabinet before settling down to sleep.

CHAPTER FIFTEEN

It was raining the next morning when Rosetta arrived, so they decided to stay indoors. Rosetta spent most of the day watching television.

Cara had to remind her to fetch lunch, and the young girl was reluctant to budge. When she eventually left the room, Cara switched off the television and hid the remote control under her pillow.

On returning with the sandwiches, Rosetta frowned at the blank television screen. 'Shall I switch the TV on?' she asked, searching for the remote control.

'No, dear, I've got a bit of a headache,' said Cara. Then, catching sight of Rosetta's disappointed expression, she said, 'Do you have any brothers or sisters, Rosie?' She felt obliged to talk to her since she had taken away her entertainment.

'No, I'm an only child. You're lucky to have a sister. I've always wanted a sister.'

Cara shrugged. 'You have Mandy. She's like a sister to you, isn't she?'

'I suppose so.'

'Sometimes friends can be better than sisters,' Cara said.

'I just feel sad that I'll never know what it's like to be so closely related to someone and grow up with them. It must be great.'

'Gloria and I didn't get on well when we were younger. I spent most of my time with my best friend, rather like you and Mandy. So you see, it's not necessarily better for people who have siblings.' Cara turned her attention to the view from the window as images of the tree house where she'd played with Beattie flashed through her mind.

'Maybe that's true,' said Rosetta. 'But if I ever get married, I'm planning to have more than one child.'

'It is nice to have family around you,' said Cara, feeling suddenly sorry for Rosetta, sensing her loneliness and isolation. She was reminded of Benjamin, who was always quite a lone figure in their family. 'Even in bigger families there can be children who don't get on with the others,' she said, speaking her thoughts.

'I suppose so,' said Rosetta, shrugging. 'Maybe it's because I don't have any, but I've just always been secretly jealous of my friends who have brothers and sisters. Although, a friend of mine, Lucy, she's an only child and she loves it. She says we get all the attention from our parents. No competition. I'm not very competitive though. My friend Edie says that she's jealous of me because she's got three sisters and her parents don't have enough money to buy stuff for all of them, so they always have to share things.'

'There are advantages and disadvantages to having a large family,' said Cara.

'How many children do you have?' asked Rosetta, after a pause.

'Three.'

'That's nice. Did they all get on well when they were growing up?'

'Two of them did. My eldest was a little different from the other two.'

'Do you see them all regularly?'

'Not as much as I'd like to, but they're busy with their lives. They've all got their own families. I have five grandchildren, and two great-grandchildren.'

'Wow!' said Rosetta.

No, thought Cara, *I have six grandchildren; Benjamin has a daughter I've never met.* Tears threatened to fall.

Wanting to unburden herself, she began telling Rosetta how Benjamin left home nearly sixteen years ago and how no one had heard from him since. She explained how his wife took their youngest daughter, Jemima, to live with her in Jersey and she had not seen or heard from either of them in over ten years. She also told her how Penelope fled from her violent husband and took Carl and Andrew to a refuge.

Rosetta listened intently.

Cara managed to tell it all without crying. Afterwards, she worried that she'd revealed too much to this young girl. Somehow, though, it came as a relief to divulge everything to someone who was fully removed from the situation, everything about her sorrow at being parted from her close family. It was as if she'd been waiting for the opportunity to arise so she could release some of the burden.

That night, when Rosetta left, Cara cried. She cried until she felt she could cry no more. She wanted her family together: to know they were all right.

CHAPTER SIXTEEN

When Cara woke up on Thursday morning, she felt a sense of unease. Sitting up in bed, she settled her pillow behind her, all the while thinking of her dream. Billy was so young and handsome in the dream; they had been in his car, both so happy, laughing and smiling. Billy kissed her and told her he loved her, but in an instant his face changed and it was no longer Billy looking back at her but Frederick. She'd melted into his deep brown eyes, then she woke up.

She remembered again that it would soon be the tenth anniversary of Billy's death. Cara visited Billy's grave regularly with Penelope and never missed the anniversary of his death. She and Penelope made an occasion of it every year: cleaning the tombstone, clearing the weeds growing around it, placing a bouquet of fresh flowers onto the grave.

In an attempt to distract herself, Cara picked up the remote control and switched on the television. Even as she watched the pictures on the screen flickering and changing, her dream remained uppermost in her mind. Why had she dreamt of Frederick?

The locket.

Her intention, on placing the locket in the drawer, had been to leave it there; it was a reminder of a time in her life she would prefer to forget. Now, though, curiosity reared its head.

Hesitantly, she reached into the drawer and took out the necklace. She'd thought it was beautiful when Frederick first gave it to her; she still thought so. Despite the painful recollections, she absent-mindedly fastened the chain around her neck and touched the locket as it lay against her chest. She could not avoid the question that then entered her mind: *I wonder if Freddie is still alive.*

Their relationship had ended so suddenly. She'd been in love with him and was left not knowing if he'd ever really loved her. His unexpected revelation—that he was married—had torn to pieces all her dreams of their future together; everything she'd hoped and lived for up to that moment dissolved into nothing. Her life moved on, but in a completely different direction.

Long after marrying Billy, she would lie awake at night and think about Frederick, and every so often, when alone, she cried over him. She longed for an answer, needed to know whether—even for one precious minute—she'd been as important to him as he'd been to her. To know this would be to know she hadn't lived a lie. But she couldn't ask him—he'd disappeared. Her question would remain unanswered, trapped in the maze of her memory.

The locket was loaded with reminders of the past, it seemed, and Cara felt guilty, as if she'd betrayed Billy by putting it on. A gift from another man containing a lock of his hair. She reached behind her neck to undo the clasp, but as she did so, Rosetta arrived. Cara did not have time to remove the necklace, so she pulled her nightdress up higher to cover the shiny locket.

'Hello, Cara, how are you today?'

Rosetta's voice brought Cara back to the present day. 'I'm fine, dear,' she said, forcing a smile.

'Are you sure?' Rosetta asked, as she placed the breakfast tray on the bed. 'You look tired. Did you sleep well?'

'Yes, I did, but I had a strange dream, that's all.'

'Really? What did you dream about?'

'Nothing. It's silly.' She wished she hadn't mentioned it.

'I've got a book about the meaning of dreams,' said Rosetta, grinning. 'I could find out what your dream meant.'

'It was nothing, dear,' Cara said with a dismissive wave of her hand.

Rosetta appeared dejected. She sat down and began switching television channels with the remote control.

Cara felt terrible for upsetting her. 'It was only a dream about my late husband. It shook me up a bit,' she explained. 'When you're as old as I am, the past can seem like a faraway place and every so often something reminds you of it.' She instinctively touched the locket, making sure to keep it hidden under her nightdress. 'It's all still there in my head. Now and then, I'll remember an event from the past and I can get a bit lost in it, I suppose.'

'Like coming back to Huddlesea?' said Rosetta. 'I bet seeing the old town again has made you remember a lot of things you'd forgotten.'

'Yes,' said Cara. 'Although, I don't think we ever really forget, we just sometimes have to be reminded.'

'So, did you meet your husband in Huddlesea?'

'Yes.' Cara lowered her eyes. 'Yes, I did.'

'That must be why you dreamt of him then,' said Rosetta.

'I do dream of him occasionally. He was a big part of my life. It's just that last night's dream...' Cara recalled the image of Frederick from her dream as the colour rose in her cheeks. She coughed to hide her discomposure. 'Um... it just reminded me that it's nearly ten years since he died.'

'Oh, I'm sorry to hear that.'

'I usually go to his grave on the anniversary of his death, but this year it might not happen.'

'Why not?' Rosetta raised her eyebrows.

'There's no one to take me.' Cara gave a wistful smile.

'I could take you,' offered Rosetta. 'Where is it?'

'Thank you for offering, Rosie, that's very kind of you, but it's in London. It's too far for you to take me.'

'London?' Rosetta narrowed her eyes in thought. 'What about your children? Can't one of them take you?'

'They're busy.'

'Too busy to go to their dad's grave? I'm sure they'd take you if you ask.'

Cara doubted Catherine or James would have the time to take her to the cemetery. They rarely went to the grave and had never gone along with her and Penelope on the anniversaries. They were too tied up with their own lives.

'Shall I ask Gloria to phone one of your children?'

'No, dear.'

'But it would be a pity for you to miss the anniversary. When is it?'

'The tenth of June. This Sunday.'

Gloria walked in. 'I'm going out, and I wondered whether you needed anything from the shops,' she said.

'No, thanks,' said Cara.

'Gloria,' said Rosetta. 'Would it be possible to arrange for Cara to see her husband's grave on Sunday? It's in London. It's the anniversary of his death.'

Gloria looked at Cara. 'I'll phone Catherine,' she said.

'Thank you,' said Cara.

'See?' said Rosetta, smiling, when Gloria had gone. 'I'm sure you'll be able to go.'

'Maybe.' Cara frowned.

Gloria returned to the bedroom a while later. 'I've phoned Catherine, but unfortunately she's already arranged to have dinner on Sunday with some old friends she hasn't seen for a while. It's too late for her to cancel, I'm afraid, but she did say she would try to arrange to take you to see the grave sometime next week, if you'd like.'

Cara could not hide the disappointment as her face took on a gloomy expression.

'I did ask for James's telephone number, but Catherine says he's away in South Africa,' explained Gloria. 'He won't be coming home until next week. Perhaps you could all arrange to go next week.'

'Yes, I suppose so; it will be a shame to miss the anniversary, though.' Cara sighed deeply.

'Don't worry, Cara,' said Rosetta, taking her hand. 'I'll ask Mandy if her uncle can drive you to London. They're going back on Sunday. She's got exams next week, so he has to drive her back there. He's coming back to Huddlesea because he's still got work to do here. I'm sure he wouldn't mind if you went with them, and it'd give me the excuse to tag along.'

'No. No, we couldn't ask him,' blurted Cara, in horror at the suggestion.

'I've always wanted to go to London,' Rosetta gushed, oblivious of Cara's objection.

'No, dear, I wouldn't want to impose,' said Cara, nervous at the prospect of seeing Benjamin again even though she'd prayed for an opportunity.

'Don't worry, it won't be any bother. We could make a day trip of it. Mandy's mum, Claire, will be going back too, and little Amy.'

'I'm sure they won't have enough room in the car for all of us, dear.'

'Cara's right, Rosie, I don't think it would be such a good idea,' said Gloria, still standing at the door. 'Mandy's uncle is a busy man, you mustn't ask him. It would be rude.'

'It's okay, Gloria, I know Mandy's uncle; he's great. He'll definitely agree,' said Rosetta.

'He might have other plans,' said Gloria. 'Don't ask him.'

Rosetta smiled at Cara as if she hadn't heard Gloria. Her eyes were misty, her head undoubtedly full of dreams of a trip to London. Cara returned Rosetta's smile, beginning to warm to the idea; at least it would give her the chance to find out what Benjamin had been up to.

Gloria mumbled a few unintelligible words and closed the bedroom door behind her.

Cara was suddenly struck by the idea that Gloria may try to stop her meeting with Benjamin. She'd been so against the idea of Rosetta asking Mandy's uncle to take them to London.

'I won't get a chance to see him,' she said, almost forgetting where she was.

'See who?' Rosetta's brow furrowed.

Cara opened and closed her mouth, unsure of what to say.

'Cara?' Rosetta pushed for an answer.

'Billy,' she replied, racking her brain. 'I meant I won't see my husband's grave.'

'Yes, you will, Cara, you will.'

Cara touched the locket and held it between her fingers. It was a habit she had, when wearing a pendant, to play with it while thinking, like someone might use a set of worry beads in contemplation.

'That's a nice necklace,' said Rosetta. 'Is it new?'

Cara's cheeks reddened. 'What? This?' she said, holding it out and hoping Rosetta wouldn't notice her discomposure: 'No, it's not new; it's quite old. I used to wear it when I was about your age, Rosie. Gloria found it and gave it back to me the other day.'

'It's lovely.' The young girl leaned forward to examine the pendant. 'It's got your initial on it. Wow, that's really nice. Is it real silver?'

'Yes, I think so.'

Rosetta took the locket between her fingers. 'If you used to wear it when you were my age, it might be an antique.'

Cara laughed. 'Just how old do you think I am?'

Rosetta blushed. 'Sorry, I didn't mean...'

'That's all right, dear. When I was your age, I thought forty was old.' She rolled her eyes. 'I am a bit of an antique, I suppose.' Her hand went up to the locket still in Rosetta's grip. Much to Cara's relief, the young girl let go of the pendant.

'Is there a photo inside?'

'No, dear.' Cara covered the necklace with her nightdress. 'There's nothing inside.' She looked straight ahead of her. 'What's on television, Rosie?' she asked, changing the subject.

⧗

That evening as Cara settled down to sleep, she felt the shiny silver locket on her chest and reached behind her neck for the clasp, eager to be free of it. 'Oh come on,' she grumbled under her breath, determined to banish this reminder of the past. It was no good, she couldn't undo the clasp on her own. Lying on the bed, exhausted from the struggle, she cursed herself for putting it on in the first place.

Thoughts of Frederick filled her mind, kindled from the ashes of her memory. Her reminiscences surprised her, as did the sentimental feelings that accompanied them.

She decided to try again tomorrow to remove the necklace and put it away somewhere it would remain hidden. Soon she drifted off to sleep, holding the locket between her fingers.

CHAPTER SEVENTEEN

The next day, Gloria entered Cara's bedroom early in the morning with the breakfast tray. 'Good morning, Cara, did you sleep well?'

'Yes, thank you. Where's Rosie this morning?' she asked, rubbing her eyes.

Gloria placed the tray on the bed and went to open the curtains. 'I'll be looking after you now. That will be nice, won't it?' She smiled and folded her arms.

'W-what happened to Rosie?'

'She's no longer working for me.'

'Oh.' Cara looked down at her breakfast tray, a sadness in her heart. She had enjoyed having Rosetta around. The loss reminded her of how Penelope had left so suddenly. The changes—people coming and going from her life—were quite hard to contend with. Rosetta hadn't even told her she was leaving. 'I did suspect that a young girl might find it a bit boring spending her time with an old woman like me,' she said. 'Hopefully she'll have found a more interesting job.' She glanced up at Gloria.

'I don't think she found it boring, Cara. She just wasn't the right person to be your carer. She's too young.' Gloria walked around the bed and sat on the chair. 'I should have known it wouldn't work out. I spoke to her last night when she was leaving and explained that she was too inexperienced. She wasn't very professional. Not what I'd expected at all.'

'You sacked her? But... You didn't mention any of your concerns to me.'

'I'm merely thinking of your best interests, Cara. Enjoy your breakfast. I'll pop in a bit later to see how you are.'

Cara watched her sister walk away, and as her mind tried to make sense of the situation she remembered the conversation she'd been having with Rosetta when Gloria interrupted them the day before. They'd been talking about Mandy's uncle. This wasn't about Rosetta at all; Gloria was trying to stop her finding out about Benjamin, wasn't she?

'Wait, Gloria!'

Gloria, now halfway out of the door, turned to face Cara.

'Rosie's such a kind, considerate girl, and I like her. Can't we give her another chance? She must be devastated.'

'She's a nice girl,' agreed Gloria, 'just not really the ideal person to look after you.' She appeared to be avoiding Cara's eyes.

'But how will you cope? I mean, it will be difficult for you to look after me.'

'I'm going to find someone to replace Rosetta, don't worry.' She took hold of the door handle.

'Gloria.' Cara made one final attempt: 'Will it still be possible for Mandy's uncle to drive me to Billy's grave on Sunday? I don't want to miss the anniversary.'

Gloria pursed her lips and looked up in contemplation. 'I'll book a taxi, and we'll go together, just the two of us.'

The walls of the bedroom felt more restrictive than ever to Cara, as claustrophobia overwhelmed her. Gloria was in control here, deciding what she could and couldn't do, who she saw and didn't see. It was hard to accept that this woman, who had been nothing more than a stranger and estranged for so many years, was now pulling the strings and dictating her life. What if her exterior friendliness was just a mask? Perhaps she was taking advantage of the opportunity to completely ruin her life. She would not be seeing Benjamin on Sunday; it was possible she would never see him again. How could she, trapped in this room?

'Is there something I should know?' The question came as Cara stared at her sister, released from her mouth absent-mindedly.

'I'm not quite sure I know what you mean,' Gloria replied, looking at her watch. 'I really do have to go.'

'About Mandy's uncle, Paul. Is there something you're not telling me?' Cara persisted.

Gloria appeared to freeze, but then turned to face Cara, her brow knitted. 'Paul is a busy man. Rosetta is too young to understand that people have responsibilities. That's one of the reasons I had to let her go, don't you see?'

Cara knew there was no point trying to explain to Gloria: having no children of her own, she would not comprehend the pain she'd felt every day of her life being far from her son with no idea whether he was alive or dead. She began to pick at her breakfast, eyes averted.

Gloria was still standing at the door. 'Don't worry, Cara, we'll go to London on Sunday. We'll visit the grave together.'

'All right,' Cara said dejectedly.

Gloria stood silently in the room for a short time.

After she left, Cara switched on the television to distract her mind as tears of frustration trickled down her cheeks.

CHAPTER EIGHTEEN

On Sunday morning, Cara woke up to the sound of hailstones pelting against her window. The dull light outside hardly brightened the bedroom at all, making it difficult to tell whether it was yet after sunrise. She lifted her head to take a look at the clock beside the bed.

7 o'clock.

As she rested her head on the pillow, a gloom that had nothing to do with the weather descended, causing a frown to form on her brow. Today she would be travelling to Billy's grave with Gloria. She dearly wanted to see the grave and feel close to Billy but dreaded the journey to London with her sister.

For the past couple of days Cara had spent long lonely hours staring out of the window at the back garden, preferring to be by herself in the room rather than with Gloria. They had nothing in common apart from bitter memories, and Cara became increasingly resentful about her sister's wilful decision making: she never consulted Cara about anything, just went ahead and made plans for her as if she were a child in her care.

The garden had not changed much since Cara was a young girl and as such it held the power to ignite her memory, taking her back to times she had thought were long forgotten. She and Beattie had spent most of their school holidays in the garden and exploring the forest that sprawled out beyond.

The previous morning, Gloria had noticed her looking out of the window as she brought her breakfast.

'I hired a gardener last month; he did a good job, didn't he?' said Gloria.

'Yes,' Cara replied, nodding, wondering—not for the first time—whether the tree house was still in the forest. Remembering her dream about Beattie, she felt a yearning to see the tree house again. If she asked Gloria about it, though, it would mean having a conversation about Beattie.

'Do you remember playing in the garden as a child?' asked Gloria.

'Yes.'

'With Beattie.'

The mention of her lost friend's name came unexpectedly, and Cara searched her sister's face for any signs of awkwardness.

Gloria smiled at her and resumed looking out at the garden.

Cara decided that in the circumstances perhaps it would be okay to ask about the tree house.

Gloria's response was: 'Tree house? I didn't know about any tree houses there.'

'Yes, we used to go through the gate at the back, to the forest. We played in it all the time.'

'Hmm... Well, a few years ago, a fire in the forest destroyed most, if not all, of the trees. They've had to be replanted,' Gloria explained.

Cara turned towards the window, a sadness in her eyes. It felt like part of her history had been erased.

⌛

The taxi arrived at eleven o'clock to take them to London. As Gloria pushed the wheelchair along the path towards the taxi, Cara couldn't help wishing she were leaving this house for good.

'I'll go and ask the driver if he'll help me with the wheelchair,' said Gloria.

When her sister had gone, Cara noticed a girl running towards her. As the girl came closer, Cara saw it was Rosetta. She looked younger than ever, not dressed in smart work clothes now but in a pair of blue jeans and a black T-shirt with a picture of a white cat on the front. Her long hair was tied up in a ponytail. Seeing her again brought a smile to Cara's face.

'Hello, Cara,' Rosetta said, standing beside her, slightly out of breath after her run. 'Are you going somewhere?'

'Yes, I'm going to London, to my husband's grave.'

Rosetta's bright smile faded. 'But this is a taxi.'

'Yes, dear.'

'But Mandy's uncle said he'd take you to London. I came to get you.'

Gloria and the taxi driver approached them.

'Could you two lovely ladies help this beautiful creature out of the wheelchair so I can put the chair in the back of the cab?' The driver winked at Cara. He was a muscular man with a shaved head, a plethora of earrings in his ears, and a tattoo of a fire-breathing dragon on his right arm.

'But Gloria,' said Rosetta. 'We don't need a taxi; Paul will drive us to London. We're all ready to go.'

'There's no need. The taxi's here,' said Gloria sternly, walking nearer to the cab.

'We don't need a taxi,' said Rosetta, grasping the wheelchair's handles and manoeuvring it away from the cab.

'Rosetta!' shouted Gloria. 'I'm sorry about this,' she said to the taxi driver, as she followed Rosetta, who was pushing the wheelchair quickly along the street.

The taxi driver pointed at his watch. 'Look, lady,' he huffed impatiently. 'I haven't got all day. Do you need a taxi or not?'

'I'll be with you in a minute,' said Gloria.

By the time she'd caught up with Rosetta, the girl was at the corner of the high street talking to a tall, slim, blonde woman, who was wearing a pink, floral summer dress. A large bag, that appeared to be made of straw, hung from the woman's shoulder. Her apparel gave the impression she was a holidaymaker, a little out of place here under the grey skies of Huddlesea.

'Rosetta,' said Gloria, catching her breath.

'Claire,' said Rosetta. 'This is Gloria, Cara's sister.'

'Hello, it's nice to meet you,' said Claire, reaching out a hand.

'There's been a misunderstanding,' said Gloria, red-faced and panting. 'I've got a taxi to take us to London.'

'No, no, you don't want to be spending money on taxis. No. My Paul will take us,' said Claire, smiling brightly. 'We'll all fit in the car, no problem. It's an estate.' She looked at Cara. 'Do you know, Rosie's been so excited about this trip to London, haven't you, love? She's never been to London before. I'm looking forward to showing her all the sights.' She pushed away a lock of hair that had fallen across her face.

'But we don't want to impose,' said Gloria, impatiently.

'Don't be silly. We were driving to London anyway, and Paul has to come back here for a few more days for work, so it's no big deal. Besides, it's Rosie's birthday on Tuesday, isn't it, love? I've told her this can be our present to her: a birthday treat. Paul said we should go without you two, especially as you sacked Rosie on Thursday, but Rosie's such a sweet girl, she didn't want Cara to miss out on seeing her husband's grave today. We decided it would be unfair if we went all the way to London without taking her.'

Gloria lowered her head. 'I still think Cara and I should go separately in the taxi. It's nice of you to think of us, but—'

'No,' said Rosetta. 'We'll take you.' Then she said, 'Cara, who would you rather go to London with? A taxi or us?'

Cara opened and closed her mouth, not knowing what to say.

'Of course she doesn't want to go in a taxi,' said Claire, taking hold of the handles of the wheelchair. Cara recognised the perfume she was wearing as the one Penelope used to wear; she associated the sweet flowery smell with her granddaughter and felt a sharp longing to see her again.

'Come on, everyone,' said Claire as she walked along the high

109

street. 'Follow me.'

'I'll have to go back and pay the taxi driver,' said Gloria.

'We'll wait for you,' said Claire, cheerfully.

'No, don't.' Gloria waved a hand. 'I was only going to London to keep Cara company. You don't mind if I don't come, do you, Cara?'

'No, not at all.'

'Well, have a good time, I'll see you later.' Gloria shrugged as she walked away.

⏳

As they approached the guest house, Cara questioned whether meeting Benjamin in these circumstances would be the right thing to do. How would he react?

'You two, wait out here,' said Claire. 'I'll go inside and get Amy and Mandy, and I'll tell Paul we're ready to leave.' She disappeared inside the house.

'Rosie dear.'

'Yes, Cara?'

'I... I should go to London with Gloria, I feel dreadful for letting her down.'

Rosetta opened her mouth to protest, but Cara continued: 'Could you take me back to the house, please?' She felt her temperature rise.

Just then, a little girl with long black hair and shining brown eyes exited the house and ran along the path: Amy. She reminded Cara of Penelope at that age.

Amy skipped and smiled, playing with the daisies that grew along the side of the pathway.

Cara could not help staring at the child.

Claire was the next person to come out of the guest house; she left the door open. Bracing herself, Cara looked into the passage of the building: soon Benjamin would appear.

'I'm really sorry about this,' said Claire as she came closer. She leaned over to speak to Cara, who was sitting almost on the edge of her wheelchair in anticipation. 'It looks as though Paul won't have time to drive us to London, after all.'

'Why?' Rosetta walked out from behind the wheelchair.

'There's a note on the fridge door; he's been called out by his office to show a house to an important client. I phoned him on his mobile and he says he'll be gone for a good few hours. I knew something was up when I saw the car wasn't parked outside.'

110

'He's working on a Sunday?' asked Rosetta.

'It can't be helped,' said Cara.

'But I have to get back to London today,' said Mandy, who was now standing beside Cara. 'My exams start tomorrow.'

'I know, love.' Claire put an arm around her daughter. 'Paul said we should get a taxi and he'll come later to bring the suitcases.'

'Maybe you should wait for your husband,' suggested Cara. 'Then you can all go to London together. It's silly paying a taxi if he's going to London later to take your suitcases.'

'But it'll be late by the time he gets back,' said Claire. 'It's not right; it's the anniversary of your husband's death. Rosie was telling me how much you were looking forward to it.'

'I'll go and see whether the taxi is still at Gloria's house,' said Rosetta, running towards the high street.

'I'll come with you.' Mandy followed her.

'Yes, hurry, you might catch him. Ask him to wait!' Claire called out after them. 'Cara, do you mind if we all come in your taxi? I mean, we could share the fare.'

'Of course, dear. The more the merrier.'

Amy approached Cara. 'Why are you sitting down?' the little girl asked.

Cara's eyes filled with tears, as she mused at how much Amy resembled Penelope... and Benjamin.

'She's resting her legs, darling,' said Claire.

Amy began playing with the frilly edges of Cara's dress, which were hanging from the sides of the wheelchair.

'Amy, stop that,' chided Claire.

'That's all right,' said Cara, smiling and wiping a tear from her eye.

'Don't worry, Cara,' said Claire. 'We'll get you to London one way or another. You'll get to see your husband's grave, I promise.'

Soon Rosetta and Mandy returned, running along the street. 'The taxi'd already gone by the time we got there,' said Rosetta, puffing, 'but Gloria has phoned for another one. It should be here soon.'

'Great!' said Claire.

Cara felt a sense of relief but also frustration. On the one hand, she remembered how nervous she'd been when she thought Benjamin would be taking them to London, but equally, there was a part of her that just wanted to get everything out in the open, to stop playing games.

⧗

'Amy, help Mandy with the bags,' said Claire as they stepped out of the taxi in London.

'Here you are, Amy, you carry the sandwiches and I'll carry the drinks,' said Mandy.

'Cara, are you comfortable?' asked Rosetta, after she'd helped her into the wheelchair.

'Yes, dear, thank you.' It was a warm day, which had made the drive to London quite intolerable as there were so many of them in the taxi.

'Amy, stop running,' called Claire, chasing after her daughter as they entered the cemetery gates.

Visiting Billy's grave had always been such a private, family occasion; it seemed wrong to turn it into a party. The others were already chatting excitedly about how much they were looking forward to seeing the sights of London. This was probably a frustrating pit stop for them; no doubt they'd be in a rush to leave. Cara usually sensed Billy's presence when she was at his graveside; it was a special feeling. Now she almost wished she had not come at all. It wouldn't be the same.

She bought a bunch of pink roses interlaced with gypsophila from the flower seller at the cemetery gates, then navigated the way to Billy's grave.

'Here it is: Billy's grave!' shouted Rosetta excitedly as they reached the tombstone, as if they'd happened upon a site of public interest.

The others flocked around the wheelchair.

'Hello, Billy,' said Cara addressing the black granite stone, which she noticed had lost its shine. 'I'm sorry it's been such a long time. I would have liked to have come sooner, but it couldn't be helped. I've brought you some flowers.' She leaned forward to place the flowers in front of the tombstone.

'Mummy.' Amy held tightly to Claire's arm and said, 'Who is she talking to?'

'No one, darling.'

'Mummy, I'm scared. I want to go home.'

'Don't be silly, Amy.'

The little girl started to cry. 'She's talking to a ghost.'

Claire leaned down and whispered into Amy's ear, then smiled at Cara. 'I'm sorry about this.'

'Don't worry, dear.'

'It's a lovely headstone,' said Claire, surveying the granite carved cross. '"William Patrick Edwards, a loving husband and father, rest in peace",' she read from the tombstone. 'He died quite young, didn't he? Sorry, Cara, I didn't mean to sound...'

'He did die young,' said Cara. 'It was a car accident.'

'Mummy, can we go?' Amy tugged at Claire's arm.

'Not yet, sweetie. Cara wants to stay a bit longer.'

'But I'm hungry and I'm scared.'

'Wait a minute, sweetie.'

They stood at the graveside in silence for a short while.

Although a wooden bench faced the grave, none of them sat down. This only reinforced Cara's belief that they would rather be anywhere else.

She noticed the weeds forming near the tombstone and a sadness descended. It looked like a grave belonging to someone who had been forgotten by his loved ones. 'We should have brought some scissors to clear these weeds,' she said, to no one in particular.

'Mummy,' said Amy, 'I want to go to the toilet.'

'Oh dear.' Claire sighed. 'We'll have to go, I'm afraid.'

Cara could feel the impatience in the air around her. She wanted to stay. The others were all just waiting to leave. She acknowledged defeat. 'All right, dear, thank you for bringing me.'

As they left the cemetery, Cara felt lonelier than she had done in years. The purpose of the trip to London had been to visit Billy's grave, but they'd spent little more than a quarter of an hour in the graveyard.

'That was nice,' said Claire, as they walked along the street.

'No it wasn't,' said Amy. 'I found it spooky. Graveyards are where all the ghosts live.'

'Don't be silly, sweetheart. There's no such thing as ghosts.' Claire giggled.

'Yes, there is,' retorted Amy. 'I read a story about one in school.'

'That was only a story, Amy,' said Mandy, laughing.

They decided to go to a nearby park to eat their sandwiches.

Claire laid out a picnic blanket and said, 'We'll go and see Madame Tussauds and the Tower of London when we've finished our lunch.'

'Wow!' said Rosetta.

Cara wished she could go back home.

⧗

At seven o'clock that evening, Claire decided that she, Mandy, and Amy would take the Tube to their house. 'It'll be cheaper than a taxi, and after spending so much on shopping, it would be wise.' She held up the multitude of shopping bags they had somehow accumulated.

Cara had presumed they would all take a taxi and drop Claire, Mandy, and Amy off at home, and she'd been looking forward to this as the day out drew to a close, curious to see where Benjamin lived. 'But how will you manage on the train with all those bags?' she asked.

'There aren't that many bags between Mandy and me. We'll be okay,' said Claire.

'Yeah, it's only a few clothes. Nothing heavy,' added Mandy.

'Do you have far to go?' asked Cara.

'No, just a few stops,' said Claire.

Cara was about to ask where they live when Claire spotted a taxi. 'I'll stop this taxi for you.' She flagged down the cab. 'Have a safe trip to Huddlesea,' she said. 'And make sure you come and see us, Rosie. You've got the address. You're welcome too, anytime, Cara.' She smiled and kissed Rosetta on the cheek. 'Have a great time on your birthday, love.'

'Thank you, Claire, and thanks for the present.' Rosetta held up the sleek black carrier bag which contained her new pair of shoes.

'You're welcome, Rosie.'

Rosetta helped Cara into the taxi. 'Bye, Mandy,' she said, getting into the cab.

'Bye, Rosie. Phone me when you get home.'

'Okay.'

'Where do they live?' asked Cara as the taxi drove away.

'In Wembley.'

Although not exactly local to Penelope's house, it would have taken less than an hour for Benjamin to visit her. Why hadn't he ever visited? A tear came to her eye.

Leaning back in the taxi seat, she focussed on the view outside the window, wanting to be free of the melancholic thoughts that were hounding her. Daylight was fading and she felt her energy waning, certain she would fall asleep if she allowed herself to close her eyes.

She tried to concentrate on the events of the day so that she wouldn't linger on Benjamin's indifference. Amy had been complaining and crying for most of the day. First, she didn't want to go to Madame Tussauds or the Tower of London, and made such a fuss in the queues that they decided not to bother. Then she wanted to buy all the toys in the shops, and burst into tears whenever Claire refused.

In the end, most of the day was spent shopping for a present for Rosetta's birthday. They had been to at least a dozen shops before she finally chose a pair of shoes. Claire had practically picked up a whole new wardrobe of clothes for herself, Mandy, and Amy, along the way.

Cara had endured a day of endless crowds of tourists and shoppers, and now all she wanted to do was sleep.

☒

Back at the house that evening, Gloria helped her into bed. 'Did you enjoy yourself today, Cara?'

'Yes, it was nice,' she said, not wanting to sound ungrateful. 'I would have liked to have spent more time at Billy's grave, though.'

'We can go to the grave together soon, if you'd like.'

The suggestion took Cara by surprise, but it pleased her. 'I'd like that if it's not too much bother. Thank you.'

'It would be a pleasure.' Gloria was sitting on the edge of her bed. She did not usually stop to talk in the evenings. 'Cara, I have to speak to you.' She paused as if unsure whether to continue, then took a deep breath: 'Perhaps I should have told you years ago, I don't know,' she said, looking at her hands.

Cara's thoughts turned to Benjamin.

'It's about Mandy's uncle...' Gloria hesitated. 'Ever since you came to stay here, I've been worried he might come to Huddlesea. He's often in town for work. The thing is, I didn't want to have to tell you, but—' She stopped.

'What is it?' asked Cara, even though she already knew what the response would be.

Gloria pursed her lips.

Unable to bear the suspense, Cara said, 'I think I already know what you're going to tell me.'

'H-have you seen him? I-I thought you took a taxi in the end.'

'Yes, yes, we did. I saw him in town the other day.'

'So, you know...?'

'What is it that I should know?'

'You said you've seen him.'

'He's Ben, isn't he?'

Gloria nodded, eyes down.

'I knew it!' said Cara. 'He had dark glasses on, and it's been nearly sixteen years, but I knew it!' Her words spilled out excitedly. Although more or less sure she'd seen Benjamin, there had been a sliver of doubt; now her suspicions were confirmed.

Gloria stood up.

'Wait. How long have you known?' Cara trembled.

'Well, from the start, I suppose.'

'What do you mean "the start"?'

'Paul... Um... Benjamin came here when he left home. He told me he needed somewhere to stay.' She sat on the chair next to the bed and recounted the events of that night.

A loud knock on the front door shook Gloria from her sleep. Switching on her bedside lamp and looking at the clock on the wall, she questioned, in her half-asleep state, whether it was really true that someone had knocked the door at this time of night or had she been awoken by a nightmare? It was just after three o'clock in the morning. Another knock followed, which sounded louder than the first; it answered her question.

Who could be calling at this hour? A drunk? Someone of unsound mind? Living alone in the big house made her feel vulnerable. She switched off her lamp, conscious that whoever was outside might see the light. A voice shouted: 'Gloria!'

It was a man. Not a voice she recognised. Fearful, she decided that calling the police would be the best option. Then she heard the voice again: 'Aunty Glor, let me in.'

"Aunty"? It must be one of Cara's sons—Benjamin or James. But what would they be doing in Huddlesea? They lived in London. And why come here in the middle of the night?

Getting out of bed, she stepped into her slippers and pulled on her dressing gown. She hurried down the stairs and along the hallway towards the front door. Had something happened to Cara?

Gloria put the security chain on the door and opened it cautiously. She caught her breath at the sight of Benjamin standing outside. There were dark circles around his eyes and his clothes were dirty, as if he'd walked all the way from London.

'Is Cara all right?' she asked, concern wrinkling her brow.

'I haven't come here to play happy families,' he said impatiently. 'Let me in, it's freezing out here.'

'Wait,' she said, closing the door to unhook the security chain. When she opened the door he charged his way through and into the living room.

Gloria followed him, wary. She hadn't seen him for many years, didn't know him. What if he'd just escaped from prison?

He appeared agitated, and she was sure she'd smelt alcohol when he'd rushed past her.

'Benjamin, it's late: why have you come here?' she asked, trembling.
He was unshaven, dishevelled.

'You've got to help me. I'm in trouble. I need somewhere to hide. Don't tell anyone I'm here.' Practically collapsing onto the sofa, he began to shake, covering his face with his hands. After a minute or so, he raised his head and glared at her. 'I think I've killed Maggie.'

Gloria shivered. He'd killed someone? Maggie? Who was Maggie? She took a couple of steps backwards. 'Er... Wh-who is Ma-Mag—'

'My wife!' he snapped. 'I think I've killed my wife.' He looked at her with hollow eyes.

She turned away, intimidated by his stare. He could be mad. If he'd killed his wife, her own life may be in danger. She crossed her arms defensively. Looking more closely at his clothing, she noticed a few dark stains: blood?

'I need you to phone my mum.'

'But it's late.'

'Not now... Tomorrow. You have to find out if Maggie's dead.' He walked towards her.

She took a few more steps back, wrapping her dressing gown tighter around her.

'No one can know I'm here, okay?'

His eyes were glazed over, unfocussed, and she could now clearly smell the alcohol on his breath.

Gloria spent a restless night, tossing and turning, fearful that Benjamin might enter her room. If he thought she knew too much, he would want to get rid of her. Her mind churned everything over, unable to quieten. Why did he come here? Was she an accessory to the murder if she kept him in the house? She felt too afraid to call the police.

The next day, Gloria dialled Cara's number on Benjamin's instructions. She hadn't spoken to her sister for years.

Benjamin was watching her intently from across the kitchen table, waiting in nervous anticipation to find out if he was a killer.

Earlier that morning, he'd explained how after he and Margaret had a row he'd thrown her down the stairs: 'She wound me up!' he said, as if justifying his actions. 'Anyone would have done it. She nags. All the time. She nags and nags.'

'Hello.' Cara answered the phone.

'Hello, it's Gloria.'

'I'm sorry,' said Cara, 'but I'm just on my way out.'

Gloria wasn't surprised by her sister's icy reception. If it had been Cara calling her, she would have reacted in the same way. 'I wouldn't be calling if it wasn't important.'

'What do you want?' Cara huffed.

'I know we haven't really spoken to each other in the past few years, but —'

'Oh, Glor, I'm not in the mood. I have to go.'

'You sound upset,' said Gloria, trying to keep her on the line, worried what Benjamin would do if she didn't get the information he wanted. 'What's happened?'

'I'm on my way to see Maggie... Ben's wife. She's in hospital.'

'W-what's wrong with her?'

'Oh... like you care! If you must know, she was taken there last night. She fell—fractured her neck.'

'Will she be all right?'

'Why the sudden concern? Have you even met her?'

'You might find it hard to believe, but I do still care about you and your family,' said Gloria.

Benjamin was drumming his fingers on the wooden table, impatiently waiting for an answer.

'I don't understand why you've called today, out of the blue. It's inconvenient.'

'I hope Ben's wife recovers soon.'

'She'll survive but might be paralysed,' said Cara on a sigh. 'Not that it's any of your business. I really have to go.' With that, Cara hung up the phone.

When Gloria replaced the receiver, Benjamin leaned forward. 'Well?'

'Your wife is fine.'

'Are you sure? You sounded concerned about her on the phone.' He narrowed his eyes.

'She's in hospital with a fractured neck. She might be paralysed, but she'll survive.'

Benjamin leaned back in his chair, pale and listless.

'You should go home, Benjamin. Your mother's worried about you,' she lied, hoping to convince him.

'They all hate me. They're better off without me. I'm not going back.' He covered his face with his hands, elbows leaning on the table in front of him. After a few moments, he looked up at Gloria, wide-eyed. 'I nearly killed Maggie. She might never walk again because of me. I can't go back there. I have

118

Cara gaped in disbelief as Gloria relayed the story of how Benjamin had fled to Huddlesea.

For years after Benjamin disappeared, whenever Cara saw homeless people or drunks on the street she would peer into their weather-worn faces praying not to see her son's eyes looking back at her. She'd always stop on the street and give these people some change, hoping someone would do the same for Benjamin. Every passing car, every man on the street might have been him. She'd been stuck in a state of constant anticipation, waiting for any news.

'Why didn't you tell me he was alive?' she asked Gloria.

'I-I.'

'Do you know how I've worried all these years? Why didn't you tell me he came here?'

'I wanted to tell you back then, the day I phoned. I didn't want him in my house. He frightened the life out of me. But I couldn't bring myself to tell you. I knew he'd be angry with me if I did. Anyway, I hoped that when he found out his wife was all right he'd go home.'

'Yes, but he didn't, did he? He stayed here with you and you still didn't tell me. Why?'

'He didn't want me to, Cara. He withdrew into himself so much that I started to worry about his state of mind. He struck me as unstable at times. He did seem really sorry for what he'd done. I got the impression he needed time to come to terms with it and straighten himself out. I wanted to give him that chance.' She appeared thoughtful, as if recalling a memory. 'I used to hear him in his room crying. He kept telling me he wanted to start a new life.'

'One phone call, that's all it would've taken,' moaned Cara. 'You wouldn't have had to tell him you'd called me. It would have put my mind at rest.'

Gloria opened and closed her mouth then frowned as she said, 'Y-you knew he ran away believing he'd killed his wife.'

'Yes, we knew that, but we didn't know what happened to him after he left.'

'He kept saying he was sure you'd all had enough of him, that you'd be happier if he kept his distance.'

'That wasn't true.'

'He told me he'd abused his wife for years and felt ashamed of himself. It took nearly killing her to bring him to his senses. He knew he couldn't go on like that and said he needed to put it all behind him. That's probably why he decided to change his name: he wanted a whole new identity.'

'I want to meet with him,' said Cara.

'Are you sure that's wise?'

'He's my son! He's been missing for years and I thought he was dead. Gloria, you've had so many chances to tell me over the years. Why didn't you ever tell me, for God's sake?' Cara struggled to hold back her tears.

'I'm sorry, I thought it was for the best,' mumbled Gloria, handing her a tissue.

'You were so wrong. You have no idea how wrong you were.' Cara sniffed and wiped her eyes.

'I'm so sorry.' Gloria looked down at her hands.

'Please, I have to see him. Tell him I want to see him.'

'I don't know.'

'You owe it to me, Glor. You have no idea how I've cried myself to sleep over the years.'

'I didn't want to interfere,' said Gloria.

'So you just let me think he was dead.'

'But... You knew he'd gone into hiding believing he'd killed his wife.'

'Yes, but when he didn't contact us for years, I started to worry that I might never see him again.'

'I'm sorry, Cara. What more can I say?'

Cara stared out of the window. 'A few years ago, Cathy and I tried to find him,' she said. 'We contacted the police, but nothing came up in the usual searches. They were going to investigate further, but I called it off. I couldn't bear it. I still wanted to have hope that he'd return one day.' She covered her face with her hands.

Gloria placed a hand on Cara's arm. 'Maybe I should have told you.'

'There's no maybe about it.' Cara glared at her sister. Then, sighing, she said, 'Oh, well, what's done is done, but now I know he's in Huddlesea, I must see him. All I'm asking is for you to tell him I need to see him. Please.'

'All right.' Gloria stood up. 'Get some sleep. I'll try to speak to him tomorrow.'

CHAPTER NINETEEN

Cara woke up the next morning with a renewed sense of hope. Her dream of all her family being reunited no longer seemed as unrealistic or distant.

She was alone in the house for most of the morning. Gloria had gone out, to talk to Benjamin.

Doubts surfaced in Cara's mind as the minutes ticked by: would he agree to see her now he had a new life with Claire?

She switched on the television to distract herself, but it didn't work. There were too many questions floating around in her head. What would she say to him? What would it be like to talk to him again after so many years? What reason would he give for not keeping in touch? Did he still care about her?

From Cara's perspective, time itself had slowed, as if it were waiting too.

At lunchtime, Gloria entered the bedroom. 'Cara, I've spoken to Paul,' she said without even saying hello.

Cara braced herself for bad news; Gloria had said "Paul", rather than Benjamin, distancing him from her.

'He'll be here at seven o'clock.'

'H-he's agreed to see me?' she gasped the words, placing a hand on her chest as she spoke.

'Yes, he'll be here at seven, but he can't stay for long.'

Cara felt herself smile; she smiled as she had not done for a long time, as though all the years of pain and worry had been washed away.

⏳

That evening, Gloria ushered Benjamin into Cara's room and then left, closing the door behind her.

The man at the door wore a grey pinstripe suit, cream shirt, and striped blue and yellow tie. He'd made an effort to dress up, it seemed; Cara could not recall ever seeing him in a suit. The Benjamin she'd known had usually worn jeans or casual trousers and shirts, even when he was working. His face hadn't changed much with time. There were a few grey and white strands in amongst his thick black hair, which reminded her how long it had been since they'd last seen each other.

'Ben,' she said, with an enormous effort not to become overemotional.

'Hello, Mum.' He sat on the chair next to the bed and, as he did so, she caught the fresh scent of his aftershave.

He studied the carpet, unable—or unwilling—to meet her eyes.

She recalled how, as a young boy, when he'd been naughty and expected to be told off, he would behave in a similar fashion. It made her want to reach out and hold him.

'Thank you for coming.' She stretched out her arm, trying to reach the tissue box on the bedside cabinet.

He pushed the box nearer to her, managing a smile.

Cara discreetly dried her eyes as Benjamin stared fixedly at the carpet. 'Ben,' she managed to say, after a brief pause. 'It's been such a long time.'

'I shouldn't be here,' he said. 'I can't deal with this.' Standing up he turned his back on her.

'Ben!'

'I have to go. I'm meeting an important business contact for dinner.'

'This is more important than a business meeting!' She tried to catch his eye but was unable to. Sighing, she added, 'That's always been your problem: you could never get your priorities right.'

He twisted around to face her, incredulity highlighting the lines on his brow. 'Why have you called me here? What good will it do?'

She felt an urge to hit out at him for all the suffering he'd caused Margaret and the girls and for the fact he had not kept in touch for the past sixteen years oblivious of her feelings. She noticed his eyes, so similar to Frederick's, the same eyes that could inspire love and break hearts and lives. 'I'm your mother, Ben, and I've waited for years for some news, to know you're all right.'

'I caused nothing but trouble; I thought you'd all be glad to see the back of me.'

'You can't just abandon your family and expect no one to care. I thought about you every day and wished you would come home.'

He raised his eyebrows. 'But I did a terrible thing: I nearly killed Maggie.'

'It was a terrible thing, but she survived and you knew that. Why didn't you ever get in touch to let us know where you were?'

'As I said, I didn't think you'd be bothered.'

'We all miss you. Cathy, Jamie...'

'I couldn't stay there and be that person. I don't have any regrets. No disrespect to you or the rest of the family, but I know I made the right decision, leaving when I did.'

'Please sit down, Ben.' It pained her to see him hover next to the chair, knowing he wanted to get away.

He sat down and twisted his watch on his wrist so he could see the time.

'Didn't you ever miss us... think about us?'

He shrugged. 'I've left the past behind. I've got a new family now.'

Cara hadn't expected that. Her dreams of a joyful reunion with her son were evaporating. He seemed to regard her as a stranger and, worse still, someone he didn't particularly care to know. He'd always been uncommunicative as a child, and she hadn't been able to get close to him even then. The wall was still there: nothing had changed.

'I'm your mother,' she said, dabbing the tears threatening to fall. 'Are you telling me you've never regretted leaving, not saying goodbye?'

'I don't know.' He stood up.

'What you did to Maggie is unforgivable, yes. She told me how you abused her for all those years, making her life a misery; I didn't want to accept I had a son capable of such—'

'Have you brought me here to dredge up the past and make me feel guilty?'

'No, please sit down, I need to talk to you. I hear you've changed, you're not the same man you were then.'

'Yes, I have changed,' he said, fidgeting.

'I can't forgive what you did to Maggie, but no matter what you've done, you're still my son and you should be with your family.'

'I am with my family: Claire and Amy, and Mandy.'

'Yes, but... I mean, the rest of the family, too. How can you so easily cut us out of your life?'

He sat back down on the chair, holding his forehead, as if he felt pressured by her questions.

Eventually, he sat upright. 'It's difficult for me to explain, but I want to forget about the past.'

'There's no reason for you to cut yourself off from the family anymore, Ben.'

'I've moved on: I've left that part of my life behind.'

'But you can't keep running away. Don't you even care about what happened to your family? Your brother and sister? Your girls?' She sniffed and placed the tissue she was holding under her nose.

Benjamin was still fidgeting, perspiration on his brow. Avoiding her eyes, he said, 'Of course I care, but everything's changed.' He reached out to touch her hand. 'I'll always love you, but I'll be risking too much if I open the door to my old life. If Claire even gets a hint of what happened between me and Maggie, she'll leave me and I'll have nothing.'

'Perhaps it's time you told Claire the truth. It's no good living with

123

lies.'

'I made a decision to cut my ties sixteen years ago because I had to: if I didn't, I wouldn't have been able to change. It hasn't been easy; I've struggled, but I'm doing all right. I'm sorry, but it's too late; I'm not risking what I have now for a past filled with hate.' He walked to the door.

'Ben—'

'Please don't call me that. My name's Paul. Goodbye, Mum.' He grasped the door handle.

'Benjamin is the name I gave you. How dare you treat me like this? I'm your mother.'

'I don't need a mother. I'm old enough to take care of myself.' He opened the bedroom door.

'You haven't changed at all, have you?' she said, practically spitting the words, and suddenly the anxiety of the past sixteen years took hold and she wanted him to feel it too.

He held on to the handle of the half-open door, his back to her.

'Keep fooling yourself you're this new, changed man. In reality, you're selfish: selfish Benjamin Edwards, who always takes the easy way out, running away at the first sign of trouble.'

He turned to her, red-faced.

'I'm ashamed to call you my son.' She took a deep breath and went on, 'You see me here, an old woman, begging you to let me back into your life in my last years, but you're just going to walk away. I'm willing to take you back into my life even after all you did to your family; Maggie, Penny, Jemima. Where were you when Penny and Jemima needed a dad? Where were you when Penny was being beaten up by her husband every day?'

'What?'

'No, go on, go. You don't want to face the past; you have a new life. You're Paul. It's a fine role you're playing: faithful husband and dutiful father. If the mask slips slightly you're afraid they'll see you for who you really are, though, aren't you? You haven't changed, Ben; you'll always be the man who nearly killed Maggie.'

'I've changed.'

'Well then, why can't you admit it to yourself?' She sniffed, battling to keep her composure. 'If you've changed, what would be so frightening about getting in touch with the rest of the family and making your peace? If you sat down with Claire and explained things to her—'

'No. I can't.' He sat down opposite her. 'Ever since I've been with Claire I've been the perfect gentleman. I'm so scared of going back to the person I was before, it's like I'm keeping myself in check all the time. I've managed to keep it up for so many years, that it's me: that's who I am.

But seeing you again has thrown me, it's made me remember what I was like—how I treated Maggie—and I don't want to be reminded of it. I shut it out for so long. Look at me, I'm shaking!' He held up a trembling hand. 'I can feel the guilt inside. It's as if I'm back there whenever I look at you.'

'That's because you ran away, Ben, and you're still running. You haven't faced up to the past. Isn't it about time you admitted to yourself that you're not that person anymore? You're not. I still love you; we all love you. You're part of the family. Put right the wrongs you did in the past and come back to us. Make us proud of you.'

'I would have to tell Claire everything.' Closing his eyes briefly, he put a hand to his brow. 'I can't, don't you see? I never told her why I left Maggie. I was so ashamed, I made up my past. I lied to her.'

'Yes, but she'll understand why you lied.'

'No, she won't.' His eyes were wide. 'She'll be afraid of me and she won't trust me. I've already missed out on seeing Jemima and Penny grow up, I couldn't survive if she took Amy from me.'

'That won't happen, Ben. Talk to Claire. It's not right that you should be so estranged from the rest of your family.'

'I told you, it hasn't been easy for me, but I made a choice. I had to choose.' Standing up, he walked over to the window. He looked out of the window for a while. Eventually, he turned around. 'When Aunty Glor told me Dad had died, it broke my heart. I couldn't go to the funeral... I wanted to. I really did.'

He sat down again at the foot of the bed.

She could see his eyes brimming with tears.

'I couldn't bring myself to drive you to London the other day, to the grave. I wanted to go so I could see the grave—that's why I initially agreed to drive you there. I didn't even stop to think about the consequences of us meeting up like that. But in the end I couldn't bring myself to do it. I was too afraid I'd cry if I saw Dad's grave. I'm sorry.'

'Billy was a good man,' she said, avoiding his eyes.

'I felt so guilty when I heard he'd died and I wouldn't get a chance to tell him I loved him. I'd disappeared from his life. I idolised him and wanted to be just like him, you know. It's his influence in my life that has helped me to become who I am today. I'll never forget him. I wish he could have known he meant so much to me.'

Cara recalled how close he had been to Billy, shuddering when she saw his tear-filled eyes and was reminded, yet again, of Frederick Johnson.

'I didn't mean to hurt you, but don't you see? I had to leave the past behind.'

'It may have been the right decision at the time, Ben,' she said, looking at her hands. 'Things are different now. I'm old. I'll be gone soon, and I want to spend my final years with all my family around me.'

He stood up and folded his arms. 'So you want me to tell Claire everything and risk losing all I have?'

'She's not all you have. Think about the way you felt when your father died. That's how you'll feel when you hear about me dying; that's how you'll feel if you hear about, God forbid, something happening to your brother, your sister, or Penny, or Jemima. Don't leave it too late to do the right thing, Ben.'

'But Amy——'

'What about Penny and Jemima?'

'Oh God.' He covered his face with his hands. 'Tell me it's not true about Penny's husband beating her up... please.'

Cara looked down at her blanket. 'It's true,' she said, 'but she's safe now. She has two sons, you know, Andrew and Carl, they're about the same age as Amy.'

'What about Jemima?' he said to his hands.

'I don't know,' replied Cara. 'She moved away to Jersey with Maggie over ten years ago. They've never kept in touch.'

'Isn't she even in touch with Penny?'

'No, they fell out because Maggie thought Penny's husband, David, was too similar to you. She didn't want her to marry him, but Penny didn't listen.'

'Looks like she was right about Penny's husband.'

'Yes.'

'I can't imagine Penny would want to know me, and I'm sure the rest of the family probably feel the same. I'm trouble. I've caused them enough pain.' He walked back to the window.

'Nonsense. I'm sure everyone would be so relieved to know you're alive. Time changes everything. They'll be pleased to see you.'

He turned to look at her. 'Come on, let's face reality: Penny has suffered at the hands of a violent husband, why would she want to see me? I used to hit Maggie.'

'That was then.'

'Where is Penny?'

'I don't know. She's at a women's refuge, in hiding from her husband.'

'Little Penny, my little girl. Amy reminds me so much of her.'

His mobile phone sounded. 'Hello,' he said. 'Yes, yes. Sorry, I'm running a bit late. I'll be there soon.' He placed the phone inside his jacket pocket. 'I really have to go, Mum. I'll think about what you've said.'

Cara sat staring at the bedroom door after Benjamin left. He'd brought the past back with him when he reappeared in her life, and their conversation had stirred up hidden emotions that were now taunting her.

She'd accused him of lying to Claire about his life. Yes, he had lied, but she too had lied, and now her lies were mocking her, asking her if she could tell the family about Frederick Johnson. Could she tell them Benjamin might not be Billy's son? Could she tell them she'd married Billy to escape her bitter existence in the aftermath of her relationship with Frederick?

Since Billy's death she'd fooled herself that none of it really mattered and that it was mainly Billy she'd deceived, but now she knew better. Benjamin had grieved over Billy's death as a son.

Even after so many years, she still felt unable to reveal her skeletons. Why? Was it because she knew she was still, and would always be, the girl who'd nearly killed herself over her relationship with Frederick Johnson?

As her conscience churned these thoughts around, Cara became conscious of holding the silver locket between her fingers. She lifted it up so she could see it more clearly. Her mind begged the question: *Am I still in love with him?* As if to hide her shame, she covered the necklace with her nightdress.

Gloria knocked on the bedroom door and entered. 'How did it go?' she asked.

Cara smiled, trying to keep her composure. 'As well as can be expected, I suppose.'

Gloria sat on the chair next to the bed.

'I think I'll get an early night tonight,' said Cara, faking a yawn, not in the mood for company.

'All right, dear. I only popped in to let you know that while you were in here with Paul... sorry, *Benjamin*, Catherine phoned. I didn't want to disturb you, so I said you were asleep. She wanted me to tell you that David went to her flat this morning and spoke to Tom. She says Tom may have told him you're living here. She asked me to pass the message on.'

Gloria was smiling as she relayed the message, so Cara realised that Catherine had not told her why Penelope and David had split.

'I'll let you rest,' Gloria said, standing up.

'Wait,' Cara said. 'If David calls here can you tell him I'm not living with you.'

Gloria knitted her brow, 'Um... okay.' She walked to the door, then turned to face Cara. 'Where has Penelope gone?' she asked.

'She had to go away for a while. Her marriage was going through a bad patch.' Cara took a deep breath.

'Right.' Gloria nodded. 'Goodnight, Cara,' she said, turning off the light on her way out.

Cara shivered, feeling sure she would not be able to sleep tonight; she'd be listening out for the slightest noise and praying David would not find his way to Huddlesea.

CHAPTER TWENTY

After he left Gloria's house, Benjamin went to his meeting with Peter James, the representative of Kington Homes, to discuss plans for a new development of properties in Huddlesea, which Peter said would make the town a more "vibrant and exciting" area. Benjamin nodded and smiled in all the right places and agreed to meet Peter again to discuss a contract when the plans for the development were finalised, but he found it hard to concentrate throughout the meeting because he'd been left in a state of confusion after seeing his mother.

She'd looked so old and frail, so far removed from the woman he'd known; it had stirred regret for all the wasted years. He hadn't anticipated that he'd feel so emotional. In hindsight, he knew he was foolish to expect she would still look the same after sixteen years, but whenever he'd thought about her during the years they were apart, the image he had of her in his head was the same, never aged.

He knew her MS must have progressed because she was bedridden. In the past, as she'd appeared to be quite fit and well most of the time, he could practically forget she had any health issues. Seeing her today, it crossed his mind that she might not live much longer.

Although she'd remained in his memory over the years, he'd believed it would not bother him too much if he never saw her again. Today's encounter had altered his perception. He wanted a chance to put things right before it was too late.

By the time his meeting with Peter was over, he'd made the conscious decision to tell Claire everything. Surely she would understand his reasons for being unwilling to reveal the truth about his life with Margaret.

On the drive from Huddlesea along the endless stretches of motorway, he found himself wondering how to explain his past life and behaviour to Claire. During his therapy sessions, many of his problems had been linked back to his childhood.

⌛

As a child, Benjamin always felt different. Both his parents were redheads and both his siblings were too. His father told him he'd inherited his grandmother's hair colour. Benjamin had seen photographs of his grandmother, a beautiful woman with dark hair and brown eyes, but he did not want to look different; he wanted to look like Catherine and James.

The problems began as soon as Catherine started school, when Benjamin stepped in to defend her after someone in his class called her a name because she had ginger hair.

'Is she your sister, Ben?' a friend asked quite innocently after Benjamin told the other boy to leave Catherine alone.
This sparked a debate amongst the pupils.
'How come she's got ginger hair?' asked one.
'His mum's got ginger hair,' said another. 'I saw her bring Cat to school.'
'Yeah,' said Edward King, the school bully. He walked up to Benjamin and glared at him with his piercing grey eyes. 'Your dad's got ginger hair too, ain't he?'
'Ben takes after our gran,' said Catherine in a small voice.
'You're adopted, aren't you?' said Edward.

The whispers persisted and things only got worse when James started school a year later. Benjamin had by then been ostracised by his classmates as they were afraid of Edward King and did not want to be seen talking to Benjamin for fear of being the next target.

It was common for Benjamin to end up in a fight with Edward or one of his cronies after school, and this gave him the reputation of being a bad boy. Although his parents were often called to the school to see the headmaster about his behaviour, he never told them why he constantly got into trouble, so everyone came to see him as a "problem child". He resented the fact that Catherine and James fitted in well and were not subjected to the abuse he suffered.

His envy of Catherine and James meant he preferred not to spend much time with them. He drifted further and further into his own world. He would spend weekends alone at the local park or arcade. There he met a gang of boys who liked to go shoplifting and joyriding. Benjamin desperately needed to fit in somewhere, so he became one of the gang. He would do whatever they asked him to do. It was a miracle he did not end up in front of a magistrate or in jail.

Not long after he joined the gang, he started drinking. The boys in the gang would take it in turns to steal alcoholic drinks from a local off-licence. J.J.—the gang leader—would initiate the group's activities. He decided where they should go and what they would do. J.J. was a tall skinny boy with a face full of acne scars and a shaved head. He wore earrings and said he had a tattoo but didn't show it to any of them. As gang leader no one interrogated him further. He behaved a lot like Edward King and he even resembled him, with similar piercing grey eyes.

This made Benjamin even more proud to be part of the gang, because he reasoned that if someone like Edward could accept him, he must be okay.

One night J.J. decided to steal a car...

'I'll get the car and bring it round here, then we'll go for a ride.' J.J. laughed, holding up the empty bottle of whisky they'd just drunk between them.

It was dark. The others (Benjamin and two other boys, Reg and Donald) waited for him behind a garden wall.

They watched J.J. zigzag his way along the avenue towards a row of parked cars.

'He's had quite a lot to drink,' said Reg, an unlikely member of the gang: he looked like a little boy with his bowl-cut shaped blond hair and thick spectacles. He constantly queried what they were doing as if his role was that of the group's conscience.

They all stooped down behind the wall.

'He shouldn't be driving,' said Reg.

'He didn't drink that much,' countered Donald, a tall West Indian boy with large muscular arms, who appeared older than his eighteen years. 'Anyway, he always drinks and drives, he's used to it.'

Benjamin, a man of few words, merely nodded.

A few minutes passed by and the boys heard the sound of a racing car.

'That'll be J.J.,' said Donald, laughing.

Reg and Benjamin joined in with the laughter. Their fun came to an abrupt halt when they heard a loud scream—a woman's scream—and the sound of a car's screeching brakes.

The laughter stopped and fear took its place.

Donald stood up slowly and peeked over the wall. When he turned back to Reg and Benjamin, his eyes were bulging, his mouth wide open.

The two boys dared to look over the wall and saw a group of people surrounding a white car; a young woman's body lay lifeless on the ground in front of the car, lit up by the headlights. The sound of police sirens filled the air. Donald, Benjamin, and Reg ran as fast as their legs could carry them, away from the scene.

J.J. was arrested and charged with multiple offences, including drunk driving and manslaughter.

When J.J. went to prison, the gang split up, and Benjamin—ashamed of his behaviour—tried his best to lead a blameless life. He met Margaret at the age of nineteen, and within a year he married her because she wanted to get married and he thought it would be the right thing to do. He still harboured a deep-rooted need to feel he belonged somewhere.

Benjamin soon found himself trying to control what Margaret could and could not do. His possessiveness became worse after the birth of their second daughter. Penelope, their first child, was born with his black hair, but Jemima's hair was mousy brown. He accused Margaret of having an affair. Even with no real basis for his suspicion—Margaret had given him no reason to mistrust her—the doubt lingered.

It was at around this time in their relationship that he began hitting her. Whenever they argued, even over the slightest thing, he lashed out. He always regretted it but did not want to admit he'd done wrong. Each time, he felt sure it wouldn't happen again. But it did.

His drinking habit resumed, and whilst out drinking one night he met up with J.J., who had by then been released from prison. J.J. still retained a lust for rebellion, and his spell in prison only served to connect him with more like-minded criminals.

Soon Benjamin began associating with another gang, a more sophisticated team of hardened thugs. He often arrived home drunk, late at night, and if Margaret ever took out her frustration on him, he resorted to hitting her. This downwards spiral led to him nearly killing Margaret by pushing her down the stairs.

The shock of what might have happened made him realise he needed to change his behaviour. Seeing Margaret lying at the foot of the stairs, made him think of the young girl lying in front of the stolen car J.J. had been driving. He'd lived with a guilty conscience nagging him ever since.

When he moved to Huddlesea and changed his name, it was a way of letting go of his old self. He attended anger management classes and sessions with a psychologist, out of town.

⌛

As Benjamin tried to make sense of everything on the drive from Huddlesea, he thought over his mother's words: he'd made a concerted effort to change and truly never intended to go back to his old ways, so why not tell Claire everything? Then he could be a part of his family again. He owed it to his daughters, and to his estranged wife, as much as to himself.

⌛

'Paul! I wasn't expecting you home tonight. Weren't you supposed to be staying in Huddlesea for another couple of days?' Claire smiled at him. She was standing at the foot of the stairs in her pink dressing gown, holding a mug of hot chocolate, when he arrived home. 'I was just about to go up to bed.'

He walked towards her, leaving his bag at the door. 'I wanted to see you,' he said, taking her in his arms.

'Watch out, I'll spill my cocoa.' She giggled.

He stood back. 'Where are the girls?'

'In bed.' She rolled her eyes. 'Where else would they be at eleven-thirty at night?' A stray lock of blonde hair fell onto her cheek and she tucked it behind her ear.

Shrugging, he went into the living room and sat on the soft white leather sofa.

Claire followed him. 'Paul, are you okay?'

He loosened his tie. 'Sit down, honey, we need to talk.'

'Has something happened?' Placing her mug on the coffee table, she sat beside him.

'No.' He took her hand. 'Nothing's happened, I just need to talk to you.' Looking into her eyes he almost lost his nerve, but he thought of Penelope and his feelings of inadequacy resurfaced: she'd suffered, and he'd not been there for her as a father. He'd been selfish, cutting them all out of his life. Somehow he felt now was the time to tell the truth and face up to what he had done. 'I saw my mum today.'

Claire's brow furrowed. 'Your mum?'

'Yes, in Huddlesea.'

'B-but... didn't you tell me your mum died?' She drew away from him.

'Yes... Sorry, I haven't really told you everything about my past.'

'Why would you say your mum's dead if she isn't?'

'I don't know where to start. There's so much I haven't told you because I thought it would be better if you didn't know the truth.'

'Why?' She shuffled along the sofa, putting distance between them. There was silence.

'Paul... If you don't explain soon, I'm going to think you've gone mad, or I've gone mad... or—' She stopped and stood up. 'Tell me this is some sort of joke and then we can go to bed and forget about it.'

'It's not a joke,' he said glumly. 'But perhaps we should go to bed. We're both tired. We can talk about this in the morning.' Yawning, he got up from the sofa.

'What?' The word exploded from her mouth as she glared at him. 'How am I supposed to get any sleep now?'

'Keep your voice down, you'll wake the girls,' he said.

'Okay, okay.' Returning to her seat, she took a deep breath. 'Look, sit down and start from the beginning. I want to know everything.'

Closing his eyes, he said, 'Promise me it won't change the way you feel about me.' He sat next to her.

'Just tell me,' she said anxiously.

'Right.' He looked at the floor. 'Sixteen years ago, I left London and moved to Huddlesea when me and Maggie broke up.'

'Yes, I know.'

'Yes, but you don't know the truth about what happened between me and Maggie.' He glanced at her then turned away. 'This isn't easy for me.'

'W-well, it's not easy hearing you've been lying to me for over nine years.'

'Sorry.'

'Just tell me what happened.'

'Oh God.' He stood up.

'What's wrong?'

'I can't tell you.'

Standing up, Claire put a hand on his arm. 'Look, Paul, we've been through a lot together. I'm sure that whatever this is, we can get through it.'

He turned around slowly. 'My real name's not even Paul.'

She pulled her hand away from him as quickly as if he'd given her an electric shock.

'I changed my name.'

She took a few steps backwards. 'Why?'

He shrugged.

'What is your name?'

'It's Paul, I changed it by deed poll, but it was Benjamin.'

'Benjamin? Wh-why did you change it?'

'I didn't want to remember the past. I hated who I used to be.'

'Did you commit a crime? Did you change your name because you didn't want to be traced?' She moved further away from him as she spoke.

'No, not exactly.'

'Why go as far as to change your name?'

'I used to drink a lot.'

'Drink?'

'Yes, alcohol.'

'You were an alcoholic?'

'No, I used to drink a lot. I used to hit Maggie.'

Claire placed a hand over her mouth.

'I didn't know what I was doing at the time, Claire, I was drunk.'

'So, she threw you out?' she asked, averting her eyes from his gaze.

'Not exactly.' He sat on the sofa. 'One night, we had a row and I pushed her. She fell down the stairs and I thought I'd killed her. I didn't know what to do, so I left London and went to Huddlesea.'

'You thought you'd killed your wife, so you ran away? What about your daughters? Didn't you think about them?'

'I didn't think about anything. I needed to get away. I ran.'

'You *were* thinking... You knew you'd be sent to prison if she was dead.'

'Claire, you look frightened. This is me.' He stood and approached her.

She backed away from him and bashed into the sideboard, toppling a photograph of Mandy, which then sent a brass ornament flying to the floor. It landed on her toes. She grabbed her foot and cursed at the pain.

'This is stupid,' he said. 'Have I ever laid a hand on you in nearly ten years?'

Ignoring his question, she asked, 'Is Maggie dead?'

'What?'

'Did you kill her? Is that why you changed your name?'

'No, thankfully, I didn't kill her.'

The relief was plain on her face as her features relaxed and colour filled her cheeks.

'We're talking about stuff that happened sixteen years ago, Claire.'

'Why did you keep it from me?'

'Because I knew you'd react like this.'

'Well, why tell me now?'

'Because I saw my mum today for the first time since I left London, and she wants to stay in touch. She's old, and—'

'What else haven't you told me?'

'Nothing. Look, I'm sorry I didn't tell you everything before, but it's because I didn't want to lose you. I was out of control back then. I'd never do that again.' He reached out to her, but she walked towards the door.

'How come you were so "out of control"?'

He looked at the carpet. 'I've had therapy since, and the therapist said it all stems from my childhood.' His cheeks reddened. 'After being bullied at school, I tried to appear tough. I fought back and got in with the wrong crowd. When Maggie complained, we'd end up rowing. I had a lot of pent-up anger about a lot of things. But Claire, it's in the past and if I could turn back time—'

'You can't change what you did. Do you ever consider the effect of what you did to her? The effect on her life, or your daughters' lives?'

He thought of Penelope and her violent husband and felt a sadness envelop him.

'I'd like you to leave, please,' said Claire.

'What?'

'I need time to think.'

'But, Claire...'

Her eyes were distant.

'Please, sweetheart, let's go to bed, we'll talk about this in the morning. You're tired. We're both tired.'

'Please don't make this more difficult than it is,' she said.

He walked over to the unit in the corner of the room and, opening the glass cabinet, took out a bottle of whisky.

'What are you doing?'

He picked up a tumbler. 'I need a drink.' He saw fear in her eyes. 'How many times have you seen me pour myself a drink over the years?'

'You said you were an alcoholic once.'

'I've already told you: I wasn't an alcoholic, I just drank a lot; there's a difference. I chose to drink a lot. I'm in control now.' He took a sip from the glass.

'I have to think of Amy and Mandy,' said Claire.

'What?'

'I want you to leave.'

'This is ridiculous.'

'Please go!' she said.

'But—'

'Get out!'

'Okay, I'm going, but I'll be back. This is my home.' He walked out of the door and as he stood on the doorstep, stunned, heard Claire securing the double bolt and turning the key in the Chubb lock.

CHAPTER TWENTY-ONE

Cara sat eating her breakfast the next morning when a loud knock on the front door shook the foundations of the old house. After a few seconds the knock came again. Her first thought was of David. She'd slept fitfully, waking up at intervals throughout the night, her mind full of anxiety as she anticipated him coming to Huddlesea in search of Penelope.

She heard Gloria shout, 'All right, I'm coming!'

The knocking persisted and became louder. Eventually she heard Gloria open the front door and could make out a man's voice. The next thing she knew, her bedroom door flew open and a man approached her at great speed. The breakfast tray and all its contents landed on the floor. Everything happened so fast, she couldn't focus.

The man grabbed her arms, and his face came into view. Cara held her breath.

David looked as though he had been living rough. His baggy beige jacket was too warm for the weather and he reeked of sweat. At least a week's worth of stubble peppered his chin, and his hair—usually cropped short—was unruly and messy, as though it had not been combed or washed in weeks.

'Where is she?' he shouted into Cara's face.

She smelt the stale alcohol on his breath and had to turn away.

'I'll call the police,' said Gloria, leaving the room.

He ran after her. 'You won't call the fuckin' police, you old bat! You'll stay right here where I can see you.' As he dragged her forcibly back into the bedroom, he warned, 'I've got a gun,' then glaring at Cara, said, 'I'll use it if I have to.' He pushed Gloria onto the chair.

'Right, Cara.' He caught his breath. 'Look, tell me where Penny is, and I'll go. I don't want to hurt anyone.' He sat on her bed.

His cheeks appeared sunken and there were dark circles around his eyes. He had lost a lot of weight. 'I... don't kn-know where she is, David,' she said, trembling, unsure what he would do next.

'Don't give me that!'

As he got up, he wobbled to one side so that Cara thought he would fall over. His hands were shaking.

'You're not making this easy for me, Cara. I don't want to hurt you, but I will if I have to.' He walked over to the bedroom door and slammed it shut. Reaching into his jacket pocket, he withdrew a handgun. 'Now,' he said softly. 'You.' He pointed at Gloria. 'Stand up and go over there.'

Gloria moved quickly towards the wardrobe as directed, not taking her eyes off the gun.

He followed her, stood beside her and smiled, before placing the weapon against her head. 'So, Cara, tell me where Penny is or I'll shoot.'

'Really, I'm telling you the truth.'

'I'll shoot!' he shouted.

'David, please calm down. Come over here. Let's talk about this sensibly.' Cara felt her heart pounding and perspiration on her forehead.

'She's taken my kids! She's left me. You can't take someone's kids away from them without an explanation. She must be crazy! She's not fit to be a mother. I'm going to find her and I'm going to get my kids back. They're my kids! She can't just take them. I have rights, you know.'

His eyes were boring into Cara's, and his hand, which was still pointing the gun at Gloria's head, shook violently.

Cara held her breath.

'Okay, wait,' he said, 'I'll make a deal with you.' Lowering the weapon, he walked towards Cara, sat down on the bed and smiled. His gaze was like that of a wild animal. 'I don't want to end up in jail.' He waved the handgun as he spoke. 'I only want to see my kids. Phone Penny and ask her if I can see them.'

'Please put the gun down,' said Cara, catching her breath.

'I will, as soon as you phone Penny.' He pointed the gun at her.

Cara gasped.

'I'm not afraid to use it, you know.'

She froze. Eyelids shut, a feeling of resignation and futility, she sat waiting for the bullet. There was nothing more she could do. There was no way to reason with him. She prayed he would just get it over with.

'Open your eyes!' he screamed.

She had been expecting the bullet, so when his voice sounded loudly out of the silence, for a split second she was sure he'd pulled the trigger. Slowly, she opened her eyes.

David lowered the weapon and placed it inside his jacket pocket.

From the corner of her eye, Cara could see Gloria still standing like a statue in front of the wardrobe. She daren't look directly at her sister in case David thought they were communicating. Perhaps if they played along with him he would calm down.

'Well?' he asked. 'Are you going to phone Penny?'

'David, I really don't know where she's gone. She ran away. She didn't tell me where she was going.'

'You're lying! She tells you everything,' he said, sitting closer to her on the bed. 'In fact, you probably put the idea in her head, didn't you? Penny would never walk out on me. She loves me. You're the one who told her to leave, aren't you?' He stood up.

'No, of course not,' she said, acutely aware that he could easily take the gun back out of his pocket.

'She can't have just disappeared.' He scanned the room, as if searching for clues. 'Someone must know where she is.' Turning to Cara, he said: 'Are you hiding her here?'

'No.'

'Okay, you won't mind if I search the place, in that case.' He kicked the chair forcibly; it fell over and skidded across the floor to where Gloria was standing, narrowly missing her feet.

'If I find out you're lying to me, I'll kill you,' he said, sneering at Cara.

Following the trajectory of the chair, he walked over to the other side of the room and pushed Gloria aside as if she were merely an object in his way: she had to grab hold of the edge of the wardrobe to stop herself falling over.

David began sifting through the contents of the wardrobe, throwing most of the clothes onto the floor in a frenzied rage.

Turning around, after finding nothing of interest, he shouted: 'Where is she?' before running out of the bedroom, trampling on Cara's clothes as he went.

The two sisters remained where they were, paralysed by fear. They could hear furniture being moved and the sound of glass breaking in the kitchen.

'I should try to call the police,' said Gloria quietly. She walked towards the bedroom door.

'Be careful,' whispered Cara.

Gloria hurried out of the room.

Cara waited. She heard the front door open and close. Nerve-racking seconds ticked by.

Eventually, David returned to the bedroom. 'Okay, she's not here, where is she, Cara? You're a bit too old to play games, and I'm getting impatient.'

'I told you, I don't know where she is. Please—'

'No. No. You won't keep it from me!' He pointed a finger at her. 'You've been a burden, Cara. It's all your fault. You told her to leave me, didn't you? We were fine until you stuck your nose in. Didn't you think I was good enough for her? Hey? Answer me!'

Cara trembled with fear. 'I never knew she was leaving until the day she left.'

'Don't give me that! Do you know what you deserve? You deserve to be shot. Yes. Shot. You've taken my kids away from me. What right do you have to take a man's wife and kids from him?' Standing close to the

139

bed, he reached into his jacket pocket.

'David, please!'

'Scared, are you?' He laughed. 'You should see yourself, you're so scared.' He aimed the gun at her, laughing.

'Don't do it.'

'Why? Why? Give me one good reason.'

'Gloria has gone to fetch the police.'

There was a moment of complete silence as he seemed to regain some control of his senses. He looked at the wardrobe where Gloria had been standing, as if just realising that she wasn't there. Dropping the gun to his side, he appeared to be backing off.

Cara managed to breathe again, but the interlude of calm did not last for long. He leaned forwards and pointed the weapon at her. His finger balanced threateningly on the trigger.

Cara stiffened, resigned to her fate.

'Do you really think I'd kill you and risk going to jail for life? I wouldn't bother. You'll be dead soon enough, you old cow. You want me to kill you, don't you? Because I'd never see Penny if I was locked up. That's what you want, isn't it? You want me to kill you, so I'll never see my kids. You're a cruel woman, Cara.'

She slowly dared to open her eyes, and watched as he paced the room waving the gun dangerously.

'F-for your own sake, p-put the gun away. The police will be here any minute.'

'I've probably got enough time to kill you and get away. I can't hear any sirens, can you?' He leaned over her again, his navy-blue eyes piercing deep into her soul.

Police sirens sounded close by and he became edgy. Putting the gun back into his pocket, he said, 'I'm going to hide here in the wardrobe. When they come in, tell them I've gone, or I'll kill you. If I don't manage to kill you today, I'll kill you when I get out of jail. Do you hear me?' He stepped into the wardrobe and pulled the doors shut.

Gloria ran into the bedroom, followed by two armed policemen.

'Where is he?' asked one of the policemen.

Cara pointed to the wardrobe.

The police officer walked over to the wardrobe and opened the door.

David fixed Cara with a searing stare. 'You told them I was in here, didn't you, Cara?'

'Are you David Truman?' asked the policeman.

'Yes, I am,' he said, still glaring at Cara.

The policeman proceeded to caution him and he was handcuffed and led away from the house.

'Are you all right, Cara?' Gloria sat on the bed and held her hand.

Tears formed in Cara's eyes.

A policewoman entered the room and explained to them that they would be required to make a statement about what David had done.

Her thoughts muddled, Cara could still see David's angry face staring at her; he'd threatened to kill her, his eyes full of malice. 'We won't be making any statements, Officer. I'm sorry we wasted your time,' she said.

'Wait! Cara, you're still in shock.' Gloria took a tissue from the box at her bedside and wiped Cara's tears. 'Of course we must make statements. He's a dangerous man.'

'No, we won't be making any statements. David is family. Officer, I'm sorry, but you can leave now.'

The policewoman frowned. 'If you're sure, madam.'

'I'm sure. It's family business. We'll sort it out.'

'I'm not so sure,' said Gloria, standing up and facing the policewoman. 'That man came into our home today, with a gun, and threatened to kill us. He's wrecked our home.'

'That's not true, and you know it.' Cara felt sure that very soon she would lose control and break down.

Gloria turned to look at her, open-mouthed.

'Now I'm really confused,' said the policewoman. 'Which one of you two ladies is telling the truth? I have to warn you, it's an offence to waste police time.'

'The truth is, it was a family argument that got a bit out of hand.' Cara could still feel the hatred emanating from David's stare. 'We don't need the police involved,'

'Fine,' said the policewoman, nodding, 'but if you change your minds, or if you have any further problems, please get in touch.'

A policeman then entered the bedroom. 'Are we ready to take statements?' he asked.

'They don't want to press charges.'

The police officers left.

'Glor,' Cara called out, as her sister followed the police out of the room. 'Don't leave, please stay, I'll try to explain.'

Gloria rolled her eyes. 'I don't know what you're thinking, Cara. He could have killed us. If I hadn't gone to get the police, God knows what would have happened. I'm still trembling, I won't feel safe in this house again while he's out there.'

'I know, I know.'

'You're in shock,' said Gloria, sitting next to her on the bed.

141

'They've taken him to the police station, but they can't hold him without any evidence. They'll release him and he'll be back here. I'm scared. Aren't you scared? What went on between you when I went to fetch the police?'

'If you hadn't returned with the police when you did, I'm sure he would have killed me.' Cara stared ahead blankly.

'So, please, help me understand. Why on earth are you defending him?'

'He threatened me, Glor. He said he'd kill me if I told the police where he was hiding. If I go to court to give evidence against him, he'll kill me. The truth is, Penny is on the run, in a women's refuge to get away from him. He's a violent man. He used to hit her.'

'Oh my God.' Gloria put a hand over her mouth. 'Why didn't you warn me about opening the door to him?'

'I was hoping he wouldn't come here. Anyway, I've never seen him like that before. I didn't have a clue about his violence when I was living with them.' Her conscience taunted her. Why hadn't she told anyone about her concerns? 'I was always upstairs in my room,' she said loudly to silence the mocking voices in her head. 'Penny didn't tell me the whole story until the day she left him.'

'But didn't you hear him shouting?' Gloria said. 'He was quite vocal today. Unhinged.'

'I asked Penny a few times about the shouting, yes. She said he had a bit of a temper, but she never said anything about the violence.'

'Poor Penelope.' Gloria shook her head. 'That man is a lunatic. He looked drunk today, or on drugs. Did you see his eyes? What makes you so sure he won't come back today when they let him go because they have no evidence? We should have given statements to the police.'

'They'll find his gun; they won't let him out straight away, he'll be charged.' Cara tried to reassure herself as she spoke.

'But what if they let him out tonight, or tomorrow? You haven't seen what he's done to the house, it's like a bomb's hit it.' Standing up, she began gathering Cara's clothes from the floor. After folding some of them and placing them in the wardrobe, she lifted the chair and put it back next to the bed, then picked up the breakfast tray and heaved a sigh.

Cara noticed her sister's hands shaking with nerves.

Eventually, Gloria sat down. 'Cara, please, all we have to do is give a statement to the police about what happened here today, then he'll be punished. Think about Penelope and her children.'

Cara felt selfish suddenly, realising she had only been thinking of herself. Making a statement against David could mean he'd be sent to prison; Penelope would no longer have to hide.

There was a knock at the front door.

'Who can that be?' asked Cara nervously.

'I'm not answering it.'

'Aunty Glor!' a voice shouted through the letterbox.

'It's Ben,' said Cara. 'Let him in.'

Gloria left the room.

Cara heard him talking to Gloria in the hallway, but could not make out what they were saying.

A couple of minutes later, Benjamin entered Cara's bedroom.

'Hello,' he said.

'Hello, Ben.' Her cheerful greeting was met with a grimace.

'What? Oh, you want me to call you Paul? I'm sorry... I can't—'

'I stupidly thought you were right—that I should tell Claire everything. I told her about you and about what happened with Maggie. I went back to London, after my meeting last night. It's all over, she's thrown me out.'

'I'm sorry.'

'You should be, it's all your fault.'

She lowered her eyes.

'I've brought my belongings. I'll be staying here for a while, with Aunty Glor.'

'I'm sure it's just heat of the moment—'

'Well, I'm glad you're sure, because I'm not.'

'Don't worry, it will sort itself out.'

'No it won't. I shouldn't have listened to you. "Tell her everything," you said. "She'll understand," you said. Now you're saying everything will sort itself out. I can't even bear to look at you, but what else can I do? I have nowhere else to go.'

'Claire will come round; give her time.'

'Time. Yes, time.' He was sitting on the chair next to the bed with his head in his hands. 'Time is all I have left. I've lost Amy. I've lost everything.'

'I'm sorry, I thought it was the right thing to do. I'll speak to Claire if you like. She seems lovely. It will be all right, you'll see.'

'Do you really think I'd let you speak to Claire?' he huffed. 'I'm not going to let you make things any worse than they already are. You ruined my marriage, poking your nose in, and now you've ruined my relationship with Claire.' He stood up and placed his face close to Cara's. 'You're a selfish, old—'

'Shut up, Ben!' she said bluntly.

He moved away from her, stupefied.

'Get out of my room, I'm sick and tired of you. You deserve to lose

Claire and Amy. If anyone is selfish, it's you. I've had a gun to my head today. Penny's husband is in town, looking for her, and he's threatened to kill me. The last thing I need is you blaming me for your inability to handle your relationships. You're an adult, you make your own decisions. Go away, I don't want you here. I wish I'd never seen you again. Now I have, and it's quite clear you haven't changed, do you know how ashamed that makes me?'

'Penny's husband is in town?'

She continued as if she hadn't heard him speak. 'You made Maggie's life a misery and Penny's husband did the same to her. You're two of a kind, and he nearly killed me today. Go away, leave me in peace. I'm too old for this.'

'No, no,' he said. He sat down on the chair again. 'Where is Penny's husband?'

'At the police station.'

'The police station? I saw a police car outside. Quite a commotion. I didn't realise... So that was Penny's husband outside talking to the police? The scruffy guy in the beige jacket?'

'Yes.' She sat in silence.

'What did he do to you?' He turned his attention to the mess in the room. 'Did he do this?' he asked, pointing at the clothing in disarray.

Anger and frustration bubbled inside Cara's mind as her cheeks reddened. David's invasion of the house that day had left her in a state of terror and anxiety, and she wanted to hit out at someone. She recalled how Margaret had appeared older than her years during the time she'd endured Benjamin's violence. Suddenly, to Cara, he represented all the men who, like David, caused women like Penelope to suffer.

'Please, tell me what he did.'

'He did what he used to do to Penny and what you used to do to Maggie; he tried to make me feel helpless, scared, intimidated.' She felt her anger controlling her speech. 'He threatened me with a gun and said if I didn't tell him where Penny was he would kill me.'

'So are they going to send him to jail?'

'I don't know.'

'Didn't the police tell you?'

'No.'

'I've got to try and see him,' he said, standing up.

'Why?' she asked, eyebrows raised.

'He's the man who beat up my daughter, why do you think?'

'So you're going to beat him up? How good of you, Ben. That's not what Penny would want, don't you see? You were the same as him. You may have changed, I don't know, but the truth is, you did exactly the

144

same thing to Maggie. What difference is there?'

'Penny is my little girl.'

'Maggie was someone's little girl too. Penny is nearly thirty years old, you haven't seen her in nearly sixteen years. All of this proves you're still the same old Benjamin: any excuse for a fight.'

Benjamin placed a hand on his forehead. 'This is different.'

'In what way?'

'I wasn't around for Penny when she was growing up or when her husband was beating her black and blue. I owe it to her.'

'If you do anything to David, you'll be in trouble. You'll go to prison. Do you realise that?'

'I've got nothing else to live for. I've lost Claire and Amy. I don't mind doing time. I have to find this man, he won't get away with what he did to Penny.' With that he left the room.

'Benjamin!' she shouted after him, shuddering as the front door slammed shut.

⧗

Gloria entered the bedroom when Benjamin had left. Her body language screamed dejection. She sat on the chair and looked at her hands. 'Cara, I've decided I'm going to make a statement against David.' Her eyes were full of tears, her voice shaky. 'I have to. I've just seen the rest of the house. He's broken things.' She rubbed her forehead and addressed her sister, eyes pleading: 'Have you had time to think about it yet?'

'Yes,' she said. 'I'll make a statement too.'

Gloria smiled and took Cara's hand in hers. 'You won't regret it. I'll call the police and let them know.'

⧗

Gloria returned to the bedroom a few minutes later, a frown on her face.

Cara smiled at her, in an attempt to break through the tension.

'They've already released him,' said Gloria, who was standing at the bedroom door.

'David?'

'Yes, the policewoman I spoke to said they didn't have any power to hold him at the police station. They couldn't charge him. All they did was warn him about causing any more trouble here and let him go.'

'But... but he had a gun,' said Cara.

'Yes, apparently it was a toy one.'

145

'A toy? B-but he held it to my face. It looked real.'

Gloria shook her head.

'He smelt of alcohol. Couldn't they have kept him there until he sobered up?' she asked. 'And what about his threatening behaviour?'

'The policewoman said he behaved himself at the police station, and they couldn't charge him without our statements. What if he comes back here?'

'Didn't you tell the policewoman he might come here?'

'Yes, she said we should phone them straight away if he does. There's nothing they can do because they've already let him go.'

'I'm sorry, Glor, I should have agreed to make a statement earlier. You wanted to. I'm so stupid.' She held her head.

Gloria sat on the edge of her bed. 'At least Benjamin will be staying here tonight so we won't be alone,' she said.

Cara nodded, but then she remembered that Benjamin had gone to find David.

⧗

Benjamin slammed the front door shut and stood outside Gloria's house. He took a deep breath, aware his inability to rein in his anger had caused so much damage in the past. Somehow it had all returned to find him like an old friend.

He tried to calm down by telling himself it was only natural that he felt outraged: he loved Penelope, and David had hurt her; any father would feel the same. He took another deep breath.

The desire to hurt David was uppermost in his mind as he made his way to the police station. As he walked towards the high street his pace was steady and firm, he felt ready for a confrontation. He thought of his daughter and, as he did so, battled between wanting to retain his control and wanting to give David a taste of his own medicine. All the lessons from the anger management classes dissolved in a tide of emotion.

As he turned the corner of Hammond Street his chest expanded and his features locked into a stern grimace, like a boxer psyching himself up for an important fight. His pace quickened and he almost bumped into a small dark-haired woman walking hand in hand with a young girl of about two or three years of age. The little girl's hair was dark, too, tied up in two neat pigtails—the woman's daughter perhaps.

He looked at the woman's face and saw her shrink back in fear. Her eyes met his and she flinched.

'Sorry,' he said, realising his gait must have been intimidating. He

loosened his shoulders.

The woman took the child in her arms.

He watched as she scurried past him like a petrified mouse.

⧖

Gloria brought the cordless telephone into Cara's bedroom. 'Catherine's on the phone for you.'

'Thank you.' She took the phone and watched Gloria walk out of the bedroom. This would be the first time she'd spoken to Catherine since meeting with Benjamin. Should she tell her she'd seen him? Perhaps it was too soon. She placed the telephone against her ear: 'Hello, Cathy dear.'

'Hi, Mum, how are you?'

'Fine, thanks. How are Tom and the children?'

'Great,' she said. 'I've been really worried about you since Tom told me David came here yesterday. Did Aunty Glor give you the message?'

'Yes, dear.'

'Tom's sorry he told David where you are. He didn't know why David and Penny split up. David lied to him, said they'd argued and Penny had run off taking the children. Tom said he was really insistent and wouldn't leave without some information. Tom felt sorry for him.' She was talking quickly.

'Don't worry, darling,' said Cara. 'I'm all right.'

'But what if David goes to Huddlesea? I wouldn't put it past him. Tom's told him Penny's not with you, but—'

'Please don't worry about me, David has already been here.'

'What?'

'This morning. He caused a scene and Glor had to call the police, but they've warned him off.'

'Are you sure you're all right?'

'Yes, dear, he only wanted to know where Penny is, but I think he's got the message that I don't know. He won't bother us again.' She recalled David's eyes so full of hatred and felt a sense of fear, knowing he could return without warning.

'I'm so glad you're okay,' said Catherine. 'I'll come to see you soon. I'll phone Jamie and ask him to come too. I assume he's back from South Africa.'

Cara had images of Catherine, James, and Benjamin being reunited. Maybe if he saw his brother and sister he would feel more able

147

to face up to the past.

CHAPTER TWENTY-TWO

'The idyllic town of Huddlesea was shaken this morning by the news of a death. The body of a thirty-year-old male was discovered at the foot of Stoneleigh Cliffs by a local man walking his dog. Stoneleigh is a renowned suicide hotspot, but suspicious circumstances have not been ruled out. The identity of the deceased is not yet being disclosed, but it is understood he was not from the local area and that he had been questioned by police yesterday in connection with a domestic argument. He was released without charge early yesterday afternoon.'

Cara knew at once: David was dead. Yesterday he'd been standing here in this room threatening to kill her. Alive. Living and breathing. The shock hit her like a bolt of lightning. 'Glor!' she shouted, frantically. 'Glor!'

Gloria rushed into the bedroom, dressed in her nightgown. 'What is it, Cara? Are you all right?'

'David is dead.'

'Wh-what? How?'

'It was on the news.' Cara pointed to the television.

Gloria turned to face the screen but saw only the weatherman as the news had by now finished. She turned to her sister, disbelief evident in her wrinkled brow. 'Cara? Are you feeling all right? Why would it be on the news?'

'He fell from Stoneleigh Cliffs.'

'He killed himself?' Gloria asked slowly, eyebrows raised.

'I don't know. Maybe.' Cara felt her cheeks burn with the memories that still managed to disturb her more than fifty years later.

Gloria sat on the chair next to the bed. 'Wh-what did the news say exactly?'

'They found a man dead at Stoneleigh this morning and he wasn't local.'

'So they didn't say his name?'

'No.'

'It could be anyone.'

'No, it said that the police questioned him about a domestic argument yesterday.'

'Hmm...' Gloria narrowed her eyes in thought. 'He definitely wasn't in control of his senses yesterday, but it would make more sense that he would have come back here rather than kill himself.'

Cara stiffened as she remembered how Benjamin had stormed out of the house. 'Did you speak to Ben yesterday when he came home?' she asked, agitated.

'Yes,' said Gloria, nodding.

'How did he seem?'

Gloria shrugged. 'Fine... Well, a little upset about Claire, but, other than that, fine. He said he'd been walking, trying to clear his head. He was tired so he had some supper and went to bed early.'

'Is he still at home?' asked Cara.

'Yes, I think so.'

Just then, Benjamin walked in.

'Speak of the devil,' said Gloria.

'Good morning. I'm off to work; it's my last job in Huddlesea for a while, so I'm going to see Claire this evening to ask if she'll let me move back home.'

'All right, dear, but you're welcome to stay here as long as you need to.'

'Thanks, Aunty Glor.'

Cara searched his face for signs of guilt or remorse.

He left the room.

⧗

Later that morning, Gloria entered Cara's bedroom followed by the female police officer who had been at the house the day before.

'I'm afraid I've come with some bad news this morning,' began the policewoman. 'There isn't an easy way to say this.' Addressing Gloria, she said: 'Perhaps you should sit down.'

Gloria nodded and sat on the edge of Cara's bed.

'Early this morning, a local man was walking his dog near Stoneleigh Cliffs and he discovered a man's body. We have identified him as David Truman, the man we questioned yesterday after you called us here.'

'We heard the news this morning,' said Cara.

'I'm sorry,' said the policewoman. She coughed. 'We will need someone to formally identify the body. It's procedural. I wonder if one of you would be willing to do that for us.'

⧗

As Cara sat in the car on the way to the mortuary, she thought about David. Although they'd lived in the same house for years, she'd never really known him.

When she first moved to Furley Avenue she'd spent some evenings in David's company, occasionally joining the family for dinner, but as time went by she remained in her room on her own for the most part and didn't associate with him.

Their last encounter was a terrifying one, but she felt sad now, in denial of the circumstances in which she found herself.

The policewoman wheeled Cara's chair into the small room where David's body lay. His skin was so white, almost translucent. As she stared in disbelief at the lifeless body, she preferred to imagine he had fallen asleep.

He bore no resemblance to the manic man who'd forced his way into the house the day before and threatened to kill her.

As she looked more closely, she recognised the slight kink in his nose, the way his hair parted to the left with a curl, and the mole on his chin. This ending she could never have foreseen. Along with the sense of relief that he could no longer hurt anyone, there pulsated a deep feeling of loss. Thinking of her own son Benjamin and how he had changed, succeeded in turning his life around, it saddened her that David would not be given that chance. She remembered him as a young man when Penelope first introduced him. She had liked him then. Cara wiped a tear from her eye.

The policewoman drove them back home.

'How did he die, Officer?' asked Gloria.

'A tragic accident, most probably. We found an empty bottle of whisky at the top of the cliff. It may or may not have belonged to the late Mr Truman; we're waiting for the laboratory test results. The most probable explanation is that he fell from the cliffs: it's a dangerous place to be walking, even if you're sober, and there was a high wind last night. We are appealing for witnesses, but so far no one has come forward with any information. Of course, we'll keep the case open until we've ascertained the cause of death. We can't rule out the possibility of someone else being involved.'

Cara avoided the policewoman's eyes.

⧗

The late news that evening contained a further story about David's death. This time his name was mentioned and a photograph shown. Cara

151

watched the news through sorrowful eyes.

Benjamin entered her room when the news had finished and found her crying.

'Mum? Are you all right?'

'Have you heard the news?' she asked.

'What news?'

'David's dead,' she said, dabbing her eyes with a tissue.

'David?'

'Yes.' She searched his face, checking again for any sign of remorse.

'Who's David?' His features exuded bafflement.

'Penny's husband.' Cara watched for his reaction. Surely there'd be clues in his behaviour if he'd been involved... He'd be anxious and agitated if he'd killed David.

'Penny's husband is dead?' he asked.

It might have been an accident, thought Cara. *Perhaps they were arguing and David fell from the cliff.* Her mind ran through the possibilities.

'How did he die?'

Was he trying to bluff her with the question?

'He fell from Stoneleigh Cliffs. The police found him this morning.' She continued to stare at her son.

'Well.' He shrugged. 'Good riddance.'

'How can you say that?'

'Mum, he threatened to kill you yesterday. He used to beat Penny up. Why do you care so much now?'

'I lived with David and Penny for five years,' Cara said, sobbing. 'I know he wasn't perfect, but I can't pretend he never existed. I had to go and identify his body today.'

Benjamin sat on the edge of the bed and took her hand. 'I'm sorry.'

She remembered the fury in his eyes just before he'd gone out the day before.

'Are you all right?' he asked.

'Yes, I'm fine.' She blew her nose and smiled sadly. 'Ben. Yesterday, y-you were so angry, and you went out looking for David.' She stopped.

There followed an uncomfortable interlude of silence.

Benjamin placed a hand over his mouth.

She glanced up at him sheepishly, and he looked at the floor. 'Wh-what happened?' she asked quietly.

'What do you mean?'

'Yesterday you said you were going to look for—'

'Oh, my God.' He stood up and swiped a hand through his hair. 'Yes, okay, yesterday I was angry when—'

'Did you see him?' asked Cara, nervously.

'You think I killed him.'

She wished she could retract her words.

'You do, don't you?'

'Maybe I thought you might have got into a fight with David. As I said, yesterday you were s-so angry, I...'

Benjamin sat down on the chair beside her bed and leaned forward, his head in his hands. Then he glared at her. 'You actually think I killed him.'

'I-I...'

'Come on, admit it. You're thinking that I caught up with him yesterday, and I beat him up and threw him off the cliff.'

'No.' She shook her head.

Benjamin got up from the chair. 'You're so quick to jump to conclusions. Now do you understand why I don't want to keep in contact with you?'

Cara hated herself at that moment. She had waited so long for her son to come back into her life.

'Shall I tell you what happened yesterday?' He sat down again. 'When I left here, I was angry. Yes, I was furious. I'd just heard that my mother had been terrorised by the brute who used to beat up my daughter. And yes, I did go looking for him, I wanted to give him a piece of my mind.' He took a deep breath and exhaled. 'Maybe I would have punched him, I don't know. But I never even saw him. Instead, I saw a woman walking in town with her young daughter; they reminded me of Claire and Amy. I remembered my row with Claire: when I told her about what I'd done to Maggie, she looked so scared.' He stopped, as if he could not go on. After a brief pause, he resumed: 'I went for a long walk and ended up standing on the edge of Stoneleigh Cliffs. I considered ending it all. I actually understood why people do it: why they kill themselves.'

Their eyes met as he revealed this.

Cara reddened, remembering her past. 'Don't say things like that!'

'It's true, Mum; I could have easily thrown myself off the cliff.'

'Ben, you're scaring me.'

'Sorry.' He raked a hand through his hair. 'It's... Well, I really thought I had nothing left to lose. I made a decision, standing on those cliffs: I'm never going back to how I used to be. I decided it wouldn't be worth trying to find David. I felt like killing him, but what would that have solved? I can't forget Claire's eyes and how terrified she looked. If I went and beat David up and she heard about it, she'd hate me— especially now she knows about my past.'

Cara lowered her eyes. 'I'm sorry I doubted you, Ben, it's just—'

'I know, you still see me as the man I was sixteen years ago.'

'No. David dying... it threw me. I wasn't thinking straight.' She smiled at him, through her tears.

'It's too late. Yesterday I came so close to becoming the man I used to be, and I'm sure it's because you've come back and brought the past with you. I thought I was cured after the therapy, but I'm not. You know, you were right when you said I'm still the same old Benjamin. I am. I can't change. I can't be someone I'm not. I got away from the things and the people that reminded me of my anger and that's how I've managed to be this other person. Yesterday, I realised that all it takes is one little thing to turn me back into my old self. You remind me of it all.'

'But you have changed, Ben; you've been with Claire for years and you've been good to her. No one can put on an act for that long. You should have more confidence in yourself. You're a good man now.'

He shook his head. 'The way I treated Maggie, it will always be there in the back of your mind, and whenever I see you, I'll always remember it. I've worked so hard to forget it all. It's best if we go our separate ways. Sixteen years is a long time, we've all moved on. It's for the best.'

He turned to leave.

'You can't just forget about us,' said Cara in a high-pitched voice. 'What about Penny? David is dead, she doesn't need to hide now. Why don't you meet her and explain everything to her? Wouldn't you like to see her again?'

He twisted around to face her. 'But you said you don't know where Penny is.'

'I don't, but we can find her. Together.'

His features were drawn, mournful. 'I shouldn't get involved.'

'But you're her father.'

'No, I let her down.'

'But if she sees you're genuinely sorry for what you did—'

'I phoned Claire today. We talked and she's agreed I can go home. I only came here to get my stuff. We're going to try to get through this.'

'But will you at least help me find Penny?'

'She'll probably come to find you.'

'But what if she hasn't heard about David?'

'Aunty Glor can help you find her.' He was standing at the bedroom door.

'Ben, you will still come and visit me, now Claire knows the whole story?'

He gazed at the floor, pouting. 'Claire's agreed I can move back

154

home, but things are still rocky between us. It wasn't easy for her to learn all about my past; we need to sort out our relationship.'

'I've met Claire; she seems nice. I'm sure she wouldn't mind us keeping in touch.'

'I'm not so sure. She feels deceived because I didn't tell her the truth from the start. I've told her I'll cut my ties with the past.'

'She doesn't have to know if you visit me. She doesn't even have to know if you see Penny. You don't have to tell her,' pleaded Cara.

'I don't want to lie to her.'

'You can't walk away, Ben; I don't know if I could bear losing you again.'

'It's not the same this time. You know I'm okay. You don't have to worry about me.'

'So, what are you saying?'

'It would be best if we don't see each other.'

'I'm your mother,' she almost screamed the words.

'I still love you,' he said. 'But it's a choice I have to make: Claire or you.'

'You shouldn't have to choose,' said Cara, impatiently. 'I'll speak to Claire.'

'No. This isn't Claire's decision, it's mine. I can't face remembering everything. Sorry.'

'I won't let you go.'

'Stay out of my life,' he said bluntly. 'I'm sorry, but I can't risk losing Amy.' His eyes were welling with tears. 'Bye.' With that, he was gone.

Cara stared at the bedroom door for a long time after he'd left, tears streaming down her cheeks. She'd been so hopeful that once he was reunited with Catherine and James things would change, but now all her dreams of them being a family again were out of reach; she had doubted him and her doubts had sent him away.

Cara felt the silver locket between her fingers and lifted it so she could see it. As she did so, a single teardrop fell onto the shiny pendant, covering the inscription for an instant before dispersing.

CHAPTER TWENTY-THREE

The days following David's death were difficult for Cara. She felt lonelier than ever, having so many hours alone to sit and think. Her most prominent thoughts were of things that made her feel upset or anxious. She couldn't help playing over in her mind the way David had charged into her room, his eyes full of desperation, seeking Penelope, and then the way he had come to such an untimely end, so suddenly and unexpectedly. The memory of his pale, lifeless face in the mortuary hung over her like a shadow, disturbing her peace, making it difficult for her to sleep. On top of that, she had to deal with remorse and regret over driving Benjamin away.

She needed someone to talk to, but Gloria remained distant and uncommunicative.

One evening, when the silence and isolation became too much to bear, Cara stopped Gloria as she walked towards the door after delivering her supper. 'Glor, why don't you sit in here with me to have your dinner?'

Gloria looked over her shoulder. There were dark shadows around her eyes. 'I'm not hungry, I ate earlier.' She put a hand against her mouth to stifle a yawn. 'I need to clean the kitchen, then I'm going to bed.' She was standing by the bedroom door with one hand on the knob.

'You look worn out. Why don't you sit here while I eat? You can clean up later.'

Gloria sighed and let go of the door handle. She sat on the chair next to the bed, smoothing the lines of her pleated pink skirt and dusting a piece of fluff off the sleeve of her white cardigan.

'I haven't really been able to relax these past few days,' said Cara, 'since everything that's happened. It's all been so disturbing.'

Gloria stood up and switched the light on, then walked over to the window. 'Yes, I know. It's going to take a long time to get the house back in order after what David did to it,' she said as she closed the thick velvet curtains. It was getting dark outside. 'I suppose you'll be leaving soon, now Penelope no longer has to hide from him.' Gloria walked towards the door.

'Wait,' said Cara. 'Has Penny contacted you?'

'No, but it's only a matter of time.' Gloria said, closing her eyes. 'You know you don't have to return to London, don't you? You could stay here with me, if you like.'

Cara smiled at her sister. 'That's kind of you, Glor, but I do want to try to find Penny, and if there is any way I can move back with her, I will. Furley Avenue has been my home for the past five years. I miss it. Even though I was stuck in my bedroom most of the time, there was always something going on outside the window. London is busier than Huddlesea. It's not that I don't like it here, I do, but when I'm here in this room there's not much to see out there. I feel as if I'm just waiting for time to end.'

'I did bring you the television to keep you entertained,' said Gloria. 'I could arrange for your bed to be moved to the front room, so you'll have a view of the goings-on in town. Of course, it's not as busy as London, but there's always someone passing by the house. Rosetta said you enjoyed your trips into town. I could take you out and about. You won't have to be cooped up in here all the time.'

'That's very kind, Glor, but I won't change my mind. I never really did like Huddlesea, even as a young girl. I was constantly hoping for a way to leave. There are too many ghosts here.'

'I see.' Gloria pursed her lips.

'That doesn't mean I won't visit. I'm sure we'll keep in touch. And you're more than welcome to take a trip to London whenever you can.' Then Cara's brow furrowed slightly as she said, 'Oh dear, I'm getting ahead of myself. We haven't even found Penny yet. I do hope we can find her soon. I hope she's okay.'

'I'm sure she's fine,' said Gloria. 'Well, I really must go and clean up. I'll come and collect your tray in a while.'

'Glor, will you help me find Penny?'

'I don't know if I can,' she replied. 'I wouldn't know where to start.'

'The police at the Hensley police station helped her escape; they probably know where she is. Would you call them for me?'

'I'll try and find the number.'

Gloria smiled, but Cara could see tears forming in her ice-blue eyes.

'I suppose I'd hoped you'd decide to stay here rather than return to London.'

Looking at Gloria, Cara could no longer feel any bitterness. True, she had not been the perfect sister, far from it, but they had become friends. 'I'm grateful for all you've done for me but, as I said, Penny's house was my home for so long, I miss being there. Thank you so much for letting me stay.'

'Oh, you would have done the same for me.' Gloria kept her eyes averted as she spoke.

'We will keep in touch,' said Cara. 'Everything's different now.'

'Yes.' A tear fell from Gloria's eye. 'Oh, I am a silly old fool,' she murmured, as she wiped the tear away with the sleeve of her cardigan.

Gloria did not mention Penelope for the next few days. She continued to behave aloofly, bringing Cara's meals and leaving the room after a few words about the weather or about the people she had met in town whilst out shopping. Then one morning she sat on the chair next to the bed, still wearing her red quilted dressing gown, her hair in a net. 'Cara,' she said, eyes down, 'I've had a call from Catherine.'

'Cathy?' Cara smiled. 'Last time I spoke to her she said that she and Jamie could come to visit. Did she mention that?'

'She said she'll be coming to see you tomorrow.'

'What about Jamie?'

'She didn't talk about him. It was just a brief call to let us know she's coming. She couldn't really talk, she was on her way to take her children to school.'

Cara beamed. 'I've missed her.'

'She said she can only pop in for a short while. I invited her for dinner, but she's too busy. Oh, and she said she has heard from Penelope.'

'Oh, how wonderful! What a relief! I knew she'd be all right. Before you know it, I'll be back in London. I can't wait to see her and little Carl and Andrew again.'

'Yes. That will be nice.' Without warning, Gloria headed for the door.

'Wait, Glor. Why do you look so... well... unhappy? Aren't you pleased Penny's free now? Hang on, is there something you're not telling me... about Penny?'

Gloria turned to face her.

'Is Penny all right?'

'I don't know, dear. I think so.' Gloria shrugged.

'Didn't Cathy say anything else about Penny?'

'No, but as I say, she couldn't talk for long, she only called to give me a message for you.'

'Glor, have I offended you in some way?'

'No, of course not. Sorry if I don't seem pleased for you. I am, but I've just got used to you being around, I suppose. This house is too big for one person. I'll miss you. I'll be fine, though.'

'Oh, I see. This was never going to be a permanent arrangement, Glor, you knew that.'

'Yes, I know. I do understand, don't worry. Penelope is your granddaughter; of course you'd rather be with her. She's your family.'

'You're my family, too.'

'I know,' said Gloria, 'but I haven't been much of a sister.'

'I didn't mean that you're any less important to me.'

'But I've been unkind to you for most of my life. I did want to make it up to you.' She slouched, looking at the floor.

'Let's leave the past where it belongs. None of us are perfect; we've all done things we regret,' said Cara.

Gloria wiped away a stray tear.

'I'll never forget what happened to Beattie, but I have forgiven you. Maybe it's about time you forgave yourself.'

Gloria gave a half smile stained with sadness. 'I'll miss you, Cara.'

CHAPTER TWENTY-FOUR

As Catherine walked into the bedroom, Cara noticed she looked thinner than usual. She had always been a slim girl, but today she appeared even more slight. Her pink summer dress, which Cara had seen her wear before, did not fit her well; it was loose around the bodice.

'Hi, Mum.' She kissed Cara on the cheek and sat on the edge of the bed, placing her white handbag on the carpet. 'Sorry I haven't visited since I brought you here, but it's so difficult to arrange for someone to look after the children.' A lock of her red hair fell onto her face and she tucked it behind her ear.

'You should have brought them with you, I would have loved to see them again. I miss them.'

'It's hard to handle the two of them on my own.'

'What about Tom? He could come with you; I'd love to see him too. I suppose he's working, though. How is he?'

Catherine touched her forehead, giving the impression she was deep in thought. 'Mum, about Tom...' She stood up and sat on the chair next to the bed. 'He's not well.'

'Oh dear, what's wrong with him?'

'Nothing life-threatening; well, not really. He's depressed. He has to take antidepressants. He's fine when he takes them, but if he forgets, it's not pleasant. He has these mood swings.'

The last time Cara had seen Tom at the flat, the night before she came to Huddlesea, he'd seemed tired; he hadn't spoken much, but it was late and she'd assumed he'd been at work all day. 'How long has he had depression?' she asked.

'It most likely stems back to his redundancy last November. He started to behave different. Moody.'

'But Tom's usually such a cheerful young man.'

'That's the problem, there are times when I don't even recognise him anymore. One minute he's his old self, laughing and joking, but he can change just like that.' She clicked her fingers. 'And I never know what to say to him.' She brushed her hair away from her face. Her green eyes were brimming with tears.

Cara reached over and handed her a tissue. 'Don't worry, dear, I'm sure he'll get better. As you say, losing his job couldn't have been easy to come to terms with.'

'Yes, that's part of it.' Catherine dried her eyes. 'But depression is an illness. It's not like you or I getting a bit upset, it's a serious condition. The doctor said Tom's been having suicidal thoughts.'

'Tom wouldn't do that,' said Cara, quickly.

'No, that's what I thought, but last month I came home one evening and found him sitting at the kitchen table with about twelve packets of paracetamol tablets in front of him. I'm sure he was planning to take an overdose. I hide all the medicines because I'm scared of what he'll do. Can't hide his depression pills from him though, he needs them.'

'I'm sorry, Cathy.'

'I'm praying he gets another job soon. He's going for an interview next week.'

'Yes.' Cara nodded. 'I'm sure he'll be fine when he gets another job and he's got a routine.' She remembered now that the last time she'd seen her daughter, she'd appeared pale and tired, but being so worried about Penelope, she hadn't stopped to consider that Catherine could have problems of her own. 'Cathy dear, if you ever need to talk, call me. You shouldn't keep everything bottled up; it's hard enough to cope without having to pretend you're fine when you're not.'

'I didn't want to worry you.'

'I know.'

'Enough about me. How are you? Are you feeling all right?'

'Yes, I'm fine. Gloria's been very good.'

'No, I mean the MS.'

'I haven't had any problems. I've got the tablets the doctor gave me, apart from that I'm the same. I'm no worse, thank God.'

'Good.'

'Don't worry about me; I've had this condition for so long, I don't really think about it. The only thing I miss is being mobile, but I'm quite well otherwise.'

Catherine smiled at her. 'That's a lovely necklace, I haven't seen you wear it before.' She leaned forward to take a closer look.

Cara had been holding the locket in her hand as she spoke, unaware. 'Er... it's a necklace I used to wear when I was a young girl. Gloria found it here and gave it back to me.'

Catherine took the locket between her fingers.

Cara held her breath.

'It's got a "C" for Cara,' said Catherine.

'Yes.'

'It's lovely. I might steal it from you, as it's my initial too!' Catherine laughed.

Watching as her daughter flicked open the locket, Cara winced.

'What's inside? Hair? Is that hair?' The strands of black hair were neatly tied together with a piece of cotton. 'Whose hair is it? It's black, like Penny's hair. Is it Penny's hair?'

'I can't remember whose hair it is.'

'No, it can't be Penny's if Aunty Glor found it here.' She frowned, as if trying to work it out in her mind.

'I think it was a lock of my best friend's hair. Yes. It was so long ago I'd almost forgotten,' she lied, taking inspiration from what Gloria had said.

'Really? You must have been thrilled to see it again.'

'Yes, I was.' She avoided Catherine's eyes.

As Catherine tried to close the locket the hair fell out. 'Oh, no, where's it gone?' She knelt on the floor. 'It has to be somewhere down here, but it's difficult to see. The carpet's dark too.'

'Don't worry, dear.'

Catherine stood up. 'It's been inside the locket for so many years, trust me to be the one to lose it.'

'Don't worry, it's not important,' said Cara, secretly hoping Catherine would find it.

After kneeling down on the carpet and searching with her hands for a minute or so, Catherine sat back on the chair and shrugged. 'It's disappeared.'

Cara decided she would try to find the hair herself later, when Catherine had left.

'I'm sorry, Mum.'

'It's okay.'

'I'll have to go soon,' said Catherine, noticing the time on the clock next to Cara's bed. 'Oh, I nearly forgot: I've got some news about Penny.'

Cara felt her spirits lift when she heard her granddaughter's name. 'Glor mentioned you'd heard from her. Is it true?'

'Yes, she called me a couple of days ago.'

'How is she? What did she say?'

'She told me David is dead. Is it true he died in Huddlesea?'

'Yes,' said Cara, bowing her head.

'I was so shocked when I heard,' exclaimed Catherine. 'It must have happened quite soon after he'd been here to see you.'

'Yes, that same night.'

'Did he kill himself?'

'There's no evidence yet.'

'It's so tragic. It doesn't help that I'm worrying about Tom's state of mind. It makes you realise how fragile our lives are. Do you think he killed himself because Penny took the children?'

'The police think it was an accident; he may have been drunk and he most likely fell.' Cara could see the imposing cliffs in her mind's eye as she spoke.

'Whatever happened, it's so tragic. It wasn't too long ago we saw him at Carl's birthday party. He was so young.'

'I know.'

'I mean, I know he didn't treat Penny well, but I didn't know about the violence. I remember a nice, quiet young man.'

'He had problems,' said Cara. 'I saw the other side of him when he came here looking for Penny. He was frightening.'

'He must have been, I suppose, for Penny to go into hiding. That's the one good thing that's come out of this: she'll be able to go back home.'

'Yes.' Cara smiled. 'Did she say when she'll be moving back to Furley Avenue?'

'No, she didn't. How have things been here with Aunty Glor?' she said, changing the subject.

'We're getting along quite well.'

'I'm so pleased. I told you things would work out for the best, didn't I?'

'Yes, dear, but I'll be glad to get back to Penny's house. I've really missed her. Will you ask her to call me?'

'I don't have a contact number for her, but if she calls me again I'll tell her to get in touch.'

Cara felt her mood darken. Why hadn't Penelope called her at Gloria's house? She could have got the number from Catherine.

'Has Jamie been in touch?' asked Catherine.

'No, he hasn't.' Cara's heart ached; she had not seen her youngest son for a few months.

'I called him last week and he said he would come to see you,' explained Catherine, 'but he didn't know when he'd find the time. He's busy planning his move to South Africa.'

'Tell him to bring Emily and William with him when he comes. I'd love to see them all before they leave.'

'Emily and William are staying in England.'

'That will be hard on them, won't it? But I suppose it makes sense they should wait until Jamie is settled in his new job before joining him. He might change his mind,' she said thoughtfully.

'Mum...' Catherine paused and looked at her hands.

'What is it, dear?'

'I don't know if I should be the one to tell you this,' she said, doubt creasing her brow.

'What is it?'

'Don't tell Jamie I told you, promise me.'

'You'll have to tell me now, or you'll have me worrying that something terrible has happened. What is it, darling?'

Catherine ran a hand through her hair. 'It's not great news, I'm afraid. Emily and Jamie have split up.'

'Split up?'

'Yes, they're getting divorced. When you see him, don't tell him I told you.'

'Divorced? But... I didn't even know they were having problems.'

'No, neither did I.'

'But Emily is such a sweet girl,' Cara said. 'It's such a shame. I must speak to him before he goes to South Africa.'

'I'll try calling him again and ask him to contact you.'

'Oh... all my family has scattered here and there and I hardly see any of you.' She thought of Benjamin.

'That's unfair, I visit you whenever I can.'

'I know, dear. Sorry.'

'You mean Ben, don't you?' she said.

Cara shivered at the mention of his name. 'N-no, not only him, everyone... Penny, Jamie...'

'Do you think we'll ever see Ben again?' Catherine asked.

'No, I don't,' said Cara bluntly.

'Well, it has been about sixteen years, I suppose,' Catherine said, shrugging.

Cara did not respond.

Catherine checked the time on her watch. 'Mum, I'm going to have to head back. I can't leave the children alone with Tom for too long. They'll be wrecking the house.'

'You should have brought them with you.'

'It's a long journey. I didn't want to tire them too much, they've got school tomorrow.'

As she watched her daughter leave, Cara wished she could go with her. She felt sad. She had hoped to return to London, but it seemed that Penelope might have other plans which did not include her grandmother.

Cara found herself holding the silver locket between her fingers again and remembered that Frederick's hair was somewhere on the floor. Lying down, she rolled onto her chest and leaned forward over the side of the bed to search the carpet. She peered at the dark brown carpet, straining her eyes; the tiny lock of hair was nowhere to be seen. Determinedly, she ran her hand along the plush fibres to no avail.

Hearing Gloria's footsteps coming up the hallway, she rolled over to lie on her back.

The door opened.

'Hello, Cara.' Gloria raised her eyebrows as she entered the room, then retreated. 'Oh, sorry, I didn't know you were tired. I'll come back later.'

'No, it's all right,' Cara said, sitting up. 'I was resting.'

Gloria walked in with the vacuum cleaner and a can of furniture polish. 'I wanted to clean the room, dear.'

Cara knew the lock of Frederick's hair would now be lost for ever.

CHAPTER TWENTY-FIVE

A few days later, James visited Cara. He looked tired, as if he hadn't slept for days, and his hair was greyer than she remembered it.

'Hello, Mum, long time no see,' he said with an apologetic smile. He kissed her on the cheek and sat on the chair next to her bed.

Facially and physically he resembled Billy, and Cara was invariably reminded of her late husband whenever she saw him. Like Billy, James usually had a cheery smile on his face, but today there was no sign of that smile.

Gazing into his deep blue eyes, she recalled what Catherine had told her and a sadness descended.

'Lovely to see you, Jamie; thank you for coming,' she said as brightly as she could.

'I'm sorry it's been so long. This past year has been a difficult one, and I've been so busy at work.'

She wondered whether she should ask about his split with Emily. 'Jamie, I've missed you.'

'Yes, I've missed you too. Has Cat told you about me and Emily?' he asked.

She felt unsure of what to say and fiddled with the bedsheets nervously.

'We've split up. We're getting divorced,' he said, before she had a chance to respond.

'I'm sorry.'

'No, I'm fine, don't worry about me. Everything's fine. It's for the best.' He looked at his hands.

'What went wrong? You two always seemed happy together.'

'We were for a while. But things haven't been good between us for a few years. These things happen.'

'I only want you to be happy, darling.'

'I am. I'll be all right.'

'Divorce is a big step. Why don't you separate for a while and see if you can't sort out whatever the problems are. You've been married for so long; there must have been something keeping you together. Isn't it worth trying to...'

James was shaking his head as she spoke. 'It's over. Don't you think I've considered all the options? This didn't happen overnight, you know; it's been a while.'

'But you loved Emily once. She's so—'

'There are a lot of things you don't know about Emily,' he said, standing up and walking to the window.

He had his back to her.

'Yes, I'm sure that's true, but whatever she's done, you have a child together. William needs both of you.'

A frown creased his brow. 'William's not my son.'

She laughed nervously. 'That can't be true.'

'She was seeing someone else behind my back before we got married.'

Cara batted away unwanted thoughts of Frederick.

James sat at the end of her bed. 'I'm sick of going over it all. My marriage is over. Can we change the subject, please?'

'But, Jamie, are you sure William is not your son? He could still be your son. There are tests you could do.'

'William's dad left her, so she married me. She lied to me about the pregnancy dates. I had no way of knowing she was lying. I loved her; she had me wrapped around her finger.'

Images of Billy flashed through Cara's mind.

'Anyway, that's not why I'm getting divorced. I've known about William not being my son for years. Emily told me a few years back: she cried a lot and said she felt guilty for lying for so long. It came as a shock, but I thought we'd work through it. I still loved her.' He avoided Cara's eyes. 'We're getting divorced because she's changed. I've changed. Oh, I don't know... There are lots of reasons. We don't want the same things. I'd rather not talk about it.'

'I'm sorry.'

'Maybe it is because I found out William isn't mine.' He shrugged. 'Yes, I suppose things might have started going wrong then.' He got up and walked towards the chair. 'I mean, it's not an easy thing to come to terms with... Trust is so important in a relationship. I found myself questioning everything she said.'

'But she must have loved you to stay with you.'

'No, she used me; she only wanted a father for her child.'

'But imagine how hard it would have been for her to tell you everything.'

'Our relationship was based on lies.'

Cara could see the sorrow in her son's face as he spoke. A tear rolled down her cheek.

'Don't cry.' He sat close to her on the bed and put an arm around her. 'Don't worry about me, I'm fine. The divorce will be final soon and I'm going to work in South Africa. I've been offered a great position over there.'

'Why are you going so far?' she asked. 'I'll never see you.'

'I'll visit, it's not that far. I'll be coming over from time to time to see William. It's just what I need, Mum; I need a new start.'

'You're not running away, are you?'

'No, I'd been planning the move to South Africa for a while, I was even going to take Emily and William with me. I'm not running from anything, I'm doing this for me. It's what I want.'

Cara smiled at him and wiped her tears. 'You must keep in touch, promise me.'

'I will.'

As she watched him leave the room, she could not help feeling that another one of her children was leaving her life for good.

CHAPTER TWENTY-SIX

'Good morning, Nan!' The cheerful cry greeted Cara as she awoke the next day. She lazily wiped her eyes, and sat up in bed.

Penelope drew the bedroom curtains, and turned to look at her. The sun shone into the room. Cara had to blink to make sure she wasn't dreaming. Standing either side of her granddaughter were Carl and Andrew, big grins on their faces.

'Penny?' Cara said, still not quite believing her eyes.

'Yes, I'm back.' Penelope sat on the edge of the bed and took Cara's hand in hers. Her smile radiated genuine joy, and her dark brown eyes were full of life. Her shiny black hair, which had been neglected for so long, was styled into a sleek bob, and there were no signs of any grey hairs. She wore a denim skirt and a smart white blouse. With her fresh, youthful appearance, no one would ever guess the horrors of her past.

Cara's heart was smiling as she observed her granddaughter. She squeezed Penelope's hand tightly and could not stop her tears from falling.

Penelope hugged her.

'I'm so happy you're here, Penny dear!'

'So am I, Nan.' She took a tissue from the box on the bedside cabinet and dried Cara's tears. 'I'm taking you back home with me.' She beamed. 'Well, that's if you want to come.'

'Yes. Yes, I do, Penny. I've been waiting for you to come back.'

⧗

Gloria stood at the door waving goodbye to Cara, who was seated beside Penelope in the car.

'Goodbye, Glor, we'll keep in touch,' said Cara.

As they drove away, she wondered whether she would visit Huddlesea in the future. Although her intentions were to see Gloria from time to time, she knew it was not within her control. Her life would be in London now with Penelope, and travelling alone wasn't an option; she knew it was possible she would never see Huddlesea again.

The car came to a halt at the traffic lights outside The Horse and Dragon public house. Cara wondered if it still looked the same inside. She felt sad that this might be the last time she'd set eyes on the building: the place where she'd met Frederick... As soon as the thought entered her mind she dismissed it, annoyed with herself. Why did she still have feelings for him? He had been the cause of so much pain in her life.

She pulled her gaze away from the pub. Penelope glanced at her and smiled as she set off from the traffic lights. Cara couldn't help thinking of Frederick again. Penelope's deep brown eyes brought the memories flooding back.

She caught herself turning around to take a final look at The Horse and Dragon, and breathed a sigh of relief when they drove out of Huddlesea leaving the ghosts behind them.

⧗

As the car turned into Furley Avenue, Cara's mood lifted. Penelope's house had been her home for so many years, and without David in the house Penelope no longer had to live in fear; they could spend more time together.

For many weeks, Penelope did not talk about the women's refuge. Neither did she bring up the subject of David's death. Cara didn't mention either of those things knowing Penelope was probably trying to forget and move on with her life, and Cara did not want to upset the children.

Penelope behaved much more like her old self, positive and bubbly. Cara was no longer confined to her bedroom: her granddaughter helped her to get around the house so that she could sit in other rooms, and she also frequently took her out and about town in the wheelchair. A sense of freedom and peace reigned in the once stifling house.

One evening, quite out of the blue, Penelope said, 'I'm looking for work, Nan. Just part-time, to bring in extra money. I hate relying on benefits; the boys need so much more now they're growing up,' she explained.

'That's a good idea,' said Cara. 'It will be good for you to meet new people. I can keep an eye on the boys for you.'

'No, don't worry, Nan, I'll find a job to fit in with the boys' school hours. Dave never allowed me to work.' She looked lost in thought for a moment, then went on, 'Now he's not here, I'm going to do what I want.'

Cara did not know what to say. It had been about two months since she'd moved back, and it was the first time Penelope had mentioned David.

A brief silence followed, then Penelope spoke again: 'You're going to think I'm cold-hearted, Nan, but when I heard he died I felt so relieved and... glad. I hated being in the women's refuge. It was like being in prison. All I would hear all day would be women talking about their violent husbands and how they were too afraid to go outside. Paranoia was everywhere. I know going to the refuge helped us get away from Dave, but the last thing I needed was to be talking to other women who'd been through the same thing. Some people might find that therapeutic; one of the counsellors told me it was good to talk about it. Maybe I wasn't ready, I don't know... but for me... I didn't want to relive it over and over.'

'Hmm... I can understand that,' said Cara.

'Plus I didn't want the boys to hear it all. I didn't want the boys being in that environment, and I hardly slept at night because I had this irrational fear that Dave would come and take them from me. I had a solicitor helping me, and I was worried he would somehow get the address of the shelter through the lawyers.'

'It's over, dear, you have to try to put it behind you.' Cara touched her granddaughter's hand.

'Yes, I know. It's over, and I want to make a new start for the boys' sake. I want them to forget about the past.'

'They're young, I'm sure they won't remember any of this,' said Cara, inwardly wondering how much the boys would remember.

'I'm not so sure, Nan. I mean, I still remember my mum and dad arguing and all the violence.'

'Yes, but you were a bit older. Anyway, you've turned out all right, haven't you? You're a sensible girl.'

'That's debatable,' she said sadly.

'Penny, soon you'll meet a nice young man and all the years you spent with David will be a distant memory, like a bad dream you once had.'

'One of the counsellors at the refuge told me I might have been attracted to Dave because he reminded me of my dad. What if that's the type of man I'm attracted to?'

'You can't think that way, Penny.'

'Looking back, sometimes I think I'm lucky to be alive.' Penelope's eyes were wide as if she were recalling a violent episode.

'He's gone, dear, he can't hurt you anymore.'

'I always remember how Mum knew, before all of us... She said he was like my dad, didn't she?'

Cara lowered her eyes as she remembered her last meeting with Benjamin.

Penelope shook her head mournfully. 'I never want to be in that situation ever again.'

'You won't. Not all men are like David. He was an exception, not the rule.'

'But, Nan, all the men I've ever known are the same.'

'That's not true. What about my Billy? He was a good man,' said Cara, echoes of her recent conversation with Benjamin playing in her mind: '*I idolised him... wanted to be just like him.*'

Penelope smiled through weary eyes. 'You're right, Nan, I'm getting things out of proportion. Sorry.'

'Everything will be all right, dear, you'll see. You'll meet someone special, someone who deserves you.'

Penelope rolled her eyes and shrugged. 'Maybe.'

CHAPTER TWENTY-SEVEN

A tall grey-haired man stood outside the front door.

'Steve! What are you doing here?' asked Penelope in surprise.

'Hello, Penny. I was just passing, so I thought I'd stop by to see how you're doing,' he said, smiling.

The last time she'd seen him had been at the women's refuge. He'd been one of her counsellors. They became friends during her stay, and she had sent him a *thank you* card the week after she left the refuge. She told him he was like the father she never had.

'I was so thrilled when I heard you'd got back on your feet, and I wanted to see you. I know being at the refuge must have been stressful.'

'Thanks, yes, it was but everything's great now. Um, come in for a cup of tea.'

'I don't want to impose.'

She giggled. 'Steve, you're too polite for your own good. I've just put the kettle on, actually; I'm having tea with my nan. Remember I told you about her?'

'Oh, yes. It would be nice to meet her.'

Cara glanced up from her position on the sofa to see a tall, middle-aged man enter the room. He was quite large, but he did not appear overweight, more well-built, his frame similar to Benjamin's. He wore a grey suit and navy blue tie and was carrying a black briefcase.

Penelope followed him into the room. 'Nan,' she said excitedly. 'This is Steve. He was one of the counsellors at the refuge. He helped me get back on my feet.'

Cara smiled at him. 'Hello.'

'Hello, Cara. It's nice to meet you,' he said warmly, reaching out an arm to shake her hand. 'I've heard a lot about you.'

Cara noticed his eyes; they were kind-looking eyes, a warm chestnut colour. There was something strangely familiar about him, but she knew she'd never met him. Perhaps he resembled someone else. She racked her brain but could not place anyone in her memory.

'I'll go and make the tea,' said Penelope, beaming. 'I'll let you two get acquainted.'

'So, you're a counsellor?' said Cara, uncomfortable alone with the stranger and feeling the need to start a conversation.

'Yes, I help out at the women's refuge where Penny was staying, from time to time.' His voice was soft and deep.

'I don't envy you. It must be a stressful job.'

'Yes, it is.' He laughed. 'That's why I've got grey hair.'

Cara laughed along with him.

'But seriously, I do enjoy the work, especially when I see people like Penny benefiting from our help. I was struck by the way she looked so unhappy when she came to the refuge, but I can see she has a sense of independence and self-worth again.'

'Yes, you do a very good job.'

'You must be pleased to have her back.'

Cara said 'Yes,' instinctively but felt embarrassed knowing that Penelope had been talking about her to this man.

'She's a lovely girl. You should be proud of her,' he said.

'Yes, I am.'

'And the boys, Andrew and Carl, they were so well-behaved.'

'Yes, they are treasures.'

Penelope entered the room carrying a tray with three mugs of tea and a plate of shortbread biscuits. She placed the tray on the table and handed a mug to Steve. 'Here you go, just how you like it: one sugar and not too strong.' She smiled.

'You remembered,' he said, laughing.

Penelope sat down next to him. 'So, Steve, what brings you to this neck of the woods?' she asked brightly.

'I'm visiting a family not too far from here. The children are being monitored by Social Services, and there's a real risk they'll be taken into care. It's quite a sad case.'

'I was saying to Steven that his job must be stressful,' said Cara.

Penelope twisted around to face her. 'Yes, I'm sure it is, Nan. But, you know, it's probably satisfying to help people who really need help.' She turned her attention back to Steve, and Cara noticed she appeared to be staring at him in awe.

'It is,' he agreed.

'Do you think I could become a counsellor?' asked Penelope.

'I don't see why not.' Steve sipped his tea. 'I could give you some details about courses, if you'd like.'

'But... I don't know,' said Penelope, waving her hand to dismiss the idea. 'How would I fit it in? I mean, I've already got my hands full with the boys.'

'There are part-time courses, with flexible hours, or you can even study from home,' he suggested.

'That sounds good. Next time you're in the neighbourhood could you bring me some details?'

'It's a deal,' he said.

Cara felt pleased her granddaughter was starting to take an interest in herself and in life again.

Steve looked at his watch. 'I have to go, I'm afraid, or I'll be late for my meeting.' He picked up his briefcase. 'Thanks for the tea, Penny.' Turning to Cara he reached out a hand to shake hers. 'Nice meeting you.'

'Yes, and you, Steven,' said Cara, shaking his hand.

'Steve, wait,' said Penelope, standing up and following him. 'Why don't you pop over for lunch this Sunday, if you're not too busy? I'm sure the kids would love to see you again.'

'All right, I don't have any plans for Sunday.'

'Bring your wife.'

'Um, I'm divorced,' he said.

'Sorry, I didn't know—'

'No harm done.' He smiled.

'No, uh...,' Penelope reddened slightly. 'Um... be here about three o'clock,' she said, walking to the door to show him out.

Shortly, Penelope returned to the living room. 'Isn't he lovely?' she said, eyes twinkling.

'Yes, dear,' said Cara, slightly concerned that her granddaughter might have developed some sort of crush or infatuation. 'I'm sure he's a good counsellor,' she said pointedly.

'He is; he helped me so much. I can't wait until the boys see him again. They got on well.'

'Yes, well, you were at a low point in your life when you met him and he helped you through, but he was only doing his job, you mustn't read anything else into it,' said Cara.

Penelope giggled. 'Nan? You don't think? Oh, no! I really like Steve, but not in that way. He's a father figure to me, a proper one, though: not the lousy one I had. He's such an inspiration.'

Cara smiled. 'Sorry, dear, but you did have me worried there for a while. I'd love you to find someone new, but he's not quite what I had in mind.'

Penelope giggled again. 'I'm not looking for another relationship just yet, I'm considering becoming a career woman. I am serious about this counselling thing; I'd be able to understand people with problems because I've had my fair share.'

'I'm pleased you're able to see the bright side, dear.'

Penelope placed the empty teacups onto the tray. 'Oh, Nan, I forgot to mention that you and Steve have something in common.'

'Do we?'

'Yes, you can talk to him about it on Sunday. He told me he used to live in Huddlesea. Is that a coincidence, or what?' She picked up the tray and left the room.

CHAPTER TWENTY-EIGHT

'Hello, Cara,' said Steve, 'nice to see you again.'

Cara, seated at the dining table, looked up at him and smiled warmly. 'Hello, Steven, how are you?'

'Fine, thank you.' Standing behind him was a little girl, maybe five or six years old. Her long blonde hair fell in unruly curls over the shoulders of her turquoise dress.

'Sally, don't be shy,' he said, placing a hand on the girl's head. 'Say hello to Cara. Cara, I'd like you to meet my granddaughter, Sally.'

'Hello, Sally,' she said, smiling at the girl. 'Aren't you pretty?'

'Yes, she is, isn't she? Takes after her granddad, of course. Her mum and dad asked me to babysit, so I thought it would be nice for her to come along and meet Andrew and Carl.'

The girl smiled awkwardly.

Cara noticed Sally's dark brown eyes, the colour of chocolate; it struck her as an unusual combination with her yellow-blonde hair.

'The food's ready,' said Penelope, popping her head through the living room doorway. 'Please take a seat and I'll call the boys.'

Steve sat opposite Cara, after helping Sally to sit on the chair next to her.

'We had a lovely drive here, didn't we, Sally?' he said to the young girl.

Sally nodded shyly and blushed.

'Do you live locally?' asked Cara.

'No, I live in Hertfordshire,' replied Steve. 'It's nice and green. I used to live in London but prefer the countryside these days. I spend quite a bit of time in London while I'm working, though. The city is too crowded for my liking, and I always feel an enormous sense of relief when I get back home. It's a different world. Perhaps I'm getting old!'

'If you're tired of London you're tired of life, isn't that how the saying goes?' said Cara.

Steve chuckled. 'Yes, something like that. But for me, it's more to do with growing up in a city and wanting a change.'

'Oh, that's interesting,' commented Cara. 'I wasn't aware you grew up in London; Penny told me you used to live in Huddlesea.'

'Yes, yes, I did,' he said animatedly. 'We lived there for a while when I was a child, but it was a brief stay. We moved back to London when I was about ten or so. We weren't living in Huddlesea, actually, just outside in a little place called Stampsley. My father worked in Huddlesea.'

'Stampsley, oh yes, I know it. It's by the old bridge,' said Cara, her mind filling with nostalgic thoughts.

'That's right: Turner's Bridge. A place renowned for s-u-i-c-i-d-e attempts, I was told.' He spelt the word "suicide" aloud to avoid saying it in front of Sally. 'Yes,' he continued, 'funnily enough, there's another place in Huddlesea itself where people go for that, isn't there? It was on the news the other week. Some unfortunate soul was found there.' He shook his head.

Cara tried to move her mouth, to say something to change the subject, but no words would come out. He seemed blissfully unaware that the "unfortunate soul" found at Stoneleigh Cliffs had been Penelope's estranged husband.

Scratching his head, he said, 'What's it called? It's on the tip of my tongue. You must have heard of it.'

'Stoneleigh Cliffs,' she said almost choking on the words.

'Yes, of course,' he said, smiling.

She forced herself to smile back. It was at times such as this that Cara wished she wasn't reliant on other people for her mobility; if she could have, she'd have made an excuse and walked out of the room. Talking about the cliffs was difficult for her, not only because it was so soon after David's tragic end but also because of the shadowy reflections from the past that haunted her mind whenever she heard the name "Stoneleigh".

'It's funny there are so many people wanting to end it all in such a small part of the country. I'm sure it can't be all that bad.' Steve giggled.

Cara knew he expected her to laugh along with his joke, but she couldn't. She closed her eyes, as if to shut out painful thoughts. Steve had innocently latched on to this subject, she told herself; he didn't mean any harm.

Penelope's footsteps could be heard approaching the dining room. Lowering her voice, Cara said, 'Steven, I don't mean to be rude, but can you try not to talk about these sorts of things when Penny comes in? It's not long since David, her husband, you know...'

'Of course. I'm sorry, you must think I'm so insensitive.'

'It's all right,' said Cara.

Penelope entered the room followed by Andrew and Carl. They were carrying the roast meal. 'Put the potatoes over there, Andrew,' said Penelope.

'I'll take those,' said Steve, helping Andrew with the plate.

'Hello, Steve,' said Andrew, smiling. He sat next to him.

'This is my granddaughter, Sally,' said Steve. 'And, this is Carl and Andrew.' He pointed at the boys.

Carl sat next to Sally.

'So, what have you two been chatting about while I've been in the kitchen?' asked Penelope.

Steve's cheeks reddened.

'We were talking about Huddlesea,' said Cara with a forgiving smile.

'Your dad used to work there, didn't he, Steve?' said Penelope.

'Yes, in the early fifties,' he said. 'Cara, when did you live in Huddlesea?'

'I was born there, and I left in the mid-fifties when I was about nineteen.'

'Huddlesea's quite a small town, isn't it?' he said. 'I remember going there once or twice; everyone knew everyone.'

'Yes,' said Cara. 'It was that sort of place.' She laughed a bitter laugh soured by her past experiences.

'Hmm... it's possible you knew my father back then.'

'Yes, it's possible, I suppose. What's his name?'

'Fred Johnson.'

'Fred John—' Cara stopped and stared at Steve. *Freddie's son?* The colour washed out of her cheeks.

'Are you all right, Nan? You look like you've seen a ghost,' said Penelope.

'I-I need a glass of water,' she said, coughing. 'Some food has gone down the wrong way, I think.'

'Andrew, fetch Nan a glass of water,' said Penelope.

Steve frowned at Cara.

She could not meet his eyes.

Andrew returned with a glass of water.

'Thank you, Andrew, bless you,' said Cara.

They began to discuss other matters, much to Cara's relief, but she remained on tenterhooks all evening worried Steve might mention his father's name again. She could not help the curiosity this sparked in her brain, and she kept searching Steve's face for some resemblance, but he looked nothing like Frederick.

Before leaving, Steve turned to Cara. 'Lovely to see you, Cara. I'll have to ask my father if he remembers you. What's your surname?'

'Edwards,' she replied.

'But it was Hughes when you lived in Huddlesea, wasn't it, Nan?' said Penelope.

'Er... yes,' said Cara, sighing. 'But I don't recognise your father's name; I'm sure I never knew him. I left Huddlesea at a very young age.' She spoke quickly.

'Well, I suppose you can't really know everyone in a town,' said Steve.

'No,' Cara agreed. 'And as you say, you weren't living in town, so...'

'That's true,' he said. 'Well, no doubt we'll meet again.'

When he left, Cara found herself fiddling nervously with the silver locket and praying Steve would not ask his father if he remembered her.

⧖

Cara lay awake that night, unable to relax. At first she found herself pondering whether it could be possible there'd been two Frederick Johnsons working in Huddlesea in the early 1950s. It was quite a common name. However, she knew that in such a small town it would be too coincidental. Besides, she'd known most people in Huddlesea and had always found it easy to spot a stranger.

Cara's mind ran through an imagined conversation between Steve and Frederick:

'Hi, Dad.'

'Hello, son, where have you been today?'

'I've been to see a friend, Penny. She's a lovely girl; she used to stay at a women's refuge, but now she's back home with her grandmother. Her grandmother used to live in Huddlesea, you know.'

'It's a small world, isn't it?'

'You can say that again! Her name's Cara. Did you know a Cara Hughes?'

Would Frederick deny all knowledge of her as she had of him? Cara found herself hoping he wouldn't, but anxiety tugged at her heart, and she prayed Steve wouldn't mention their meeting.

No matter how hard she tried to think of other things, her thoughts went round in circles. Every time she was about to drift off to sleep, she woke up, different scenarios of Steve talking to Frederick playing out in her head.

She found she was able to remember quite a lot about Frederick—the way he used to raise his eyebrows when he spoke, the intensity of his stare. Steve had inherited those characteristics, which was—she now realised—why she'd thought she recognised him when they'd first met.

In the end, to stop the repetition in her mind, she deliberately

180

imagined a conversation between Frederick and his son, in which Frederick denied knowing her.

Cara drifted off to sleep, the silver locket clasped tightly between her fingers.

CHAPTER TWENTY-NINE

One afternoon, a few days after Steve's visit, when Penelope returned from collecting the boys from school she ran straight into the living room. 'Nan, guess who I just bumped into?' she said, beaming.

Cara was engrossed in a daytime soap opera.

'Steve,' Penelope said, sitting down next to Cara on the sofa.

'That's nice.' Cara had hoped they would not be seeing any more of Steve. She looked back at the television.

'And, guess what? His dad remembers you!'

Cara felt the colour rise in her cheeks.

'Steve thinks it would be nice if we all meet up for a meal, so I've invited them next Sunday.'

Turning to her granddaughter, Cara said, 'I don't think that would be a good idea, Penny.'

Penelope's smile faded. 'What do you mean?'

'I don't want to see Steven's father.'

'Wh-why not?'

'It's a long story.'

'But, Nan, you said you didn't know Steve's dad.' Penelope's brow wrinkled in confusion.

'I lied.'

'Why?'

'As I say, it's a long story.'

'I want to hear it,' said Penelope.

Cara pursed her lips.

'Why don't you want to see him?' asked Penelope after a pause.

'We used to know each other, but we didn't part on good terms. I'd really rather not discuss it,' said Cara, quickly.

'What happened?'

'I was young when I met him and I... fell in love with him, but it didn't work out.'

'You had a relationship with him?'

'Yes, but I'd rather forget about it.'

'You're talking as if it happened yesterday. It must have been fifty-odd years ago; you must have been no more than teenagers. What harm would it do to have a meal together?'

'I don't want to see him,' said Cara. 'You'll have to cancel the arrangements.'

'A whole lifetime has passed since you last met. Aren't you even curious to see what he's like now? You might even laugh at your failed relationship.'

'You're not listening to me, Penny.'

'Nan, I'm going to make us a cup of tea and then I want you to tell me exactly what happened back then. You're acting as if I've invited a mass murderer to dinner.' She walked out of the room.

When Penelope returned with the tea, she sat on the sofa and, using the remote control, turned off the television.

'Hi, Nan,' shouted Andrew.

Carl ran after him into the living room and immediately switched on the television.

'Carl, Andrew, go and play in your room. Nan's tired.'

Penelope switched off the television again.

'Oh, Mum!' the boys cried in unison.

'Just go!' said Penelope.

The boys ran out of the room and could be heard running up the stairs.

'Right.' Penelope handed Cara a cup of tea. 'I want to hear everything, from the beginning.'

Cara wished she could stand up and leave the room.

'What could Steve's dad have done that was so bad?' asked Penelope after Cara's unbroken silence. 'Just because you hated him as a teenager is no reason to refuse to see him now.'

'I didn't hate him,' Cara said. 'Well, maybe I did. I don't know. It was so long ago.'

'Exactly! It was ages ago, so why can't you forgive and forget?'

'It's not that simple.' Cara stopped, reluctant to say more, feeling uncomfortable talking about him. The meeting with Steve had awoken emotions inside her, emotions she had thought were dead and buried.

'How long did your relationship last?' asked Penelope, interrupting her reminiscence.

'Only a couple of months.'

'Can't you just let bygones be bygones?'

'No. Sorry.'

'Steve's become a good friend of mine, Nan. I don't want to let him down. Can you please explain why you won't see his dad?'

'It's personal, Penny.'

'I told you everything about my problems with Dave. That was one of the hardest things I've ever had to do. Whatever happened between you and Steve's dad, I'd like to feel you can tell me.'

'I've never told anyone this before. Not even Billy.' An image in her mind of the last time she'd seen her husband taunted her and caused her to sigh deeply. 'I didn't want anyone to know,' she stated morosely.

'It might do you good to talk about it.'

Cara looked at her granddaughter and then closed her eyes again. On opening them, she said, 'If I tell you, Penny, it goes no further. Can you promise me you won't tell anyone?'

'Who would I tell, Nan? I don't go anywhere or see anyone. Oh, okay, yes, I promise.' Penelope shrugged.

'Oh, I hope I don't regret this.' Cara looked up to the ceiling and then said, 'It's possible... Well, I-I think my relationship with Freddie resulted in me becoming pregnant.'

Penelope frowned. 'What do you mean you "think"?'

'I wasn't sure.'

'You either got pregnant, or you didn't. I don't understand.' Penelope took a tissue from the box on the coffee table and blew her nose. 'Oh, I get it. You lost the baby. That's what this is all about.' Her eyes were distant.

Cara remembered Brenda telling her that Penelope had lost a baby girl.

'You don't want to meet Freddie because it brings it all back.'

'No, dear, I had the baby.'

Penelope gaped at Cara. 'You had a baby with him? Wh-what happened to it? Did you have to give it away?'

Cara looked at her hands. 'Your father might be Freddie's son.'

'What?'

'I always told myself he must be Billy's child, but he looks so much like Freddie...'

'I'm... I don't know what to say.' Penelope blinked exaggeratedly. 'Who else knows about this? Does my dad know?'

'No, no one knows.'

'My dad didn't know?'

'I didn't know for sure; it's only a suspicion I have. He could be Billy's son. I've never really been sure, Penny.'

'How could you not have known? Were you seeing both of them at the same time?'

'No, I met and married Billy within a few weeks of splitting up with Freddie.'

Penelope stood up and walked towards the window. She turned to face Cara. 'So you've kept this secret for so long? If I hadn't met Steve, no one would ever have known.'

'I didn't want to upset Billy or your father, and Freddie had gone. I had no idea where.'

'Why did you and Freddie split up?'

'He was married at the time.'

'You had an affair with a married man?'

'I didn't know he was married. I fell in love with him. I was swept away: it was truly love at first sight. In my eyes he could do no wrong. He was my first love.' Shaking her head, she added, 'So young and so naive.'

Wrinkles of confusion formed on Penelope's brow. She returned to the sofa and sat next to Cara. 'If you're not sure about any of it, why are you still refusing to see him?'

'Ben always looked different from Cathy and Jamie; he reminded me so much of Freddie. He has the same dark hair, and dark brown eyes.'

'So, Steve's dad might be my granddad. I'd say that's more of a reason to invite him to lunch. I want to meet him.'

'No, Penny, please. I didn't tell him about the pregnancy. I never knew until I married Billy. It's best left in the past.'

'I wonder how my dad would react to being told he's not Grandpa Billy's son?'

Recalling her conversation with Benjamin about Billy's death, Cara said, 'Your father loved Billy. Idolised him. He was heartbroken over his death.'

'Nan, my dad wasn't around when Grandpa Billy died, how do you know—' She stopped, then staring at Cara she said, 'Nan, do you keep in touch with my dad?'

'No, of course not.'

'Well, how did you know he was heartbroken over Grandpa Billy's death?'

'Um... Glor told me.'

'Aunty Gloria? Has she seen him?'

'Yes, in Huddlesea.'

'Does he live there?'

'No, he lives in London, but he goes to Huddlesea for work from time to time.'

'Did you see him when you were in Huddlesea?'

Cara couldn't be sure whether Penelope wanted her to say yes or no. 'I suppose you have a right to know. Yes, I saw him briefly in Huddlesea, but it's not worth mentioning, dear. I won't be seeing him again, so there's nothing to concern yourself about.'

Penelope took another tissue and wiped a tear from her eye. 'Sorry, Nan, I don't know why I'm crying, I'm all right really.' After a brief pause, she continued, 'How is he?'

Cara looked at her granddaughter, trying to work out why she had asked the question. Did she care? Had she forgiven him? 'Um... he's all right, I suppose,' she said.

'Is he still the same?'

'He still looks the same, a bit older but—'

'No, I mean, does he still behave the same?'

'He's really sorry about the way he behaved back then.'

'Did he ask about me and Jemima?'

'Yes, he loves you; he never stopped caring about you.'

'Why did you say you won't be seeing him again?'

'It's complicated. He has a new partner. She's only just found out about how his relationship with your mum ended and it shocked her. He's totally reinvented himself. He calls himself Paul. Claire, his partner, doesn't want him to keep in touch with me.' The truth was too painful to relate.

'Are you sure it's *her* who doesn't want to, or *him*?'

Cara remembered how Benjamin told her he didn't want to stay in contact with her. She'd tried to shut it out, but she felt an ache in her heart, realising he'd written himself out of her life for good. 'I don't know, Penny, but either way, we won't be seeing him again.'

'It's probably for the best,' said Penelope, drinking the rest of her tea in silence.

Cara was reminded of the girl she'd known before: the girl who had lived with David. She was ashen-faced, her eyes devoid of hope. 'I didn't mean to upset you, Penny.'

'It's all right, Nan, I'm glad you told me this. I needed to know.'

The two women stared straight ahead. They were looking at nothing in particular, like two strangers in a waiting room.

Penelope walked back to the window, then turned to face Cara. 'One of the girls I met at the refuge was going through a divorce. Her husband tried to claim she'd had an affair and that the child wasn't his. Her solicitor arranged a blood test. My dad and Freddie can have a blood test.'

'No.' Cara shook her head.

'Why not? It makes sense.'

'Penny, please, I've already told you, this is a secret I've kept for most of my life and I don't want anyone else to know.'

'This is important to me, Nan, can't you see? I thought my granddad died, but he might still be alive. Steve might be my uncle. I've got this whole new family I didn't know about. It's been so hard these past few years, not having any family beside me that I could rely on—'

'I've been with you.'

'I don't mean you, Nan; I mean my mum deserted me. I haven't seen my sister for years. My dad... well, you know the story. If they'd been around, maybe all this with Dave wouldn't have happened.'

Cara felt the stab of guilt again over keeping her suspicions about the violence to herself.

'I just think finding out about this new family has come at the perfect time for me, when I'm starting to rebuild my life.'

'Your father doesn't want to know me,' said Cara. 'I can't see him agreeing to this.'

'I'm sure he'd want to know if his real dad is still alive.'

'It's not a good idea. Your father admired Billy. He told me he inspired him to put his past behaviour behind him and change. I don't know how he'd react to this news.'

'My dad must be about fifty years old. I'm sure he'd be able to handle it. He doesn't need a dad at his age, but I'm sure he'd be interested in finding out that his family history is a bit different from what he was led to believe.'

'It's all speculation. I shouldn't have said anything. He might still be Billy's son, so what's the use rocking the boat at this stage? We're all old.'

'I want to know,' said Penelope.

'I understand why you're curious, Penny, but this isn't something to go rushing into. As I told you before, Freddie never even knew I was pregnant when we split up; you can't just go and ask him to have a test after all these years to see if he's your grandfather. You're getting carried away with this because it sounds exciting. You're young, I know why you'd look at it that way, but it's complicated. What good could it do anyone to find out now?'

'It's better for people to know who they're related to, isn't it? Medical issues, that sort of thing. There are lots of things that run in families.'

'It doesn't matter anymore, too much time has passed.'

'It matters to me. I have two young sons. I want them to know their family. I'll speak to Steve and see what he thinks about it; I mean, he's a counsellor so he'd know if it's a good idea to bring all this out into the open.'

'I'm too old for this.'

'Nan, I'll deal with it. You don't have to do a thing,' said Penelope, taking her hand.

⌛

Cara could not sleep that night. Frederick remembered her. She felt excited, unable to wait and see what happened next: would he be told their relationship resulted in her becoming pregnant? How would he react to the news? She surprised herself with her thoughts.

Cara knew and could not deny that her love for Frederick had been all-consuming. She'd loved Billy, but that was another kind of love, more of a companionship. Shutting her eyes, she asked herself why she'd allowed her feelings for Frederick to be rekindled.

How would his wife take the news? Was he still with his wife?

Shaking her head, she attempted to put an end to the overthinking. *Do I still love him?* Her heart rate quickened.

As she questioned herself, she became aware of the reality: her relationship with Frederick remained an unfinished chapter; she'd never really stopped loving him, simply filed it all away at the back of her mind. Their union ended suddenly and unexpectedly. She'd believed she would marry him and have his children. She'd imagined they'd be together for ever. Those filed-away feelings had been there all along and were now being opened and re-examined.

CHAPTER THIRTY

Cara's parents were confused when she first introduced Billy as her boyfriend.

'Didn't you say your boyfriend's called Freddie, dear?' asked her mother, bewilderment evident in her frown.

'He was only a friend,' replied Cara, blushing.

'But—'

'No, Mother, Billy is my boyfriend now.' Cara had to resist the urge to cry as thoughts of Frederick flashed through her mind.

'People will start talking about you, young lady. You'll get a reputation if you're not careful.'

'I'm happy with Billy,' she muttered.

'You were brought up properly. You'll bring shame on the family; you know how people talk in this town. Only last week you were telling me how much you love Freddie, but now you bring Billy home...'

'Billy saved my life,' said Cara, trying to make sense of the situation.

'Yes, and I'm grateful to him, but what are you going to do? Are you going to marry Billy? You should be finding a good man to settle down with at your age. You shouldn't be giving your heart to every man you meet. You were going to introduce us to Freddie last week. What went wrong?'

Cara could not bear to speak about him. She felt dizzy suddenly and started to cry.

'Cara! Cara!' Her mother put an arm around her and helped guide her to a chair.

'I'm all right,' said Cara. 'I'm just tired.'

Her mother stared at her then. Just stared, didn't say a word. Then, narrowing her eyes before closing them for a brief moment, she said, 'I'll make you a cup of sweet tea.'

Years later, Cara often remembered the way her mother's eyes had burned into her soul then, as if she were reading her innermost thoughts. Something told her that her mother had known more than she herself knew at the time: about the pregnancy.

Billy's proposal of marriage came unexpectedly, only a couple of weeks after they met. Cara had thrown herself into this new relationship, wanting to dispel the horrible hollowness that took over after Frederick's rejection. She knew Billy loved her. Nothing else mattered. When he proposed, she smiled and said yes automatically, certain that would be the best way to forget about Frederick.

Since last seeing Frederick, she'd spent her nights crying herself to sleep and her days waiting for him to come back. She wanted him to tell her it was all a lie, or that he'd left his wife for her, but as each day passed with no sign of him, her anxiety increased. The way he disappeared so completely made her wonder whether she'd dreamt him, whether their relationship had been just an illusion.

Billy became her lifeline throughout the turmoil of those days. She did not love him, not in the way she loved Frederick, but Billy brought a sense of equanimity to her life. She could not quite comprehend *why* he loved her but she knew, without doubt, that he did.

As she walked down the aisle on the day of her wedding, Cara cried. It was not out of the ordinary for a bride to shed a few tears of joy, but her tears were of heartache and remorse. What would everyone do if she just turned around and ran out of the church? She felt an urge to run. Far away.

On reaching the altar, she saw Billy standing beside her, smiling; he appeared blissfully happy. She couldn't do it to him. If she walked out on him, she'd hurt him, break his heart, just as Frederick had broken hers. It was over a month since she'd last seen him, and it was unlikely she would ever see him again.

Wiping her tears and blanking her mind, she went ahead with the wedding.

Instead of being one of the happiest days of her life, to Cara her wedding day was like a public function she had not particularly wanted to attend.

CHAPTER THIRTY-ONE

'I've made an appointment at the solicitors' so we can arrange the DNA tests,' said Penelope, sitting next to Cara on the living room sofa.

Ever since the revelation of her relationship with Frederick Johnson, Cara had suffered a constant sick feeling inside, a churning in her stomach. The past had finally found its way to her door.

'Someone will have to contact my dad,' said Penelope.

'Penny, I've already told you what I think about involving your father in all of this. He doesn't want to keep in contact with me.'

'Everything's changed now; this is important.'

'Can't we just forget about it?'

'Nan,' Penelope narrowed her eyes, 'I have to admit, I did change my mind last night after I'd had time to think about things, but Steve rang today to tell me his dad suggested we go to his house for dinner on Sunday instead of them coming here. I told him you didn't want to meet up with his dad, then ended up telling him everything. Sorry. I got so used to telling Steve all my problems at the refuge, it just came out.'

Cara placed a hand over her mouth.

'Anyway,' said Penelope, 'he's keen to find out the truth, because he'd like to know if he has an extended family. He said he'd pay for the tests to be done. So, as I say, I've made an appointment at the solicitors' to get the ball rolling.'

'Well, I don't know where your father lives, dear.'

'Doesn't Aunty Gloria know?'

'I don't know, maybe...'

'I'll give her a call,' said Penelope.

Penelope spoke to Gloria, and she agreed to contact Benjamin. Arrangements were made for them to meet at Gloria's house.

'Nan, I feel a bit nervous about going to meet my dad on my own, will you come with me?'

'Let's forget about this paternity test,' said Cara in a final attempt to escape the past.

'We can't: Steve wants us to do it, and I suppose it would be for the best. He's probably told his dad about it, and I'm sure he'd be interested to know if he's got a son he never knew about.'

Cara shifted uncomfortably in her seat. Everything was happening irrespective of her own wishes, like a river surging on.

'Nan, it would be better if *you* explained it all to my dad. He still thinks Grandpa Billy was his dad, I'm sure it'll come as a shock to him to find out he might not have been. You should be there.'

'I don't know,' said Cara.

'We're supposed to meet at Aunty Gloria's house tomorrow. I never thought I'd see my dad again.' Penelope's eyes were wide. 'Please say you'll come with me, Nan.'

Cara felt she had no choice but to agree to accompany her.

Ironically, they were going back to Huddlesea, where it all began, for the truth to be told. The long drive was monotonous, the rain relentless. The weather mirrored Cara's inner mood.

Benjamin initially suggested to Gloria that they meet at Penelope's house. He didn't want to meet at his house, fearing Claire's reaction. Penelope flatly refused to have the meeting at her house; she remembered her father as a drunken, violent man who used to hit her mother, and she had no desire for such a person to ever enter her home.

The only neutral place they could think of meeting was at Gloria's house.

'But isn't it a bit far to go to meet your father, considering you both live in London?' Cara had asked.

'Well, we can't meet in a public place, not to tell him this; we don't know how he'll react. It has to be somewhere private, so Aunty Gloria's house is the best option.'

'But Huddlesea?'

'Apparently, my dad has to go to Huddlesea tomorrow for work, so it's convenient. It's not that far, Nan, only an hour or so if we take the motorway.'

So here they were on the motorway, on the way to tell Benjamin something she should have told everyone years ago. *How different would it have been if Billy knew everything back then?* Would he have stuck by her? She knew the answer: *Yes.* Billy was a good man and he loved her. Somehow, knowing *that* made her feel worse. He'd have forgiven her and it could have been out in the open long ago, but she chose not to tell him and consequently ended up in this position today: worried, anxious, frightened.

She remembered the last time she'd seen Benjamin, when he told her to stay out of his life. A sadness had haunted her ever since, but she understood his reasons: he feared becoming a bad person. He'd said he still loved her, and that was some comfort. She'd been left with hope that maybe one day, when he regained Claire's trust and felt more secure in himself, he'd come back to her. Now though, what she was about to tell him was life-changing. When he found out she'd kept the truth about his father from him, would he be able to forgive her? This could signal the end of their relationship.

The rain lashed against the car window, falling heavy and hard. The splattering raindrops were like long, thin, watery fingers pointing at her, blaming her. She prayed for the journey to end.

⏳

Benjamin was already at Gloria's house when they arrived. He stood up to greet them.

'Penny.' His eyes were full of tears as he moved towards her, arms outstretched.

Penelope ignored him and studied the carpet.

Bowing his head, he sat back down on the sofa.

'Shall I make tea for everyone?' asked Gloria.

Penelope did not respond, but remained standing at the entrance to the living room as if debating whether or not to enter.

'Tea would be nice,' said Cara.

'Please, sit down, Penelope,' said Gloria.

Penelope sat on the armchair furthest away from the sofa and Benjamin.

Gloria moved Cara's wheelchair nearer to Benjamin.

He looked at Cara but his eyes were distant.

Gloria left the room.

'It's nice to see you again, Ben,' said Cara apprehensively.

He avoided her eyes. 'I'm glad you decided to come, Penny,' he said, trying once more to communicate with his daughter.

Penelope sat stiffly and did not respond.

'Are you all right, Penny?' Cara felt worried that seeing her father again after so long may have been too much for her, especially as the last time she'd seen him had been a traumatic experience.

'I'm fine, Nan,' she said, seeming to regain consciousness.

'I can understand if you hate me, Penny,' said Benjamin softly. 'I admit I was a terrible person when I lived with your mother. I'll never forgive myself for what I did, but I'm not the same man. I couldn't control myself when I'd had too much to drink. I only drink occasionally now, hardly ever. I'm so sorry for everything.'

193

Penelope stared, trancelike, at the floor as he spoke. Then, suddenly snapping out of her stupor, she said, 'The sooner you tell him why we're here, Nan, the sooner we can leave.'

Gloria walked into the room. 'Here we are,' she said. 'A nice cup of tea for everyone.' She placed the tray on the table in the centre of the room.

No one moved.

Gloria appeared embarrassed to be there, her cheeks and neck flushed. She picked up a cup and offered it to Cara.

'Thank you, Glor.'

'Penelope, Paul, help yourselves.' Gloria smiled at them.

Silence followed, broken only by the sound of china cups clinking on saucers.

'Look how grown up you are, Penny,' said Benjamin, disturbing the lull. 'I hear you have two sons of your own. I've missed so much. It was all my fault, but it doesn't have to be like that...'

Cara watched Penelope as he spoke, and saw her face had reddened.

Penelope placed her cup back in the tray and sat down. She sighed. 'Nan, can we just get this over with?'

Cara felt all the eyes in the room upon her, as if everyone were waiting for her to confess to a crime. 'Ben, there's something I have to tell you.' She stopped and coughed nervously, then turned to Penelope, her eyes pleading. 'I can't do this.'

'Please, Nan. For me, please.'

'But it was so long ago,' said Cara. 'When Billy died, I thought I would never have to tell anyone.' Her voice broke slightly. She shifted in her chair, feeling uncomfortable.

'Do you want me to tell him?' asked Penelope.

'No.' Cara knew she was the only person who could break this news to him.

'Do you want me to leave the room?' asked Gloria as Cara caught her eye.

Cara remembered how Gloria had aired her suspicions about Benjamin's paternity so openly at their cousin Ada's wedding, years ago. The Gloria from back then would have been revelling in excitement, being proved right about her sister's infidelity; but as she looked at Gloria, she realised life had changed her—she would not be so quick to judge. 'No, you can stay, Glor, you'll find out eventually, anyway.'

Cara coughed again. 'Ben, before I married your father, I had a relationship with a man called Freddie.'

He shrugged. 'Okay, so why are you telling me this now?'

'Because, it's possible... There is a chance...' She glanced at Penelope.

Penelope nodded by way of reassurance, urging her to carry on.

'I had a suspicion that you might be Freddie's son.'

'Is this some kind of joke?'

'I—'

'It doesn't make sense.' Benjamin's eyes were wide.

'Well—' She struggled to continue. What words could she possibly find to make everything all right?

'But you've never mentioned it before.'

'I didn't know for sure.'

'Why now?'

'You've been missing for years—'

'Yes, but I was in my thirties when I left home; you had plenty of opportunities to tell me your suspicions.'

'I—'

'And...' He got up and shook his head in confusion. 'I saw you a couple of months ago, and I told you how heartbroken I was over Dad's death and you just sat there. You had the chance to tell me then. Why are you telling me now?'

'You could still be Billy's son,' she said, in an attempt to soften the blow.

'We want you to have a DNA test to find out if you are Freddie's son,' said Penelope.

He turned to face her. 'A DNA test?' Then he addressed Cara, 'Do you know how old I am? I'm forty-nine years old, and you're telling me now that the man I thought was my dad wasn't my dad.'

'I'm sorry,' said Cara.

He sat back on the sofa. 'I don't know what to say.'

'If you have the test, we'll know for sure,' said Penelope, impatiently.

'All those times people used to comment about me looking different to Cat and Jamie, you didn't say a word.'

Cara blushed.

'Did Dad know about this?' he asked.

'No,' she said, her heart skipping a beat.

'You've been lying to everyone for years.'

'Ben, please...' started Cara.

'Will you have the test?' asked Penelope.

'Why are you asking me to have this test? What does it matter if Dad's dead?'

'Steven, Freddie's son, knows about it, and he wants the test done

195

so we can be sure,' explained Cara.

'His son? Do you still keep in touch with "Freddie"?' Benjamin glared at her.

'No, no. Penny knows his son; he was a counsellor at the refuge she was staying at. He told her his father used to work in Huddlesea. I only found out last week that Freddie is his father.'

'So this Freddie knows about me?' asked Benjamin.

'No... Well, not as far as I know,' replied Cara.

'Will you do the test or not?' asked Penelope, agitated.

'Why should I?' he spluttered, then appeared to regret his response, closing his eyes. 'Sorry I snapped at you, Penny. This... Today... T-this news was totally unexpected. If you want me to do the test, I will.'

Penelope stood up. 'You'll be hearing from our solicitor.' She walked over to Cara. 'Come on, Nan, let's go.'

'But aren't you going to finish your tea?' asked Gloria.

'Sorry, Aunty, we'll visit again soon.' Penelope wheeled Cara towards the door.

'Penny,' said Benjamin.

She stopped walking.

'We must keep in touch. My daughter Amy looks like you, you know. I'd love you to meet her.'

'I hope you treat her better than you treated me and Jemima. If you've really changed, she's lucky, but I hope you'll understand that I don't want to know you.'

'Penny, please give me a chance to prove I'm not the man I used to be.'

'It's too late.'

'What about your children? I'm their granddad.' He followed them out of the house. 'I'd love to meet the boys.'

'We don't need you; we're fine as we are, thanks.'

'It doesn't have to be like this,' he pleaded. His voice was getting louder. 'I love you, Penny; you and Jemima. I've never forgotten you. Please don't leave.'

Penelope helped Cara into the car and picked up the wheelchair to put it into the boot.

'Let me help you,' said Benjamin, taking hold of the wheelchair.

'Let go!' shouted Penelope. 'I don't need your help!'

Cara could not recall ever seeing her granddaughter so angry.

Benjamin took a step back.

Penelope stood facing him. She looked into his eyes where tears were forming. 'In sixteen years, you've never even phoned. What kind of dad is that? You never cared about us, so don't fool yourself!'

'I did care about you. I do care, Penny.' He wiped his eyes.

'You walked out on your two daughters when you thought you'd killed our mum. Do you expect me to just forget that?'

'I don't expect you to forget... or even forgive me, but please let me be a part of your life. I'll show you I'm not that man anymore.'

Penelope slammed the boot shut and sat in the driver's seat.

'Penny.' He ran to the side of the car. 'Please, don't leave yet. Let's talk.'

'Goodbye,' she wound up the window.

'Penny, don't be so hard on him, he regrets his past behaviour.' Cara stared at her son through the car window, wishing she could comfort him.

'Leopards don't change their spots, Nan, that's one thing I've learnt.'

Cara noticed tears in her granddaughter's eyes. 'Everyone deserves a second chance.'

'He's got his second chance; he's got a new family. It's more than he deserves,' sneered Penelope as she pulled away from the kerb.

Cara could see Benjamin watching the car. He didn't take his eyes off them.

Soon they turned the corner and he disappeared from view.

'Penny, your father came to see me when I was staying with Glor, and I met his new partner, Claire, and his little daughter, Amy. He's really changed. He's nothing like his old self.' A tug of guilt reminded her of the accusation she'd made over David's death.

'I can't forget what he did,' said Penelope. 'I didn't realise it would be so hard for me to see him again. If I'd known, I would never have come here.'

Penelope switched on the car radio and hardly said a word for the rest of the journey. She concentrated on the road and listened to the soft music playing on the radio, not wanting to think about the meeting with her father.

⧗

On walking into Gloria's living room, Penelope's mind had flashed back to her last memory of her father, and scenes had appeared in front of her eyes, like those in an old home movie—unfocused snippets of action taking her to an era long since gone. Her mother's screams rang clear in her head then, as if she were present in the room: Penelope witnessed a

197

replay of that terrifying moment when she—as a twelve-year-old—stood at the top of the stairs in her pyjamas and saw her mother lying on the floor covered in blood, her guilty-looking father standing over her. It had felt as though she was losing her grip on reality, standing there in Gloria's living room, her mind being bombarded with palpable recollections of the past.

Penelope had heard of flashbacks, and in the past after waking up from nightmares, images raging through her head, she'd thought those were flashbacks. Never before had she experienced anything as frightening as what had occurred today in Gloria's living room—visions, sounds, smells, so real, as if she'd actually been transported to that night.

As soon as her father got up from the sofa to greet her, her mind had gone back to the horror of the last time she'd seen him, when he'd said: 'Oh my God, she's dead, I've killed her,' before leaving the house and slamming the door behind him.

CHAPTER THIRTY-TWO

Life after the revelation of Cara's secret carried on as normal. The world as she knew it did not come to an abrupt end, and no one treated her any differently. It was anticlimactic; at least if Penelope or Benjamin shouted or were angry with her, it would justify why she'd kept it a secret for so long. Penelope only seemed concerned about making sure the paternity test was organised, and mainly because Steve said he wanted it done; Benjamin's concern centered around re-establishing contact with his daughters.

Perhaps there would be a delayed reaction to the news. Maybe Penelope and Benjamin were in denial, both holding on tightly to the hope that the test would prove Cara wrong.

⌛

The day after the trip to Huddlesea, Penelope went to see a solicitor and returned home late in the afternoon. 'The solicitor says you have to take part in the DNA test too, Nan,' she said. 'I'm going to arrange an appointment at the doctor for you, and the solicitor is going to send away for the laboratory tests to be done.'

Cara turned pale.

'Nan? Are you feeling all right?'

'Yes, a bit tired, that's all.'

'I know this is really stressful and I'm sorry to put you through it, but now Steve and his dad know, there's no going back.'

'I know, dear.' Cara took a deep breath. 'Penny?'

'Yes?'

'Will Freddie have to have the DNA test at the same time as me?'

'No, he'll be making a separate appointment with a doctor.'

Cara breathed a sigh of relief.

'Don't worry, Nan, I'll ask Steve to arrange it. The solicitor will be sending the details to my dad. Apparently, it takes about five to ten working days for the results to come through once all the samples have been taken.'

'That soon?' Everything was happening at breakneck speed. Once the results were known, Frederick would be here wanting answers. Cara didn't feel ready to see him again.

⌛

A few days later, Penelope received a phone call from Steve.

'Nan, Steve says his dad's been to the doctor and given his DNA sample. He's suggested we all get together for dinner. Freddie wants to see you.'

Cara shifted uncomfortably. 'You know how I feel about that.'

'Well, once the test results come through, you'll have to see him.'

'Why? Why will I have to see him?'

'If it's proved my dad is his son, they'll want to get to know each other, won't they?'

'Your father is fifty years old, he doesn't need a dad. And Billy was the best dad he could have asked for. I didn't want this test done in the first place, Penny. I don't see how it will benefit any of them. Why would Freddie want to meet a son he never knew existed, at his age? As far as I can see, Steve is the only one who wants this test done. It'll all be yesterday's news soon enough. So what if Freddie is Ben's father? I don't care.'

'Nan, there's more to it than that.' Penelope sat down beside her on the sofa. 'According to Steve, his dad has fond memories of your relationship. He'd like to get to know you again.'

Fond memories? Cara felt the colour rush to her cheeks. 'It wasn't even a proper relationship,' she protested, 'just a fling I had when I was a foolish young girl. I regret meeting him. I don't want to see him. Do you ever want to see any of your ex-boyfriends to talk about old times?' She looked directly at Penelope.

'This is a bit different: you had a child together.'

'That hasn't been proved.' Cara averted her gaze.

'But you said it's a strong possibility. Doesn't that make your relationship with Freddie a bit more than a fling?'

Cara pursed her lips.

'Aren't you even curious to know what he did in his life after your relationship?'

'I know what he did: he went back to his wife. I was in love with him, but he was just having an affair.'

Penelope screwed up her nose. 'You're still holding on to a lot of resentment. If you meet up with him and talk things through, it might help you come to terms with the past and put it all in perspective. You're still seeing him as the man who betrayed you all those years ago, but he's an old man. He can't hurt you. You're hardly a young, innocent girl anymore.'

'I know you want to help, dear, but betrayal is not an easy thing to forget.'

'I know what betrayal feels like,' said Penelope. Sighing, she went on, 'I just think this is your chance to resolve something for yourself. Your past has been hanging over you. It must've done, I suppose, if you thought my dad wasn't Grandpa Billy's son.' She raised her eyebrows. 'Wow! Thinking about it, how did you get through that?'

Cara looked at her hands. 'As I said, Penny, I never really knew for sure.'

'No, but it must have played on your mind over the years.'

'Maybe.'

'You not wanting to see Freddie, after all this time... that proves my point: it's been bothering you for a long time, and you still haven't forgiven him, have you?'

'Perhaps I haven't.'

'If you meet him and talk, you might be able to finally forgive and forget. I'm reading a book that says if you don't let go of blame you can't really move on in your life, you'll always be stuck. It's good advice.'

'Maybe for a young girl like you, but I'm old; I've got nowhere to move on to.' She laughed drily. 'I've lived my life. I think I moved on from Freddie—I married Billy, I had my children and my grandchildren.' She touched her granddaughter's hand gently and smiled.

'But Nan, you still seem so angry with him. That's not right.'

'Penny, it's not always easy to forget the past. You of all people should know that. When we saw your father the other day in Huddlesea, I dearly wished we could try to be a family again, but I understood you were still angry with him. You're unable to put that behind you, so we're probably never going to have a proper relationship with him. I feel exactly the same way about my past with Freddie.'

'What? My dad nearly killed my mum, how can I forget that?' Penelope stood up.

'Please, Penny, don't get upset. I'm only using it as an example—'

'Huh! It's not a good example,' she said, twisting around to face Cara, hands on her hips. 'Having a violent drunk for a dad and not being able to forgive him is a bit different from splitting up with your boyfriend and holding on to it for the rest of your life!'

Cara opened and closed her mouth, unsure what to say. 'S-sorry... All I meant was... Well, you said you can't move on until you put the past behind you; you have to forgive and forget. Are you willing to do that with your father?'

'Why is this conversation suddenly all about me and my dad?' Penelope slouched and walked over to the window. She stood there, her back to Cara for a short while.

When she turned around, Cara could see she had been crying.

Penelope sat down next to her. 'I know I have issues that I have to resolve,' she said drying her eyes. 'Who knows? Maybe someday I'll forgive my dad. Maybe I'll even forgive Dave. But it's all too recent; it's going to take time, that's why I'm getting counselling.'

'I'm sorry for upsetting you, dear.' Cara held her hand.

'It's all right, Nan.'

They sat in silence.

Eventually, Penelope spoke. 'I'm sorry to keep going on at you about meeting with Freddie, but as it's been over fifty years since your relationship—' She shrugged.

'It's hard to explain.' Cara looked into her granddaughter's deep brown eyes and was once again reminded of Frederick. She turned away. 'Have you ever been so in love with someone that you didn't want to exist without him? Have you ever felt that you had to be with him, and only him, and that no one else could ever be good enough?'

'I can't say I have,' said Penelope. 'All that true love stuff, I don't know if it really exists. I thought I loved Dave, but it was more of a feeling that we had things in common.'

'One day you'll meet the right man and you'll remember my words,' said Cara, her eyes distant.

'I get it, he was your first love, but you fell in love with Grandpa Billy later.'

'Freddie was always on my mind, even then.'

'It must have been hard for you to forget him because you knew you were pregnant—'

'No, at the time I met Billy, I didn't know I was pregnant, but I still loved Freddie. Over the years, it became easier to live with, but I never forgot him.'

'But what about Grandpa Billy? You loved him, didn't you?'

'Of course, but not in the same way as I loved Freddie. Billy was the kindest man I've ever known, steady and reliable, but Freddie stole my heart.'

'So when you married Grandpa Billy you were still in love with Freddie?' The surprise in Penelope's voice was audible.

'Yes,' said Cara, her mind drifting back to her wedding day. 'I denied it for a long time, but as you get older you'll realise there's no denying the truth and there's no point trying to hide feelings. Having said that, I haven't thought of Freddie for years... decades.' She felt herself blush.

'I still don't understand why you won't see him.'

'It took me years to get to the stage where I didn't wake up every morning and immediately think of him.'

'Are you saying you might still be in love with him?'

'Don't be silly.' Cara laughed but was unable to meet her granddaughter's eyes. Smoothing her skirt with her hands, she said, 'I don't want to be reminded about everything. Tell Steven I don't think it's a good idea for us to meet up.'

'But when the test results come through—'

'We'll cross that bridge when we come to it.'

⧖

That night as Cara lay in bed, habitually holding the silver locket between her thumb and forefinger mulling over the day's events, she was unable to dispel the sense of mortification. She'd spilled her heart out to Penelope. Something had snapped inside her as soon as she'd heard Frederick wanted to see her again. *I must have sounded like a lovesick fool. Why did I gabble on for so long?* Ever since she'd revealed the truth to Penelope and Benjamin about the relationship, all her repressed emotions—dormant for years—had been battling for freedom.

Why did he want to meet with her? Was he not content with lying to her, stealing her innocence, breaking her heart? To him it had been just another relationship and he remembered it with "fond memories", disregarding the bad bits.

Even after so much time had passed between them, and from such a distance, how could he still have this effect on her? She wished she could go back to their first meeting in The Horse and Dragon: she would not fall for his smile or for those eyes but would simply walk out of the door.

She prayed the days would pass quickly and the result of the paternity test would soon be known, then they could put it all behind them, go their separate ways. Even as she prayed, however, she knew it wasn't going to be that simple; it wouldn't all just go away. Frederick had returned.

On closing her eyes, she envisaged his smile, his deep brown eyes, and remembered his touch... his kiss...

CHAPTER THIRTY-THREE

The following morning, Cara sat gazing out of the window in the front room as Penelope got the children ready for school. A man approached the house: he was grey-haired and quite tall, but she couldn't see him clearly as he was facing the door.

Penelope opened the door on her way out, before the man had a chance to ring the bell. Cara heard them talking but could not hear what they were saying.

A moment later Penelope ran into the room. 'Nan, I don't know how to tell you this, but Steve's dad is here. He's come to see you.'

Cara peered out of the window. *Freddie?* Her cheeks reddened. 'You know I don't want to see him, Penny,' she said in a half-whisper.

'But he's come all this way—'

'I don't want to see him,' Cara repeated, peeking through the net curtains.

He looked in her direction.

She shrank back, then stole a quick glance at him. He was facing the front door; the curtains must have obscured his view. Cara caught her breath.

By that time, Penelope was already at the front door. Cara watched as Frederick nodded politely and walked away towards the gate.

'I'm off, Nan. I've told him to come back later, when I'm here. See you soon,' shouted Penelope from the front door. 'Come on Carl, Andrew, we'll be late.'

Cara found herself wondering whether she'd done the right thing. She recalled Frederick's face—the glimpse she'd caught as he'd stood at the door—the emotions that had stirred within her were the same ones she'd felt as a young girl; her heart had reached out to him as he turned to leave, not wanting him to go.

Although much older, he was still handsome; his eyes retained that dreamy quality. She knew now, for certain, that the love she'd felt for this man in her youth was alive and well. Her whole life she had been trying in vain to forget him, wanting to hate him.

Cara was still looking out of the window when Penelope returned, almost half an hour later.

'Hi, Nan.' Penelope smiled at her. 'I just about managed to get the boys to school on time!' She sat next to Cara on the sofa. 'So what are we going to do about Freddie? He must want to talk to you quite badly to have come all this way on his own, especially after I told Steve last night that you don't want to see him.'

'Why did you ask him to come back later, Penny?'

'So we can sort this out once and for all. He obviously wants to discuss the paternity test and about finding out he's got a son he never knew existed. He'll want answers.'

'Why now? He disappeared fifty years ago.'

'You should talk to him so he can get whatever he has to say off his chest. You're probably nervous of meeting him because of the way you split up. It'll be good for you to see him; you'll realise he's an old man. Your life has changed completely since you last saw him. You might even become friends. You can tell him you don't want to see him again if that's what you decide.'

'Don't let him in when he comes back,' said Cara. She knew she could not risk a meeting with him. Her feelings for him were the same—misguided or not, they were there: the attraction had survived the decades.

'Nan—'

'I won't see him.'

Later that afternoon, Cara was left alone in the house when Penelope went to collect the children from school. Would Frederick make another appearance? It felt almost as if she were waiting for him. She tried to focus on the television but her mind wandered.

Soon Penelope returned from her brief trip, with the boys in tow. 'Hi, Nan.'

'Hello, dear.'

'Guess who I saw when I was parking the car?'

'Who?'

'Freddie.'

Cara's eyes widened.

'Don't worry, I told him you didn't want to see him.'

'Good,' said Cara, not sure if she meant it.

'I felt a bit sorry for him, actually,' said Penelope. 'He seems really nice and he was disappointed when he heard you wouldn't see him.'

Sadness embraced Cara. Her mood was shifting erratically. One minute she never wanted to see him again, the next she desperately needed to talk to him. 'I don't know why he came,' she said, to drown out sorrowful thoughts. 'I could have been dead for all he cared all those years ago. Let's hope the results of the paternity test come through quickly, then I can forget about all this.' She settled her gaze back on the television.

'It could be even worse after the results arrive, Nan. I mean, if he's that eager to see you when we don't know anything for sure, what will he be like if he finds out my dad is his son? I don't think he'll just go away.'

Cara's mind drifted back to their relationship and she recalled that they'd talked of having children, or was it only her who had talked about it? One particular evening came to mind, when they were lying in each other's arms in the midst of the late summer of 1952. As she shut her eyes the memory became clearer...

'I love you so much, Cara,' said Frederick, sighing as he regarded her with his deep brown eyes.

'I love you too,' she said, blushing deep scarlet. 'I wish we could stay like this for ever.'

He smiled and ran his fingers through her hair.

'We belong together,' she said. 'Do you ever think about what we'll be doing in five years' time?'

'Let's not think about the future, let's concentrate on now,' he replied, kissing her face and neck passionately.

'Come on, Freddie, it's fun trying to predict the future: what do you think we'll be doing in five years?'

'Cara, my love, no one can tell what the future will bring.'

Cara leaned up onto her elbow and stroked the fine hairs on his chest. 'Do you think we'll have children by then?' she whispered.

He did not reply.

'I'd love to have children,' she gushed. 'I'd love to have a son who looks exactly like you.'

He laughed and took her in his arms again.

Later that night, as she lay beside him watching him sleep, she felt peaceful, content, and happier than ever.

CHAPTER THIRTY-FOUR

The days dragged and life seemed to be put on hold for Cara as she waited for the results of the paternity test. Frederick did not visit again, but she lived in a state of constant anticipation knowing he could reappear at any time.

It came as a disappointment to her that he'd accepted so readily her refusal to meet with him. Why hadn't he protested and refused to leave without seeing her?

He'd be back when the test results revealed he was Benjamin's father, and knowing this only intensified her hope he would return before the results of the test were revealed: if he did, it would mean he wanted to see her, not that he was just coming back because he'd found out he had a long-lost son.

Cara could not shake the reawakened emotions and noticed she spent an unhealthy amount of time thinking about Frederick. She found herself wondering whether his life since their relationship had been lived in turmoil, and maybe that was why he'd come here. Perhaps he'd gone to Huddlesea searching for her after she'd left for London with Billy. What if he'd spent a lifetime trying to find her and, now that he had, she had turned him away so coldly?

However, as the days rolled by with no further sign of him, Cara began to feel foolish. It became clear he wasn't interested in her and only wanted to know if Benjamin might be his son. If she was wrong about Benjamin's paternity, she knew she would never see Frederick again. He'd be gone: just like the first time.

⧗

One morning, Penelope brought Cara's breakfast tray into the room as usual, but she didn't walk out of the room as she usually did after a brief chat about how much trouble she'd had getting the boys ready for school; instead, she sat on the bed.

Penelope blew her nose and wiped her eyes.

'What's wrong, Penny?' asked Cara, the test results weighing on her mind. Had they arrived?

'I-I received this today.' Penelope put her hand into her jeans' pocket and produced an envelope.

Cara tensed, bracing herself for the news. Years of doubt, secrets, and denial flashed through her mind.

As the envelope dangled from her hand, Penelope opened her

mouth to speak.

Cara could see the sadness in her eyes, an apparent need to say something, but the words weren't there. 'Penny, is it the results of the test?'

'No, Nan,' she said, holding the envelope closer to Cara as if it spoke for itself.

Cara saw it was addressed to "Penelope Truman", in unfamiliar handwriting.

'It's from Jemima,' explained Penelope, placing the envelope back into her pocket.

'Jemima?' Cara put a hand over her heart. 'I-I didn't know you two still keep in touch.'

'We don't. I'm not sure how she got my address...'

'What does it say?'

'I'm so confused, Nan. I need your advice.' Penelope wiped a tear from the corner of her eye.

'What's happened, darling?'

'I haven't heard from Jemima or Mum since they left for Jersey. Jemima says Mum's ill.' She paused. 'She's dying. She hasn't got long; the doctor says she'll only survive a few weeks, maybe not even that long.'

'W-what's wrong with her?'

'She had a stroke.' Penelope lowered her eyes. 'She's in hospital.'

Cara's eyes welled with tears.

'Mum's been living in London for the past few years.'

'In London?'

'Yes.' Penelope lowered her gaze. 'I wonder why she never got in touch after she moved back. It makes me so sad to know she was living in London and didn't try to contact me.'

'Hmm... Maybe she tried to get in touch. She wouldn't have known where you'd moved to.'

'Jemima's written to me, so they knew where I live.'

'Maybe they—'

'Stop making excuses for them, Nan. They didn't want to get in touch and now I get this!' Penelope stood up and took the letter out of her pocket again waving it in front of her.

'Calm down, Penny dear. People don't always do the right thing until something like this happens. When death comes to someone's door, that usually makes people come to their senses. They've probably realised that they should have got in touch earlier. Don't hold it against them. This is your family and they love you.'

Penelope's tears were flowing freely. 'They... l-l-love me so-so much that they were there for m-me—' She stopped to take another tissue and wipe her nose. 'Where were th-they when I needed them?' She sat back on the bed and looked at the envelope, which she'd placed on her lap.

'This has come as a shock to you, Penny. Take a deep breath. Everything will be okay, you'll see.'

'You... You should eat your breakfast, Nan: it'll get cold.'

Cara started to pick at her breakfast keeping one eye on her granddaughter.

'Jemima wants me to go and see Mum. I don't know what to do,' said Penelope.

'It's so sad we all lost touch for so long. So many years.' Cara's eyes were misty: long-forgotten memories of Margaret and Jemima floated through her mind.

'What should I do, Nan?'

'Penny... I think you should—*we* should go.'

'I never forgot about her, you know,' Penelope began. 'I thought about her a lot, especially in the last few years when life got hard with Dave. There were times when I really needed her.' She stopped, her eyes battling unshed tears. 'I wanted... I-I suppose I wanted her to get in touch with me; it would have been proof that she loved me. I thought she hated me, because I didn't listen to her and I married Dave. But I loved him...' A tear escaped and trickled down her cheek.

'Don't upset yourself.'

'How was I supposed to know things would go so wrong?'

'No one could have known, Penny.'

Cara handed her another tissue.

'Mum shouldn't have left; she should have stayed. Maybe if she'd been around, things wouldn't have got so bad. Dad had already gone. Nan... I had no one.' Penelope's brown eyes were darker than ever. 'She should have supported me. All I ever wanted was for someone to love me. I wanted her to love me.'

'She did love you, Penny. She loved you too much; she didn't want you to go through what she'd been through with your father.'

Penelope sniffed and dried her eyes. 'Wh-why didn't she try harder to get thr-through to me? She never even tried.'

'Think back,' said Cara softly. 'Would you have listened? As you said, you were in love with David, and none of us knew what he was really like. None of us.'

'*She* did,' said Penelope, wiping the never-ending tears from her eyes.

'We must go and see her,' said Cara, after a brief silence. 'I'd like to see her again, Penny. It's been too long.'

'That's what upsets me, Nan. In all these years she hasn't kept in touch and now I feel so guilty, as if it's me who should have contacted her.'

'We're all to blame for not keeping in touch.'

'Maybe you're right. I suppose we should go and see her if she's dying...' Her voice trailed off into almost a whisper.

Cara felt tears in her eyes.

'I don't want to get the boys involved, though,' said Penelope, standing up. 'I'll take them to school and then we'll go.'

'Today?'

'Yes, Nan. It might be our last chance.'

Jemima had sent Penelope the details of the hospital where Margaret was receiving treatment. The drive took about an hour. Penelope hardly said a word throughout the journey, and Cara noticed her hand was trembling as she reached to change gears. When they arrived at the hospital ward, they were told that Margaret had discharged herself the day before.

'She must be all right if she's discharged herself. I don't think we need to be too worried,' said Cara, feeling brighter as they drove away from the hospital.

'Maybe, but the nurse said she discharged herself against the doctors' orders.'

'Yes... but... well, she can't be very ill if she's able to make those sorts of decisions.'

'I hope you're right, Nan.'

Soon they arrived at Margaret's house. Penelope parked the car outside and sighed deeply. 'I've brought a present for her,' she said, reaching over to the back seat of the car and picking up her handbag. She opened it, and took out a small velvet box. 'There's something I've never told you, Nan.' Penelope took a deep breath and said, 'A year or so before you moved in with me, I was pregnant... a little girl. The due date was seventeenth of December: Mum's birthday.' She opened the velvet box, took out a gold cross on a chain and held it out to show Cara. 'I had it engraved; it says "Margaret" on the back. That's the name I'd chosen for my daughter. Wanted to name her after Mum.' Pausing, as if unable to continue, she placed the cross into its box. 'I want to give this to Mum.'

Cara remained silent, unable to speak. Penelope telling her the story about the lost pregnancy made it more real, erasing all doubt. She didn't explain why she'd lost the baby, and Cara did not ask.

When the front door opened. Cara recognised Jemima at once. She'd always resembled Margaret, with her round face, green eyes and wavy brown hair. Cara couldn't help the tears that came to her eyes. The last time they'd seen each other, Jemima had been fourteen years old: a child. Now a woman stood at the door.

Placing a hand in front of her mouth, Jemima stared at Penelope, then she looked at Cara.

Penelope let go of the wheelchair and walked over to her sister. The girls hugged and started to cry.

Cara's eyes filled with tears as she watched them.

Eventually, Penelope wiped her eyes on the sleeve of her cardigan and walked over to Cara. She took hold of the wheelchair's handles.

Jemima turned her attention to Cara. 'Hello, Nan, it's good to see you again. I'm so glad you've come.'

She invited them in and led the way through the narrow hallway into the living room. Cara took in the small room with its pale blue wallpaper. A pretty border halfway down the wall, embossed with small cream-coloured flowers, caught her eye. The carpet, a dark navy blue, matched the velvet curtains. There was a brown three-piece suite in the middle of the room and a coffee table made of the same dark wood as the stand for the large television.

Penelope scanned the room as they entered. 'Where's Mum?' she asked.

Jemima's face stiffened.

'Jemima?'

'I think you should sit down, Pen.'

'Okay.' Penelope sat on the edge of the sofa.

'Mum died yesterday,' said Jemima, looking straight ahead towards the window as she explained, 'It was sudden. She'd just got back from the hospital. The doctor told me she wanted to come home; he wasn't happy about discharging her, but she insisted she didn't want to die in hospital.' Jemima reached for a tissue from the box on the coffee table. 'Sorry,' she sniffed, 'It's still all very raw.' She wiped away the tears that streamed from her eyes.

'I'm so sorry, dear,' said Cara. It pained her to see her granddaughter's sorrow.

'Th-there was nothing more they could do for her.' Jemima's voice sounded distant.

'When did she become ill?' asked Cara.

'A couple of months ago.'

211

'It must be so hard for you.' Cara reached out and touched Jemima's hand.

'I'm all right.' Jemima smiled sadly through her tears.

'I wish we hadn't lost touch,' said Penelope.

'She loved you, Pen. She talked about you a lot and wondered what you were doing. She nearly contacted you a couple of times, but...' Jemima shrugged.

'I should have tried to get in touch,' said Penelope. 'I'll never see her again.'

'I tried to get in touch earlier,' explained Jemima, 'but I didn't have your address. I wrote to your old address when Mum had the stroke but I didn't get a reply, so I thought you didn't want to see us. The letter came back in the post the other day, so I got in touch with Aunty Gloria and she gave me your new address. She gave me your phone number as well. Maybe I should have phoned you, I don't know. But I felt too nervous. It was easier to write it down.'

'I used to have this fantasy that Mum would get in touch with me,' said Penelope, a wistful look in her eyes, 'and tell me she'd never forgotten me, and that she wanted to come back but for some reason...'

'She really wanted to see you again,' said Jemima.

'Yes, but it's too late,' Penelope said in a small voice.

Jemima sat next to her and put an arm around her.

'I shouldn't have been so stubborn,' said Penelope. 'I should have tried to get in touch with her.'

'Don't blame yourself, dear,' soothed Cara.

'Yes, there's no point in worrying about it, Pen,' said Jemima 'There's no need to feel guilty. Really.'

Penelope nodded, forcing a smile.

'I just wish we'd had a chance to say goodbye to her,' said Cara, her eyes full of tears.

'When's the funeral?' asked Penelope.

'I'm going to arrange it today. It'll probably be next week,' replied Jemima.

'Please let us know the date,' said Cara.

'I will, I'll phone you.' She smiled through tear-filled eyes. 'I'll go and make us some tea.'

'I can't believe Maggie's dead,' said Cara, when Jemima had left the room.

She noticed a silver-framed photograph on top of the television set. Margaret was smiling in the picture and didn't seem to have a care in the world; her expression showed how far removed she was from the unhappy life she'd led with Benjamin.

As if picking up on her thoughts, Penelope walked over to the television and picked up the photograph. 'Mum looks happy here.'

'Yes,' said Cara.

Penelope carried the picture with her to the sofa and sat down, without taking her eyes off it.

'She looks so peaceful there, doesn't she?' said Cara.

'I should have listened to her. She knew Dave was just like Dad.' Penelope gazed intently at the photo. 'Why didn't I listen to her? Why?'

'Don't upset yourself, dear.'

'She really loved me, Nan, I realise that now.'

'Of course she loved you, Penny.'

Penelope placed the framed picture back on the television, then took a tissue and dried her eyes.

Jemima returned to the room carrying a tray of tea and biscuits.

'Jemima, it's been so long since we last saw you,' said Cara, trying to lift the mood. 'Now look at you, you're all grown up.'

'Yes.' Jemima laughed, her eyes sparkling.

'We've got so much to catch up on,' said Penelope.

'Yes,' agreed Jemima. 'How is David?'

Penelope coughed nervously. 'Um...' She looked to Cara as if for assistance.

'David is dead,' said Cara.

'I didn't know. Sorry, Pen, I didn't mean to upset you.'

'Don't worry, we'd already separated when he died.'

Jemima served the tea and biscuits, then sat next to Penelope.

'Are you married, Jemima?' asked Cara.

'Yes, Nan, I'm married to Mike. He's a vet. We've been married for four years. He's in Jersey. We still live there, but I've been staying here for the past couple of months to help care for Mum. I've got a daughter, Georgia. She's three years old. She's upstairs sleeping.'

Cara felt sad she had missed out on so much of her granddaughter's life. 'We must keep in touch, Jemima,' she said.

'We will keep in touch.' Jemima smiled at them both.

CHAPTER THIRTY-FIVE

Cara woke up early on the day of Margaret's funeral. Six o'clock. The room was shrouded in shadows. She sat up, knowing that she would not be able to get any more sleep.

As her eyes adjusted to the dim light, she noticed the old photograph album on the bedside cabinet and it took her back to the evening before when she and Penelope had spent a few hours flicking through old photos of Margaret and reminiscing. The imminent funeral had made them both feel a need to reach into the past and perhaps recapture some of the moments that seemed to have been lost for ever. They'd laughed and cried over the photographs as they remembered the precious times spent with Margaret.

Cara picked up the album and began looking through it again in the half-light, tears in her eyes.

The bedroom became brighter as the morning sun filtered through the curtains. Cara drew the curtain nearest her bed and peered out of the window, through bleary eyes. The sky was grey, although the sun had begun to break through cracks in the clouds. No sign of life could be seen in the avenue below.

She heard Penelope walk out of her bedroom and into the bathroom. Silence resumed and served to magnify her sense of loss.

She watched as the postman strolled along the avenue delivering the mail, and she heard the sound of the letterbox flapping open. Every morning, for the past few days, she'd waited, holding her breath from the time she heard the letterbox open to the time Penelope brought her breakfast tray into the bedroom. Today, although she did immediately wonder whether the DNA test results might have arrived, she didn't dwell on it: everything was trivial in comparison with the grim promise of the day that lay ahead.

In the back of her mind, she'd always held out hope that she'd meet Margaret again, that somehow their paths might cross and they'd be friends as they were before, their differences forgotten.

She was riddled with regret. If she'd known Margaret was going to die, she would have done everything in her power to see her just one more time.

Cara hoped that if Margaret could see her from some other world, she'd understand her reasons for being so estranged.

Cara heard the front door open and close as Penelope left the house with the boys. She watched them walk along the avenue with the other parents taking their children to school. The familiar small green car parked up across the road just as it began to rain. The mother helped her two children out of the car whilst holding up a big red umbrella. Scurrying over to the pavement, the little girl with the coffee-coloured hair opened a bright pink umbrella: her brother opened a bright blue one. The family walked along the avenue, the vibrant colours of their umbrellas temporarily distracting Cara from the grey surroundings, but soon they were gone and only the grey remained.

Life outside the window carried on as normal. Inside, Cara's heart was breaking.

The rain was falling more heavily and a storm cloud threatened in the distance. Cara hoped the weather would improve, the day ahead would be hard enough to face.

Shortly after Penelope returned from taking the boys to school, she entered Cara's bedroom, carrying the breakfast tray. As she placed it on the bed, Cara noticed an envelope in the tray.

'Nan, the test results have come,' said Penelope, her face stiff.

Cara put a hand to her throat, bracing herself.

'I haven't opened the letter yet. I'm too nervous. I thought maybe you could do it.'

'Yes... I mean. Oh... all right, dear. But... Um... How do you know it's the results?'

'I don't, but it's from the solicitor, so it must be.' Penelope sat on the edge of the bed.

Cara stared at the envelope that sat innocently alongside her toast and coffee. *Why today of all days?*

Penelope drummed her fingers on her leg, impatiently. Then she began biting her nails.

Cara didn't move. She wanted to start eating her breakfast but was too afraid to put her hand near the tray in case Penelope then expected her to open the envelope.

'Oh, this is silly,' said Penelope, with a nervous laugh. 'I'll open it.'

Cara gaped helplessly as her granddaughter took the envelope from the tray. 'Penny dear,' she said, anxiety evident in her high-pitched voice. 'Do you think you should open it now? Wouldn't it be more appropriate to wait until after the funeral?'

'Oh.' Penelope looked at Cara and then at the envelope. 'Yes, you're right. Sorry, Nan.'

'That's all right, dear.' She watched as Penelope placed the letter on the bedside cabinet.

'I'll leave it here till later,' she said.

Cara breathed a sigh of relief.

⧗

Cara had not expected to see so many people in attendance at the funeral; there were at least fifty people at the church by the time they arrived. She did not recognise anyone, apart from Jemima, and Margaret's parents. It was proof of the sorry fact that she hadn't seen Margaret for over ten years; their mutual friends were no longer the people who had been important in Margaret's life.

'Nan, will you be all right sitting on your own for a minute?' asked Penelope. 'I just want to let Jemima know we're here.'

'All right, dear.' Cara sat quietly in the dimly-lit church.

A large middle-aged woman with dyed blonde hair, seated in front of her, chatted to a grey-haired man who appeared overwrought with grief: 'I'll miss her,' said the woman.

The man blew his nose.

'We're all thinking of you, Eric; our prayers are with you. It's a terrible loss, but I believe Maggie is here watching us, and she wouldn't want you to be sad.'

Eric nodded and the woman took his hand. 'I remember one day when we were talking about a relative of mine who'd passed away,' she said, 'and I'll never forget what Maggie said to me; it stayed with me. Maggie said, "We should celebrate the lives of those who've gone, rather than mourning them." At the time, I thought she was just trying to find some way of comforting me, but later it struck me that there's so much truth there, isn't there? I mean, we're all going to die one day. Maggie was very positive about that sort of thing. I remembered those words when I heard she had passed, and it helped me. Made me smile.'

'Maggie always found the right words to say,' said Eric, sniffling.

'She was such a lovely woman. She'd wish you all the happiness you deserve,' said the woman.

'Thank you, Glenys,' he said.

Cara took a tissue from her bag and wiped her eyes.

A young woman with curly brown hair scurried over to Glenys and Eric. 'Hello,' she said, worry lines etched into her brow.

'Hello, Julia,' said Eric. 'Thank you for coming.'

'Eric, how are you?'

'Trying to put one foot in front of the other, take one day at a time,' he replied.

'I'm so sorry. It must be hard.' She touched his shoulder. 'I've been speaking to Jemima. She's dealing with it all very well, considering.'

'She's been great. I don't know what I would have done without her,' said Eric. 'She's been a great help, looking after Maggie towards the end. I couldn't bear to see her so ill.'

'Our thoughts are with you, Eric. It happened at the worst time, but you must focus on the future. Maggie wouldn't want you to mourn. She'd want you to be happy.' She sat next to him.

'Yes, that's what I said,' said Glenys.

Who is this man? wondered Cara, noticing how everyone was so worried about him.

'But I can't help asking myself *why*. Why Maggie? She was so young... And why now? We had such plans...' His voice trailed off.

'Don't upset yourself, Eric,' said Glenys.

He blew his nose. 'It was so good of you to come over from Jersey,' he said to Julia.

'Maggie was a very popular woman,' she replied. 'When I worked for her at the florist's I noticed how she had this gift for making friends with everyone. Most of her customers became her friends. I recognise a few of them here; they've all flown over from Jersey to be here.'

'I really should go and sit with her parents,' said Eric. 'It's so sad. I've never even met them. I'd been looking forward to meeting them; they were planning to come over next month to help with the preparations for the wedding. Life can be so unfair. The first time I meet my fiancée's parents is at her funeral.' He stood up. 'I'll see you both later.' His face was drawn, greyer than the weather.

Cara wiped a tear from her eye. She watched as he approached Margaret's parents and shook their hands.

Cara recalled meeting Margaret's parents at Benjamin and Margaret's wedding. How different the circumstances were today. She felt pained seeing them in tears at their daughter's funeral, remembering her own unbearable torment when she'd thought Benjamin might be dead, during the lost years. The way she'd dealt with the trauma was by telling herself he was still alive. She watched these two parents sitting next to their daughter's coffin and did not even want to begin to imagine the despair they were feeling. Should she go and speak to them? What could she say? There were no words that could help.

Penelope returned and sat next to her. 'I didn't get to speak to Jemima—there are so many people here—but I waved to her so she knows we're here.'

'All right, dear.' Cara noticed the sad faces around her. Margaret had touched so many people's lives.

Eric took his seat on the bench in front of them. Cara whispered into Penelope's ear: 'This man was your mother's fiancé.'

Penelope's eyes widened.

'Maggie's parents are devastated,' said Eric to Glenys and Julia. 'I didn't know what to say to them.'

'You have to try to take comfort from the positive things, Eric,' said Glenys. 'Maggie loved you. She lived a full life and found true happiness with you. Some people may live to old age and never be truly happy.'

'But it's all so unfair,' said Eric. 'Maggie had another daughter too, you know; she hadn't seen her for over ten years. She talked about her all the time, and she wanted to get in touch with her. We were going to invite her to the wedding so it could be a starting point for them to get to know each other again. Instead Jemima had to invite her to the funeral.'

Penelope's mouth opened in surprise as she listened to Eric. She turned to Cara, tears in her eyes.

Cara held her hand.

⧗

After the ceremony, the congregation made their way out of the church and into their cars for the journey to the cemetery. Margaret was to be buried in the same cemetery as Billy.

The cars moved slowly behind the black hearse along the busy London streets. Outside, people were laughing, running, talking, as they got on with their daily lives, oblivious of the black funeral cars passing them by. Cara felt encapsulated in a different world sitting in the car following the funeral procession. Laughter didn't exist here. Only gloom could be found.

The cemetery looked like an abandoned wasteland when the funeral party arrived. For miles around there were only rows and rows of headstones in all shapes and sizes, many adorned with photographs: the faces of people who were once as alive as those who were filing out of their cars and walking along the gravel path. Flowers, candles, cards and such, were strewn on graves marking the resting places of people who were once so important to someone but were now only memories.

The procession of mourners all dressed in black, walked towards the site that had been marked out for Margaret, about one hundred yards from the spot where Billy was buried.

Cara listened to the sound of the crunch of the mourners' shoes as they walked on the coarse ground. There was no other noise, as if they were the only survivors on a barren planet. She glanced over in the direction of Billy's grave, as Penelope pushed the wheelchair along the path. Cara gasped as she spotted somebody sitting on the bench next to the grave. She blinked and strained her eyes to try to see who it could be. 'Penny,' she said, 'there's someone sitting on Billy's bench.'

'Probably someone just resting their legs. Oh no, it's... what's he doing here?' Penelope sounded agitated.

'Who?'

'My dad.'

'Ben?' Cara said in surprise.

'How dare he come here?' Penelope huffed.

They reached the spot where Margaret was to be buried. The congregation gathered around as the coffin was placed on the ground. The priest started reading the service.

Cara's mind was elsewhere. Why had Benjamin turned up here? How did he know about the funeral? The thought suddenly occurred to her that he, too, would have received the results of the paternity test today. Maybe he came here to confront her, angry she had lied to him for all these years. However, gazing out at the crowd of people standing at the graveside, all with dejected and tear-stained faces, she became aware that this was not the time to think of her own problems.

It began to drizzle.

On the other side of the grave, Jemima wept, holding tightly to a little girl. A young man had his arms around Jemima. Cara presumed he must be her husband.

She could hear Penelope crying behind her. Her heart felt heavy as she listened to her granddaughter's sniffles. Cara watched as Eric threw a black rose into the grave after the coffin had been lowered; he fell to his knees in tears. Another man comforted him. Then she saw Penelope go to the graveside, holding the velvet box containing the gold cross engraved with Margaret's name.

Penelope dropped the box into the grave and wiped her eyes on the sleeves of her coat before returning to Cara. The rain persisted, as if the angels were also grieving.

The ceremony over, the crowd slowly dispersed back to waiting cars. The rain was getting heavier.

Penelope opened her umbrella over the wheelchair.

Cara and Penelope stayed there for a while longer, watching as everyone said their last goodbyes.

Jemima approached them, with her daughter. 'Hello,' she said. 'I'm sorry I didn't get a chance to talk to you at the church; there were a lot of people.'

'No problem,' said Penelope.

'Thanks for coming,' said Jemima, as though she were talking to strangers.

Cara felt sad realising that in many ways they were strangers.

'This must be Georgia,' said Cara, smiling at the child.

'Yes,' said Jemima, her expression becoming brighter. 'Yes,' she said again. Then: 'Georgia, this is your great-grandmother, Cara. Say hello.'

'Hello,' said the girl, shyly.

'Hello, dear, it's lovely to meet you.'

'And this is your Aunty Penny.'

'Hello, Georgia; don't you look pretty in your dress?' said Penelope.

'I'm going to have to go, I'm afraid,' said Jemima. 'Mike, my husband, is waiting in the car, but please keep in touch.' She held a piece of paper towards Penelope. 'This is my address and telephone number in Jersey.'

Penelope took the paper from her.

Jemima started to walk away.

'Hello,' said a voice from behind them. Benjamin. 'Jemima, wait,' he said.

She turned around.

'I knew it was you,' he said to her. 'You always did look so much like your mother.'

'Who are you?' Jemima took a step towards him, but her eyes were narrowed in apprehension.

Cara looked at Penelope and saw her face was flushed.

'I'm your dad.' He smiled.

Jemima raised her eyebrows; she did not seem angry, more shocked.

'Wh-what are you do-doing here?' she stammered.

'I came to pay my respects.'

'Respect!' Penelope could no longer keep control of her temper. As she turned to face him, she automatically rotated the wheelchair in that direction.

Cara could now see his face. He glanced at her and she saw his dismay at Penelope's reaction: his eyes were wide, his mouth open.

'Why do you care if she's dead? You thought she was dead sixteen years ago, but you wouldn't have tried to come to her funeral then. Oh, sorry, you couldn't have because you would have been done for murder, wouldn't you?'

'Penny,' said Cara. 'Please calm down.'

220

'I can't change what happened,' said Benjamin. 'When I heard she died, I wanted to come here to make sure you and Jemima were all right.'

Jemima was staring at him.

Georgia was holding tightly to her mother.

'All I want is a chance to make up for everything. I'm still your dad. You can't change that,' he said calmly.

'We know we can't, unfortunately,' said Penelope. 'If only we could.'

'Penny dear, there's no need—' began Cara.

'He shouldn't be here,' Penelope insisted.

'Let's all go home where we can talk sensibly,' said Cara. 'Let's get out of the rain.'

'Yes, we need to talk,' agreed Benjamin.

'We'll go back to Penny's house,' said Cara.

'All right, give me the address and I'll meet you there,' he said.

CHAPTER THIRTY-SIX

'I thought Dad was missing,' said Jemima, who'd been very quiet since the meeting with Benjamin.

'He was,' said Penelope. 'But Nan met him again a few months ago. I didn't want to have anything to do with him, though.'

'Penny, can we go and see Billy's grave before we leave?' asked Cara.

'Of course.'

'I'll just go and tell Mike he can leave, I'll be back soon,' said Jemima. She led Georgia by the hand.

Penelope pushed the wheelchair towards Billy's grave.

'Sit down, dear,' said Cara.

'The bench is wet, Nan.'

'Oh, okay.'

The two women remained there in silence for a while, then Penelope spoke: 'Why did you give him my address, Nan?'

Cara saw she was crying.

'After all I've been through—all the violence—I wanted to get away from all that. You say he's changed, but how do you know? I'll probably have to move somewhere else, so he can't find me.'

'Your father loves you, he wouldn't hurt you.'

Penelope did not respond.

Jemima returned a few minutes later, alone.

'We'd better be going soon,' said Cara.

'I can't bear the thought of him being in my house after what he did to Mum.'

'To be honest, I can't remember much about Dad,' said Jemima. 'He came across as quite genuine, though. Maybe he really regrets the way he used to behave.'

'Jemima may be right,' said Cara. 'He has a new family, and he doesn't drink; why don't you give him one more chance?'

'Because, I spent most of my life giving Dave "one more chance". He never changed. I'm sorry, Nan; you and Jemima can meet Dad, but I couldn't care less if I never see him again.'

'We really should be going,' said Cara after a few moments of silence. 'Your father will be waiting for us.'

'All the more reason to stay here,' said Penelope. 'With any luck he'll get fed up waiting and he'll go away.'

They headed back to Penelope's car.

‘It'll soon be time to collect the boys from school,’ said Penelope, as she parked the car in Furley Avenue.

Cara could see Benjamin outside the house.

He approached them, smiling. ‘Hello,’ he said to Penelope as she got out of her car.

She did not respond.

‘Hello, Ben,’ said Cara. ‘Have you been waiting long?’

‘No, I just got here.’

Penelope avoided any conversation with him as she helped Cara out of the car, behaving as though she had not even seen him.

Jemima smiled awkwardly as she walked past him.

They entered the house.

Penelope wheeled Cara's chair into the front room and helped her onto the sofa.

Jemima sat next to her.

Benjamin sat opposite them on an armchair.

‘Right,’ said Penelope. ‘I'm going to collect my boys from school.’ Then addressing Benjamin: ‘I'll be gone for about fifteen minutes.’

‘Okay,’ he said, nodding.

‘When I get back, I expect you to have gone.’

‘But—’

‘Bye, Nan, Jemima; I'll see you later,’ she said, ignoring her father.

‘She hates me,’ said Benjamin, tears in his eyes, as the front door slammed shut. ‘Do you hate me, Jemima?’

She avoided his eyes.

‘I'm a better man now; I'm ashamed of what I did. If I could turn back time, I would. I never meant to hurt you or Penny. I wanted to come here to try to explain how much pain I feel when I think you both hate me.’

Jemima sighed. ‘I don't hate you. To tell you the truth, I can't remember you; I was only about eight years old when you left. Pen remembers more. She was older. But I'd say we have a right to hate you for what you did to Mum.’

‘It was all so long ago,’ he said. ‘I've got a young daughter, Amy; she's only a few years older than your little girl. That was your daughter at the graveyard?’

‘Yes.’ Jemima nodded.

‘She looks like you at that age. Beautiful.’

'Thank you.' Jemima lowered her eyes.

'Look, I really have changed,' said Benjamin, 'I'm a devoted dad; I wouldn't hurt Amy, and I've never laid a hand on my partner, Claire.'

'What you have to appreciate,' Jemima gazed up to the ceiling as if trying to think of the right thing to say, 'is that me and Pen only remember you from those days. Pen remembers the violence. I remember more of the effect it had on Mum. In fact, I only recognised you today because I've got an old photograph of you with Mum and Pen.

'Mum used to have a photo album, and one day she threw away all of the pictures with you in them. She was sitting at the kitchen table, crying, and tearing out all of the pictures of you. She threw them in the bin. I rescued a few of them, because they had Pen in them; I really missed her. Mum found them one day. She was furious. She asked me where I'd found them, saying she thought she'd thrown them away. She tore them all up. I only managed to save one.' Jemima reached over to her handbag and opened her purse. 'I've always kept this in my purse.' She took out an old black and white photograph. The edges were frayed, and it was faded in parts.

Benjamin reached out and took it from her. He smiled and fought back tears.

'What you did to Mum is unforgivable,' continued Jemima. 'When you turn up here asking us to welcome you with open arms, we can't. It's like saying it doesn't matter what you did to her.'

'But,' he held the photograph out in front of him. 'You kept this... so I must have meant something to you.'

Shrugging, she took the photograph back from him. 'I was a little girl when I first put this photo in my purse. I wanted what all children want, I suppose: a happy family, a mum and dad. A dream. I had this stupid idea that if I kept this photo in there it meant everything would be all right, you know? Like there was some hope in the world. I suppose it became a superstition after a while, and whenever I'd get a new purse I'd always put this photo in it. A picture of my family. I didn't want to let it go.' She paused. 'What you have to realise is, I've never really known you. This photo—this smiling man, proud to be with his wife and daughter—this is the "fantasy dad" I had. Not you. You were gone. You let us down.'

'I know,' he said, looking at the floor. 'It's just—'

'It's also bad timing, you turning up today at Mum's funeral. It's so... I don't know, so inappropriate. You shouldn't have come here today.'

'I have to say, I agree,' said Cara. 'The girls don't need to be reminded of the way you treated Maggie, especially on a day like today.'

'I'm sorry for what I did,' he said. 'That's part of the reason I came to the funeral. It sounds stupid, but I needed to be there. I suppose I hoped, in some way, Maggie would know I was sorry for what I did to her. It was my last chance.'

'Okay, so you've made your peace with Mum, but what do you want from me and Pen?' asked Jemima. 'You stayed away for so long and you've got another family. Why are you here?'

'I want the chance to make up for the past. I didn't know the harm I was doing to your mum or you in those days. I can see clearer now I'm watching my Amy grow up. I want you to know I'm here for you. I love you. Both of you.'

Cara could not help feeling sorry for him; he appeared so distraught.

'I'd love you to meet Amy.'

'I'm not sure,' said Jemima.

'Take your time, but promise me you'll think about it. I'll give you my phone number, my address. You can visit.'

Jemima shrugged.

'Penny will be back soon,' said Cara.

'I need to speak to her.'

'I don't think today is the right time, Ben.'

'But... you don't really think she meant it when she said she wanted me to leave, do you?'

As much as Cara sympathised, she knew Penelope would be livid if she found him here when she returned. 'Please, Ben, you've had your chance to explain everything. You should leave. The girls will contact you when they're ready.'

'I want to speak to Penny, though; I need to help her understand.'

'If you care about Penny at all, you'll leave now,' said Cara.

The doorbell rang.

'I'll get it,' said Jemima.

Shortly, she re-entered the room. 'Nan, it's someone to see you.'

Frederick walked into the room behind Jemima.

Cara felt paranoid, imagining that Jemima and Benjamin could see her innermost feelings rise to the surface. At first sight of his face, a deep-rooted yearning blossomed in her heart. She recalled how helplessly in love with him she had been in her youth, unable to imagine life without him. Recently, the long lost desires were creeping back.

'Hello, Cara,' he said. He was frowning. 'I need to speak to you.'

'Freddie,' she said, unable to speak further. Her mind was whirring.

Jemima sat back down on the sofa.

Frederick remained standing.

Taking a deep breath, Cara managed to say, 'What are you doing here?'

'I should think that's obvious,' said Frederick, suddenly seeming to notice that there were other people in the room. 'Cara, is there any chance we could talk privately?'

'No,' she said defensively, her cheeks reddening. 'Whatever you have to say can be said in front of my family.'

'I got the test results this morning,' he said, and waited for her to speak.

'The test results,' she said, suddenly remembering the envelope sitting on her bedside cabinet. Judging by his demeanour, her suspicions were right and Benjamin was, beyond doubt, his son.

'I need some answers,' he said.

'Do you want us to leave you alone?' asked Jemima, standing up.

'No, dear,' said Cara quickly. She prayed he would leave, but equally she could not help staring at him as if he were some kind of idol. The duplicity of her emotions scared her, as did the way she virtually lost control of her senses in his presence.

'Why didn't you tell me this sooner, Cara? Why didn't you tell me I had a son?'

Why did he care? He hadn't cared about her all those years ago when he left her stranded, left her to choose her fate, after cruelly leading her halfway to paradise and abandoning her in a desert to fend for herself.

Benjamin stood up. 'This is my dad?' he asked.

'Y-yes,' she stammered.

'What?' Jemima's brow furrowed.

'Well?' said Frederick, looking at Cara and then at Benjamin and then back at Cara. 'Why didn't you tell me I had a son?'

'I didn't know I was pregnant until I married Billy,' she said, trying to find her bearings as she spoke.

'What did you tell your husband?'

'That's none of your business.'

'I had a right to know.' Frederick's cheeks reddened.

She hadn't seen this aggressive side of his personality before—it helped her to separate him in her mind from the young man she'd fallen hopelessly in love with years ago. She no longer felt so in awe of him. 'How could I contact you? I didn't know where you lived,' she said, rolling her eyes. 'And besides, I never knew for sure he was your son.'

'You must have known,' Frederick said bluntly. 'He even looks like me.' He pointed at Benjamin.

'As far as I'm concerned, Ben is Billy's son, I don't care about the test results.'

'So this is my dad?' said Benjamin, repeating himself, as if stuck in

226

a time warp.

Cara jumped, having almost forgotten there was anyone else in the room. 'Er... yes, Ben, yes,' she said impatiently.

The two men nodded awkwardly at each other.

'And, what would you have done, if you'd known he was your son? You were already married, remember?'

'I would have stood by you,' said Frederick.

'In what way would you have stood by me?'

'I cared about you, Cara.'

She blushed, then became annoyed with herself for letting him get to her. 'You didn't care about me,' she huffed. 'You've only ever cared about yourself.'

'I did care about you,' he said. 'I *loved* you. I was married when we met, what could I do? I couldn't just leave my wife and children; you know what people were like back then.' He sat down on the armchair next to her.

Her eyes met his. Those eyes—inherited by Benjamin and Penelope—had stayed with her as a reminder and ensured she could never forget him. Looking at him now, she wanted to trust every word he said. She averted her gaze. How could he still have such a hold on her?

'I'm sorry I hurt you—'

'You weren't sorry back then, were you?' accused Cara.

'Of course I was. I tried to contact you, but you refused to meet with me.'

'What do you mean?'

⏳

Frederick was unable to stop thinking about Cara. She haunted his sleep. He hated himself for letting their relationship go so far without telling her the truth and needed to speak to her, to explain his reasons. The feelings of guilt and pain were too much to bear.

As he stood in front of her house and hesitated at the door edged with trailing ivy, he wondered whether she had told her parents about what had happened. Taking a deep breath to calm his nerves, he knocked on the front door.

When the door opened, he was greeted by a pretty girl with long red hair. 'Hello.'

She resembled Cara. Frederick surmised she must be her sister.

'Hello.' He smiled at the girl. 'I've come to see Cara.'

'She's not in, I'm afraid. What's your name?'

'I'm Fr...a friend.' He thought it best not to mention his name; her family would not take kindly to his visit if she'd told them about him.

'I'm her sister; I could pass on a message.'

'Yes, please.' Having anticipated the possibility Cara would refuse to see him, he'd prepared a note he could leave for her. 'Please would you give her this note? It's important she gets it today.'

'Yes, of course,' said Gloria, taking the envelope. 'I'll make sure she gets it.' With that, she closed the front door.

Once inside the house, Gloria studied the envelope. Expensive paper, sealed with a wax seal. The man had looked very distinguished in his suit. He was handsome.

Gloria felt curious as to why this young man had come to see Cara; she was engaged to Billy. Gloria first began to doubt Cara's integrity when Beattie became pregnant, on the basis that the two girls spent most of their time together and therefore had to be alike.

Gloria opened the envelope and read the note:

Darling Cara,

I'm so sorry. I didn't want to hurt you. I now realise how much you mean to me. Meet me at eight o'clock in The Horse and Dragon. We have to talk.

All my Love, Freddie xx

Just as she had suspected, her younger sister was apparently living a less than innocent existence. She knew Cara had been dating a man from out of town, called Freddie, before she met her fiancé. Was she still seeing him? How could she be so blatantly deceitful? Gloria tore the note into tiny shreds and threw the confetti-like pieces into the open fire in the living room, her forehead tense with anger as she watched the remnants of the letter turn to ashes.

Frederick waited hopefully at The Horse and Dragon that evening. Cara did not appear. He ended the evening on his fourth double whisky, telling himself he should have known this would happen. How could he expect her to let him back into her life after what he had done?

☒

'I was really upset when you didn't turn up,' he said.

'Glor never gave the note to me,' said Cara, feeling a strange sense of loss. 'Not surprising; we hated each other back then.'

'I went to your home again a few weeks later. Your father answered the door. He told me you were getting married. It broke my heart, I didn't want you to marry anyone else.'

Cara raised her eyebrows. 'You knew I was getting married?'

'Yes, I even went to the wedding, with the intention of stopping it.' He laughed drily.

☒

'Cara's getting married?' Frederick felt awkward as he asked the question.

'Yes, my little girl is getting married on Sunday,' said Cara's father proudly.

'This Sunday?' Frederick knitted his brow.

'Yes, at St Mary's Church. The same church her mother and I were married in twenty-six years ago.'

'I'm sure it will be lovely,' said Frederick. 'I'll catch up with Cara another time.' He turned to walk away.

'But wait,' her father called after him. 'If you're an old friend of Cara's, I'm sure she'd want you to be there.'

Frederick continued to walk back to his car.

He sat in the vehicle for a while, shellshocked. Cara was getting married? It had only been a few weeks since their last meeting and she'd been so in love with him then.

She would be making a terrible mistake. He would have to try to stop her.

☒

Frederick stood across the road from St Mary's Church and watched the wedding cars arrive.

The groom stepped out of a grand white car, grinning. Everyone cheered.

Frederick told himself he could not let Cara go ahead with the marriage. She couldn't be in love with him one minute and marry another man the next; it was irrational.

Shortly, another car arrived. Cara stepped out wearing a long, flowing white dress, holding a bouquet of white roses.

Frederick stepped forward to see her more clearly, making sure to stay out of sight of the wedding party. He had never seen her looking quite so beautiful.

Soon everyone went into the church, and Frederick proceeded to cross the road. He knew what he would say as soon as the opportunity presented itself.

Entering the church, he walked close enough to the front of the aisle so as to have a good view of Cara.

Dressed smartly to blend in with the guests, he wore a false beard and moustache, his hair slicked back to alter his usual appearance.

Soon the priest started the ceremony. Cara turned around and smiled at her parents.

Frederick bowed his head—afraid she would recognise him—but then, remembering his disguise, felt brave enough to look at her. He noticed her hand go up to her eye to wipe away tears as she swivelled back around to face the front of the church.

He watched the groom take her hand and smile. With a sense of shame, Frederick recalled the many times had he looked at her with love in his eyes and lied to her so easily.

Slowly he realised that as soon as he'd told her he couldn't marry her, he'd lost her for ever; she didn't want to meet him to discuss it, didn't respond to his letter.

Cara appeared so content; happiness radiated from her core. Frederick doubted he'd ever be able to make her so happy.

He'd planned to turn the wedding into a dramatic scene—she would fall into his arms, he'd carry her away—but he felt unworthy. Tears of frustration burning in his eyes, he turned on his heel and left the church.

Gloria was sitting on the steps outside the church. He scurried past her and she glanced up at him, a spark of recognition in her eyes.

He ran down the rest of the steps and out of the churchyard.

⏳

'Y-you were at the wedding?' Cara put a hand in front of her mouth.

'Yes.' Frederick nodded.

'You were at the wedding?' She repeated the words, remembering how her thoughts were of Frederick as she'd stood next to Billy at the altar.

'Only briefly.'

'I can't believe what I'm hearing. I suppose you went home to your wife afterwards, did you?'

'My marriage wasn't working, I was only keeping up appearances for the children's sake. She left me for another man the year after. She left me to bring the children up on my own.'

'You probably deserved it,' Cara sneered. 'Why are you here, Freddie? If it's to see your son, he's here. You can do what you like. It's all in the past, and as far as I'm concerned it belongs there. I never asked for this paternity test to be done.'

She couldn't let him know she still cared. All the things he had just told her were spinning around in her mind. Coming back down to earth, she noticed Jemima had left the room. It had happened again, just as it used to whenever she was with Frederick; the rest of the world became secondary, invisible.

Noticing Benjamin was still there staring fixedly at Frederick, Cara said, 'You should be going, Ben.'

Benjamin stood up, slowly. 'I'd like to keep in touch,' he said.

'Goodbye, Ben,' she said.

He smiled awkwardly at Frederick.

Frederick watched him leave the room.

She felt strange being alone with Frederick, tempted to call Benjamin back. She couldn't allow the door to her old emotions to open up, afraid of what she might find.

'Cara, if I'd known we had a son, I would have taken care of you. I really loved you. Why didn't you tell me? I thought you loved me.'

I did love you, Freddie. I loved you more than I've ever loved anyone. I still love you. She heard the words in her head and battled to keep them from her lips. Her heart fought with her head. She wanted him to leave, but she wanted him to stay. *Go away, Freddie!* she was screaming inside, wishing she could stand up and leave.

'Let me tell you one thing,' she started. 'You wouldn't have had a son if it wasn't for my Billy.' She avoided his eyes, and continued: 'Ben would have been dead, and so would I: because of you.' Her cheeks reddened. Since Billy's death, she'd sworn she would never reveal this secret to a living soul.

'What do you mean?'

'The night you told me you were married, I wanted to die. I couldn't imagine my life without you. I'd built so many dreams around me and you, and I thought we'd be together for ever. You betrayed me.'

He put a hand on her arm.

'I was only a young girl. A stupid girl.' Turning away from him, she said, 'I tried to kill myself. Billy saved me and gave me a reason to live. If

231

he didn't save me, Ben would have been dead. So you see, that's why I consider Billy to be his father.'

Frederick held his head in his hands. When he looked up at her, she saw tears in his eyes.

'Cara, it was me...' He stopped as if unable to continue.

'What do you mean?'

'I saved you.'

'Wh... what are you saying?'

'I followed you. I saw you jump from Stoneleigh Cliffs.'

Cara put a hand to her throat.

'I jumped in after you,' he confessed. 'I pulled you to safety. I called someone over to stay with you while I phoned for an ambulance. That must have been Billy.'

'You're lying. It can't be true.'

'It is true,' he said.

'But you never said anything at the time. I assumed Billy...' She cast her mind back to that night, her recollection hazy. Billy hadn't claimed that he'd saved her life—he'd just happened to be the first person she saw when she found herself on the shore at Stoneleigh. They never spoke about the incident in any detail. She, in particular, feeling foolish whenever she remembered what she'd done, preferred not to talk about it.

⏳

Frederick waited at the far end of the stony beach, near the road, for the ambulance to arrive. Why were they taking so long? The minutes dragged. He hoped she'd be all right. Her body was limp when he'd pulled her out of the sea.

He rubbed his arms to get the circulation going. His clothes were soaked right through so that they clung to his skin. It must be worse for Cara, *he thought.* She'd looked so fragile, like a lifeless doll. The fall took so much out of her. *He willed the ambulance to arrive quickly, at the same time keeping an eye on the distant sight of Cara lying on the beach. At least she had someone with her—wasn't alone.*

Finally, he saw the ambulance approaching. Flagging down the driver, he called out, 'Over there!' pointing to the two lone figures on the beach.

He watched as the ambulance drove towards them. The lights of the vehicle cast a spotlight on Cara and the young man by her side.

Frederick kept his distance. Part of him wished he could accompany her to the hospital, but his mind told him it would be wrong. He'd led her on enough already.

232

His watch, full of water, had stopped working. He would have to go home.

By the time he reached the top of the cliffs where his car was parked, the ambulance had already left. The dark, treacherous sea struck an imposing sight. Frederick knew he would never have jumped if he'd thought about what he was doing before he leapt, but he'd felt an urgency to save Cara. He had jumped to follow her, not thinking of the consequences.

It made him dizzy staring down at the sea below, aware of what could have happened. They could both have died. He took a few steps back.

As he gazed out over the cliff edge, he could not deny that when he'd jumped in after her, nothing else had mattered but Cara.

⧗

Cara's heart began to beat faster. Frederick had jumped into the sea after her and risked his life to save her.

'All my life, I thought it was Billy who saved me.'

'I'm sorry, Cara.'

She stared into his eyes.

He took her hand.

Just then, the front door opened and closed. Penelope ran into the living room with Andrew and Carl to see Cara and Frederick seated side by side on the sofa.

'Nan?' Her raised eyebrows indicated her surprise.

'Hello, dear,' said Cara, stunned by the events of the past few minutes. She drew her hand away from Frederick's, feeling embarrassed.

Penelope acknowledged Frederick with a polite nod of her head. 'Hi, Nan. Where's Jemima?'

'I'm not sure, dear; she might have gone into the kitchen.'

'Right. Come on boys, let's go and meet your aunty and get some tea.'

'Is this Granddad?' asked Andrew.

'No,' said Penelope, her cheeks reddening slightly. 'Come on, let's go into the kitchen, Nan wants to be alone with her friend.'

'But I wanted to see Granddad,' said Carl.

'You said he was here,' said Andrew, sulking.

'Don't worry, boys,' said Cara. 'I'm sure you'll see him soon.' She smiled at Penelope who nodded awkwardly and quickly left the room, pulling the two boys behind her.

Cara was still smiling when she looked back at Frederick. She averted her eyes self-consciously. They were alone again.

His hand touched the locket resting against her chest. 'I can't believe you still wear this,' he said. 'Do you remember what you said to me when I gave you this locket?'

She held her breath and shook her head.

'You said because there was a lock of my hair inside, we'd always be together.'

'Did I? I can't remember,' she lied.

Taking the pendant between his fingers, he opened the clasp. His joyful expression changed to one of disappointment. 'It's empty.'

She wished his hair was still inside but then felt annoyed at herself for being so enrapt with him.

He sat on the armchair opposite her.

She noticed how the years had not taken away his looks, and he was still tall and strong. He wore a brown suit. She wondered if he'd dressed smartly especially for her.

'Did you ever think about me, Cara?' he asked.

'Now and then,' she said, wary of meeting his gaze.

'I often thought about what it would have been like if we'd married and had children,' he said. 'It's quite ironic really, finding out Benjamin is my son. He seems like a good lad. We should all keep in touch.'

He stood up and her heart reached out to him. She didn't want to say goodbye yet.

'Do you have a pair of scissors, Cara?' he asked.

'Scissors?' Her brow creased into a frown. 'I think they're in the top drawer of the unit over there,' she said, pointing.

He walked over to the unit and rummaged around in the drawer, then she saw him take out the scissors.

'Close your eyes,' he said.

'Why?'

'Trust me,' he said, winking.

She half-closed her eyes so she could still see him, and watched as he cut off a bit of his hair and placed the scissors back into the drawer.

'Okay, you can open your eyes.' He approached her and knelt down in front of her. Opening the locket, he placed the hair inside. When he'd closed it, he looked into her eyes. 'I hope this will mean that we'll never be apart, Cara,' he said, smiling.

Once again, she lost herself in his dark dreamy eyes, feeling as though she was back in the late summer of 1952.

www.ingramcontent.com/pod-product-compliance
Lightning Source LLC
Chambersburg PA
CBHW051643260626
47170CB00004B/1313